THE NUBIAN PRINCE

THE NUBIAN PRINCE

A NOVEL

JUAN BONILLA

TRANSLATED BY ESTHER ALLEN

Metropolitan Books

Henry Holt and Company   New York

Metropolitan Books
Henry Holt and Company, LLC
Publishers since 1866
175 Fifth Avenue
New York, New York 10010

Metropolitan Books™ is a registered
trademark of Henry Holt and Company, LLC.

Originally published in Spain in 2003 under the title *Los príncipes nubios*
by Editorial Seix Barral, Barcelona.

Library of Congress Cataloging-in-Publication Data
Bonilla, Juan.
   [Príncipes nubios. English]
   The nubian prince : a novel / by Juan Bonilla; translated by Esther Allen.
      p. cm.
   ISBN-13: 978-0-8050-7781-0
   ISBN-10: 0-8050-7781-2
   I. Allen, Esther, 1962–   II. Title
PQ6652.O56P7513   2006
863'.64—dc22   2005058390

First American Edition 2006

Designed by Kelly S. Too

Printed in the United States of America
1 3 5 7 9 10 8 6 4 2

To Mónica Martin and Toni Munné,
for all the proper names and all the laughter

THE NUBIAN PRINCE

ONE ▐▋▋▋

My job was to save lives. It was that simple. You may think I'm exaggerating, trying to impress you. You can think what you like; the fact is I was paid to save lives, and the more lives I saved the more money I made. My existence was a kind of tennis game in which one of the players—me—never ventured far from the house, the living room with the big-screen TV, the darkroom where I'd spend whole days developing pictures, the neighborhood where I had everything I needed to be happy: a bar where I ate long, peaceful breakfasts, a small bookshop where I could get whatever book caught my eye, a fruit stand run by a big, toothy woman who'd set aside the best grapes and most tempting peaches for me, a barber shop I'd duck into a couple of times a week, and even an Internet café where I'd spend hours surfing the Web. Meanwhile, the other player—also me—would zigzag across half a continent, which was the zone I'd been assigned. He might be setting off for the Cádiz coast; he might be arriving in Sicily. I could usually decide for myself where this other player was to be found, but occasionally circumstances decided things for me. A huge transport of Albanians arriving in Brindisi would have me on the next flight to Rome, renting a car, and racing to the city where my partner in this tennis match would be waiting for me.

You may well be wondering what sort of work I did, what I mean by "saving lives." Well, I wasn't saving people the way firemen or lifeguards do; all they really save are bodies. I've never known a fireman to rescue someone from the flames and then offer him a new and better life, something beyond dragging him down the fire escape to the street and providing a little emergency medical care. I've never heard of a lifeguard giving mouth-to-mouth to a half-drowned swimmer and then saying, "Marry me." My job was to seek beauty, to plunge my hands into the world's muck and bring up pearls. I cleaned those pearls, made them presentable, prepared them to acquire the value that was rightfully theirs. I traveled to places where poverty had hidden these treasures; I searched them out with infinite patience and rescued them. That's what I mean by saving lives.

Look at me now, for example, here on a beach near Gibraltar with the sun reluctantly sinking below the horizon while the trees, stiff with cold, lean forward as if attempting a graceful bow. A few dozen Africans have just arrived in pitiful, flimsy boats. They drag themselves along the beach in their dripping rags, following orders, fearful of the eyes that are watching them: the Guardia Civil has been waiting for them to land and immediately arrests them. Many seem about to faint; others would give their lives for a glass of water; most can't stop trembling. But the Guardia Civil doesn't do a thing for them, just herds them together to keep them under control. Some have managed to hang on to a few possessions carried in backpacks held together with duct tape. The police won't bring out the water bottles and clean towels and start pampering the refugees until the TV cameras arrive. That's how it usually is: cameras first, then the paramedics. In between, they'll call me, if I happen to be in the area. Well, actually, the only one who calls me is a lieutenant into whose palm I occasionally slip a wad of bills. He wakes me at dawn with a whispered, "Half an hour from now at such and such a place." And I'm off. When I get there, he always says,

"You've got fifteen minutes," and allows me to inspect the merchandise. I give the newcomers a quick once-over and if there's a piece that convinces me, I signal to the lieutenant, who says, "OK, stop by the station in a couple of hours."

I get there right on time, and the lieutenant has set her aside for me, the one in the pink track jacket and pants that long ago were some light color, the one with the eyes that say, "Please don't hurt me." She's been spared the medical inspection and served a cup of coffee instead. Some guy who's just seen a movie celebrating human goodness may even have bought her a doughnut. I hustle her out the door, doing my best to make sure no one sees us. Even though she's been captured, she still isn't mine; I have to be charming and radiate friendliness, make her grateful. I've bought her a sweater and tennis shoes at a twenty-four-hour store. She's certain to ask where I'm taking her, what's going to happen to her family—there's always a father or brother who gets left behind—and that's when I have to tell her the truth. I'll begin by confessing why I'm saving her while all the others who made the crossing with her will be sent right back where they came from without arousing the faintest twinge of remorse in the hearts of the enforcers of the law. If she doesn't speak English, as is often the case, I can simplify matters by hiring a translator who knows how to explain the situation quickly and forcefully. If she does speak English, I can handle things on my own and convince her she has very few options besides trusting me and allowing me to save her. I even bring along the phone numbers of some of the various gorgeous specimens—both male and female—I've saved in the past; one will probably turn out to be from the same place she is; they'll talk for a while, and when the newly captured piece hangs up she'll have no arguments left. Then it's up to me to clean her up, heighten her exquisite features, accentuate her extraordinary appeal. In a couple of days she'll be ready to visit

Club headquarters, where management will look her over. I always know in advance whether a piece I've collected will be accepted outright or will have some trouble passing the exam. In this case, there'll be no objection whatsoever. They won't stand there gaping; they're not in the habit of feeling or expressing astonishment. But they will be delighted to have Nadim—that's the name I gave her the moment I saw her; she told me her last name but for some reason refused to give me her real first name. They'll immediately schedule a photo shoot, and the resulting portfolio will be added to the Club's magnificent menu. Then they'll transfer her to a city where she'll work under some local branch manager. But I won't have any part in that; all I do is save her. Once she's assigned to a branch, she'll start earning money: 20 percent of every service. (As a rule, she'll be required to perform a service every three or four days.) The full price of the service is astronomical, of course. To put it bluntly, the proof that her life and beauty will soon be worth much more than they are now is that if I wanted to enjoy her body—which prior to her examination by Club management would not be at all an impossible thing (and I must confess that on more than one occasion I've been guilty of doing just that with the pieces I've captured)— at the Club's going rate I'd have to pay almost as much as I'll earn for having saved her. The Club offers no discount to its own scouts.

You must be wondering how I got this job. Well, the story is not without its charm. The most basic element of any story—I imagine we can agree on this—is the thing that compels someone to tell it; that's more important than the content of the story itself. Why does someone decide, suddenly, to tell a story? There are thousands of answers to that question, maybe as many answers as there are stories, I don't know. I still haven't managed to come up with an answer of my own, though I suspect it must have something to do with the circuitous route that brought me here.

I could begin by saying: I had travelled to Bolivia as part of a band of saintly crackpots sent by a nongovernmental organization to put on clown shows and acrobatic routines for the miserable children who live in the immense garbage dump on the outskirts of the capital. I was twenty-three years old, an age at which you can still fool yourself into believing that this sort of gesture will save the world. I had just finished college with a degree in dramatic arts, and to what more noble use could I put my certified knowledge, incorruptible audacity, and scant talent?

This first part of my story, however, immediately demands a somewhat deeper foray into my past—though I promise my explanation of how I landed this job will require no tedious rummaging through my deepest childhood memories in search of the one shining nugget that will illuminate all that follows. When I read a biography, I always skip the chapters about the subject's childhood; I'm sure they're only there so the author can show off all the backbreaking research he did to discover the names of the boys who waited outside the schoolyard one rainy day to settle a score with our hero. As soon as anyone starts telling me things about his childhood, both my legs go to sleep, and for that same reason I try never to tell anyone anything about mine.

I remember a certain spring night at home, watching a movie on TV with my parents and brother. The movie was *Magnolia,* a collection of shocking dramas woven together with enviable skill and copious histrionics. Suddenly one of the characters—a pathetic former TV child star who's had braces put on his teeth in order to seduce the muscular waiter he's fallen for—bursts into tears after getting his face cut open in a spectacular fall. Between sobs, he cries, "I have so much love to give." I don't know what went through my mind when I heard that line, but I completely lost it and burst into tears myself. To my mother's astonishment, my brother's bewilderment, and my old man's stone-faced indifference, I started repeating the character's line over and over. My mother got up and came over to me but couldn't think of anything to do except throw the afghan she'd had in her lap around my shoulders. "That's right—make him look even more ridiculous," my brother said.

"I think the best thing would be just to change channels," my father declared. "Either that or take him to the emergency room. With any luck, they'll decide to keep him in the hospital a while."

I got up, still wrapped in my mother's afghan and wiping my eyes on a corner of it, and went to the bathroom to look in the mirror and try to figure out what the hell was going on. Behind me, I heard my mother say, "That boy is going through a lot. He should see a psychologist. Even better, we should take him to Padre Adrián."

My mother was fascinated by psychologists and therefore also by priests. In fact, her sole preoccupation in life was to find an appropriate name for what the rest of us called "her little thing," and which she, therefore, had no choice but to call "my little thing." It might come up in any conversation, with a neighbor lady or a relative, with the owner of the corner store, or, occasionally, with a fellow passenger on the bus. Whenever her spirits darkened and she left the kitchen to sit in front of the TV until all hours, voraciously consuming carton after carton of ice cream, my brother and I would say to each other, "Mother's got her little thing again." My mother was obsessed with finding the correct name of her "little thing"; she was certain that the moment she knew exactly what was happening to her—if, in fact, it deserved to have a name (if, that is, it was something that had happened to other people in the past and would happen to still more people in the future)—her obsession would disappear. Of course everyone in the family knew that Mother's condition was a banal mixture of boredom with her empty life, resentment of my father, disgust with herself, and, finally, an uncontrollable urge to put an end to the whole thing—a combination that did not fail to present an interesting philosophical conundrum. Here was a cocktail of woes topped off with an ingredient whose essential purpose, in addition to giving the brew its own distinctive flavor, was to eliminate the cocktail itself.

During the phases when she wasn't feeling so low that she had to remain prostrate most of the day, she would valiantly pursue the label that could reduce her problem to a few syllables. First she went back to finish up her interrupted bachelor's degree, enrolling in night school, where her classmates were an impressive crop of slow but determined learners. She lasted less than a year. It was true, she said, that she'd learned things about Ferdinand and Isabella and the causes of the Spanish Civil War, that she had recovered a certain taste for mathematical formulas—Ruffini's theorem struck her as "enchanting," and its derivatives inspired rapturous commentary—and had confirmed that chemistry remained as uncouth and insufferable a subject as it was when she was in college. But something was missing. She hadn't managed to strike up a friendship with any of the students in her class, and it wasn't for lack of drinking lots of coffee with the ones who seemed most interesting. She decided that what was missing was exercise. Why wasn't gym a required subject in night school? She could answer the question herself simply by imagining most of her classmates in workout clothes. That same week she put all her class notes away in a drawer and rushed off to enroll in a sports club.

My brother maintained that what my mother really needed was a lover. It's true that when women who are inordinately bored with their families and the dull routine of their lives find something to focus on so as to escape to a better place, they experience an upsurge in mood and looks that is in direct ratio to the neglect with which they then punish their families—and during her fitness period my mother managed to get a little closer to that better place. I don't know whether she actually did have a lover during those months (I hope she did), but it would have been difficult even to ask the question; the "upsurge" had lifted her so high above us that we would have had to scream just to get her attention. And it wouldn't have been a good idea to arouse my father's suspicions. He was contemptuously dismissive of my mother's attempts to save herself and find a name for "her little thing."

There was no doubt the daily visits to the gym were doing her good, but she suddenly decided that no, this wasn't the place she was going to find herself either; some element of soul was missing in that sports club packed with bodies. Yes, that was it, what she needed were words, not push-ups. Maybe the lover who'd helped her love herself a little more grew tired of her constant doubts and rigorous self-examinations, deliberately intended to fuel her sense of guilt. In any case, the gym days were followed by a brief period of prostration. Then, I imagine, she had an idea: given the impossibility of finding a name for her problem in Spanish, it might be easier to try finding it in some other language. She enrolled in a language school. My brother suspected that my mother's decision to study German rather than English could only be a kind of secret tribute to her lover's nationality. (You see how, without knowing anything for certain, we were able to conjecture a rather odd sequence of events in order to explain something that undoubtedly required no explanation.) Whatever the case, it was the worst decision she could have made. If she'd chosen English, she might have managed to finish the course, but with German her chances were a lot slimmer. Before the end of the second semester my mother abandoned her declensions and once more took refuge in silence, serving up boiled potatoes for dinner with a vacant stare, spending hours each day in front of the television, and, on the days when she felt worst, buying colossal quantities of entirely useless things.

Finally, my brother, who is much more candid than I am and consequently wound up working as a gas station attendant despite his newly earned master's degree in journalism (he later got his honesty under control, learned not to say what he was actually thinking at any given moment, and landed a position doing PR for the Department of Education and Culture, where he was soon writing speeches for the executive director and even the minister)—finally my brother uttered the fateful word, pronouncing each syllable distinctly and separately, as if trying to downplay its force and drama: psy-cho-an-al-y-sis. Of course my mother had been giving that option a lot of thought for a long time, even before she went back to finish her degree, before she joined the gym, before she studied German, and before she'd gone to the local YWCA, where she learned to make rag dolls while telling the other women in her group about her life, and where she attended several lectures. (The proof that none of them did her any good is that she came back to us, whereas, according to my brother, a lecture is worth sitting through only when you leave the auditorium and decide never to go home again.) But opting for psychological treatment would mean burning her bridges and acknowledging that she was sick—that is, that the name of her little thing was going to be the name of an illness. And she much preferred to exhaust all other possibilities before risking having a doctor tell her that her little thing could be cured by pharmaceutical means.

My brother understood that the only way my mother could be saved by a psychiatrist or psychoanalyst was for there to be *transference,* which is the technical term for when the patient falls in love with the doctor. The earliest sessions seemed to yield some results. After her hour on the magical couch where she gradually scraped away the dark incrustation of her fears to arrive at the core where the sacred name of her ailment was emblazoned in glowing letters, my mother would come home feeling better. But after two months of treatment, her state of mind took another steep dive. We didn't want to ask, but we couldn't help noticing that she was spending hours watching television, that we had to say her name two or three times before she would notice, that she was putting salt in the coffee and sugar on the salad, and that she was buying nothing at the supermarket but jumbo cartons of ice cream. My brother pithily summed up the situation: "It's clear that there has been transference and she's gone and fallen in love, and it's also clear that the doctor has told her not to come to him anymore but to start seeing someone else." There was nothing left for my mother but to seek solace in religion. At least God and his representatives on Earth would not be as unfeeling as that psychoanalyst, who, instead of allowing himself to be adored in exchange for a thick stack of bills per session, had wounded my mother by sending her off to some colleague she would never visit even once.

When I had that crying fit, my mother thought it was time for her to do something about me, so she made me come with her to church. The visit to a psychologist could always wait until after the priests had failed, if only because priests are cheaper than psychologists. She left me in a confessional where my voice, muffled by my own incredulity, enumerated the reasons I considered it entirely useless for me to seek consolation from a God in whom I had not believed since the time when, as a child, I'd prayed to Him to make my team, the Real Betis Balompié, league champions, and he'd never given my prayer the slightest heed. The invisible priest who heard my confession must have thought he wasn't being paid enough to concern himself with the blabberings of an atheist and, as my only penitence, told me never to set foot in his church again.

At that time in my life I was obsessed with freeing myself from an obsession. In fact, I still have it; which means I'll always have it; there's no way for me to get rid of it. Ever since I first had to memorize my name and address as a boy, so that in case I got lost I could walk up to any trustworthy-looking person and ask to be taken home, the first thing I think upon waking up in the morning is this: my full name, Moisés Froissard Calderón, my old address (where no one lives anymore, or at least no one I know), La Florida 15, apartment 3B, and then my age, my profession (saver of lives, naturally), and some trait that characterizes my identity or my present circumstances, the only variable element in this daily mantra. I thought that if I could only stop this compulsive behavior, this recitation of my identity, this linguistic tattoo by which my consciousness activates itself, then my life would change, I would succeed in becoming *someone* and stop falling apart over stupid things like a ridiculous, tender scene in a movie that had no effect on anyone else. And I came away from that priest—from confessing to him that I couldn't confess anything to him and that I might have been better off with a pretty personal trainer or charming foreign-language instructor— telling myself: you have to do it, you have to learn to forget your name, your address, your age.

Somehow I had to save myself. I couldn't imagine a worse fate than the stagnant life my friends were living. Like lots of people my age, I'd tried to do whatever traveling I could with the help of summer internships and student discounts. Occasionally I'd earn some money handing out flyers, working as a lifeguard at a swimming pool where the pink of Seville's lumpenproletariat fried themselves to an even brighter scarlet, or donating sperm at the hospital—no big deal. Some friends and I were always on the lookout for ways to generate income with none of the usual headaches. The girls had it easier: the private clinics would give them close to a thousand euros for a single egg, while our sperm was only worth thirty or forty euros, depending on the demand. We were constantly sharing information: a movie that needed extras was about to start shooting; a new TV show was paying audience members to be jeered at and insulted. A few of us even tried our luck at a modeling agency, but they barely let us off the elevator. When we found out we could earn good cash by acting as basketball statisticians, we headed straight for the league headquarters to apply. On Sunday afternoons, for an hour of recording personal fouls and keeping track of each team's posses- sion time, we pocketed the staggering sum of thirty euros. We looked at other sports leagues as well, and dreamed of becoming ping-pong statisticians, tennis statisticians, handball statisticians, volleyball statisticians, or whatever—but we never had the same luck again.

Every night before I fell asleep, I used to grant myself interviews. Sometimes I'd won a grand slam; other times I'd saved fourteen people from dying in a fire. Sometimes a famous Hollywood actress was madly in love with me, or I was the only photographer to get a clear image of the pope's head the instant the bullet smashed into it. Any social welfare psychoanalyst—and any first-year psychology student and probably any department store sales clerk—could have told me: muchacho, you're suffering from delusions of grandeur; all you want out of life is to be famous. Something in your past—your parents' indifference?—is driving you to do great things, things that will make you immortal, make people recognize you wherever you go. Nevertheless, most of the interviews I conducted with myself confirmed my suspicion that my greatest talent lay in bringing out the worst in everyone around me. I believe I spoke those very words at some point during every one of the interviews, as if this were a virtue worthy of praise, as if my real mission on Earth were not simply to be the first man on Saturn, win the Tour de France, marry a millionaire, build the fanciest airport in Asia, uncover the remains of Jesus Christ, or discover an infallible cure for depression, but to serve as a funhouse mirror for everyone who got near me. In fact, I always ended up convincing my hypothetical interviewers—whom, of course, I also invariably wound up seducing—that however impressive the achievement they were interviewing me about was, what lay below it, which they'd find if they scratched the surface even the slightest bit, was a disturbing image of themselves, reflected in my unusual temperament.

I once mentioned this to my brother, at one of the rare moments when we were being serious, or at least, I was being serious—some college philosophy course or youthful romantic mishap would occasionally drive me to wax philosophic. Where-upon he, with a sidelong glance and a suppressed laugh—he was very good at suppressing his laughter; he understood that much of the impact of his jibes lay in keeping their bite undulled by a chuckle or a "just kidding"—said, "You get that from Papa." This remark had a considerable effect on me because we hadn't called the old man "Papa" since before we started high school. It was as if we'd been exchanging views on the pope and my brother had referred to His Holiness as "cootchi-cootchi." It felt pornographic.

It was my brother who took the crucial step that led to my doing something I'd never had the nerve to do: make a decision. He introduced me to a friend of his who earned a living as an administrator for Artists Without Borders.

"Maybe you can do something for him. I think he needs a little shaking up," my brother, reeking of gasoline, as ever, said to his friend.

"Would you be willing to go to Bolivia? We're sending a team there a month from now, and we need actors, clowns, pup-peteers, acrobats—things like that."

He explained everything, and I didn't even need time to think it over. That night before falling asleep, I granted myself another interview. Having just received the Oscar for my role in a biopic of James Dean, to whom I bore a remarkable physical resem-blance, I reminisced about my entire career and confessed that I was particularly proud—and also much admired though I didn't get into that—of having gotten my start in show business by bringing joy and laughter to helpless, poverty-stricken children.

I left for Bolivia like someone going off on a weekend camping trip with friends. The morning after my arrival I woke up angry, for even though I had a new address now and innumerable rea-sons to forget my name and everything else, to become nobody, just another clown, I still had to repeat to myself, in order to greet the day, or rather to be greeted by the day: Moisés Froissard Calderón, La Florida 15, apartment 3B, twenty-three years old, world-class idiot.

Half an hour after my first visit to the vast garbage dump on the outskirts of La Paz where thousands of small children lived, I went on another crying jag. Then I got over it. What else could I do? We put on a couple of shows a day, with lots of improvisation and not much juggling. The children crowding around us were wildly delighted by our ghastly little puppet shows; to them, hearing a puppet speak was miraculous. "The clowns are coming, the clowns!" they would shout when they saw us climbing toward them up a mountain of garbage. They spent all day, dawn to dusk, rummaging through the immense mass of refuse for something they might be able to sell on the streets of the city. At night, to stave off hunger, they covered their faces with glue-soaked rags and hallucinated. More than one of them had climbed a telephone pole, thinking he was an eagle, and thrown himself to the ground, or electrocuted himself by grabbing a live wire. Almost all of them had stooped shoulders and faraway eyes. Grandparents were highly improbable; it was unusual for anyone to reach forty, but I did meet a man who already had several grandchildren at the age of thirty-two. The missionaries who had ventured there to sooth the unbearable agonies of the body with balms for the spirit were opposed, naturally, to the distribution of condoms that might alleviate the overpopulation problem. But there would always be more garbage than garbage pickers, no matter how many were born. According to census figures someone in my group claimed to have seen, there were about fifty thousand people living in that dump. I can't begin to describe the stench that choked the air not only at the dump itself but for ten kilometers all around. It was a jungle of garbage, ruled by the law of the jungle. If a six-year-old girl found something of even the slightest value, she'd have to have learned a great deal in her short life to keep others from immediately grabbing it away.

The glue corroded their brains but gave them access to other regions where they could breathe or become soccer stars or drive fast cars. And in every shack on the dump an image of some virgin or saint presided over the single room where the whole family lived crammed together. Every time I left the dump, the stupefied children's applause in my ears, I would swear never to go back. Then I'd proceed to spend the evening getting drunk in some filthy dive and letting the other members of my group persuade me not to give up. I'd ask them if they really thought what we were doing was of any value at all, if they really thought that with a few quick hugs and some clown noses and white face paint we were going to save anyone. And instead of taking me to task for even asking such questions, they were naive enough to try to answer them.

I'd been there three weeks, putting on shows for adorable and all-too-easily-pleased audiences, lending a hand here and there, helping build some wooden huts that could house a few families, giving math classes if the teacher needed a day off, when I met Roberto Gallardo, a red-haired immaculately clad Argentine in his thirties whom I'd occasionally glimpsed roving across the garbage dump and had initially taken for a member of our group. But he wasn't. He showed up one evening at one of the dingy haunts I retreated to every day the instant the sun went down, in urgent need of benumbing my consciousness and manufacturing a little dose of sleep for myself. (Those days I was falling asleep without granting any interviews; there wasn't time for even a single question.) Roberto asked if the stool to my left was free, and I gestured for him to sit down. He delivered the kind of opening line that's typical of someone who has his speech well prepared, something like: "Life's tough around here, isn't it?" Then came a minutely detailed inquiry into my past and what it was that had compelled me to do what I was doing, followed by a lengthy evaluation of the likelihood that my work was doing any good at all for the public it was intended to serve. He told me the La Paz dump was a Garden of Eden compared to certain Mexico City barrios where the police charged a very high price indeed if anyone called for their help. He waxed explicit about scenes he had personally witnessed in those barrios, smothered under a layer of greasy smog above which the sun itself was nothing but a filthy piece of small change. Death was routine and came as a welcome salvation to the fortunate few who met with it before suffering too much. One night some kid would collapse headlong into the rag he'd soaked with all his liquid assets, never to wake up; the next morning they'd stick him in a cardboard box, and if the priest had nothing better to do, he'd stop by to repeat exactly what he'd said the day before at another kid's burial, and the story ended there without anyone even wondering what the kid had been alive for in the first place.

Finally, his smiling eyes working hard to establish the camaraderie his awful stories had not managed to elicit, he asked, "Don't you think we could do more for them?"

"Not all of them, of course," he hastened to clarify, "but for a few, for the best of them." I soon learned that the best of them meant the best-looking. And there he cut off his narrative, ceding the role of interviewer to me. Of course he had my full attention at that point; there were moments when he seemed like a politician who carries a thick pack of cards in his wide sleeve, so as to pull out exactly the right one at any given moment. I need hardly mention that the question that obsessed me from the start and even long after I'd grown inclined to accept the new world-

view Roberto was proposing was: why me? Was I so transpar-
ently out of place among the performers who went to the dump
every day that even a complete stranger could spot me unerr-
ingly? When I found out what Gallardo did for a living, I thought
he was a criminal who deserved to be hung. That was after I'd
discarded the possibility that he was making the whole thing up
to try and impress me. We've all been heroes and villains in our
late-night bar talk; we've all told tall tales, climbed high mountains, or hunted lions on the strength of information gleaned
from a back issue of *National Geographic* idly leafed through
long ago in a dentist's waiting room. I found myself claiming to
be the leader of a small band of neo-Nazis one night as I tried to
cast my spell on a Valkyrie who was wearing a silver swastika
pendant. When Roberto told me his job was to save lives, to sink
his hands into the muck and rescue nuggets of pure gold, I
sighed. Then he came out with an energetic speech about the
kind of ultra-Catholic misgivings that cloud our minds and keep
us from a commonsense appreciation of the greatness of the
organization he worked for.

"If children break their backs harvesting tea or go blind making athletic shoes, you'll accept that as normal—an outrage, yes,
but far preferable to their working as prostitutes. And bear in
mind that as prostitutes they'll work in absolute safety, there will
be no abuses, they will be paid what they're worth and not some
miserable pittance, they'll have doctors when they need them,
and they'll soon be able to save enough to quit doing that kind of
work if they're not happy with it. But that horrifies you; anything
involving sex strikes you as appalling. The TV can run a thousand ads selling suicidally fast cars, and no one protests. But if a
close-up of a naked man appears on the screen in an ad for refrig-
erators, or a beautiful woman is shown stroking herself between
the legs in a pitch for Persian carpets, then everyone screams for

Parliament to do something about it. A man may be losing his soul working twelve hours a day with shit for wages, but he's still an honorable man. But if he makes in half an hour what you make in a month by letting himself be pawed by some drooling imbecile who comes the minute he touches him, well then, honor is out of the question. Take any one of those handsome boys and beautiful little girls who are out there scrabbling around in garbage and shit all day long; bring out their beauty with the right kind of clothes, teach them a couple of tricks that will drive the clients wild, and in half an hour they'll have knocked out any one of the drooling imbeciles and be stowing a nice pile of money in their wallets. Ask them which outrage is greater."

His sermon seemed a little weak in points, but I preferred not to challenge it with a sermon of my own. I said only, "We all have to make a living as best we can."

And then: "Why are you telling me all this? What do you want from me?"

He told me he was having a hard time finding his way around the garbage dump. He'd been trying for days but never managed to get where he wanted to go. He'd once spotted a lovely little girl rummaging through the garbage but hadn't managed to approach her. When he finally reached the place where he'd seen her through his binoculars, on a hill of trash, accompanied by five or six other children, she'd already taken off. She was the only worthwhile piece he'd seen here. He asked me to find her for him, and said that if, during my visits to the dump, I saw any other piece that was lovely, very lovely—the pieces had to be *exceptionally beautiful,* he told me—would I please do him the favor of recruiting her, or him. He'd pay a thousand dollars per head for all pieces who met with his approval.

"Beauty is such a subjective thing," I said, my patently idiotic words sounding like a pretext for rejecting the proposal.

"Amigo," he said, "beauty is a very simple thing for a man to define."

"How?"

"Beauty is whatever gets you hard."

I laughed. And asked the obvious: "Why me?"

He told me I was different from the others, that this was clear from a mile away; I was out of place; I simply didn't belong to the new breed of lay missionaries who are spreading out across the world to improve the Kingdom of God and correct its imperfections.

That same night, sharing a cot with Virginia—something I did from time to time, always when she felt like sleeping in someone's arms, never when I was the one who felt like it—I told her about Gallardo's offer. She got out of bed and said, "You need a shave." My beard was taking over my face. And then: "We've got to turn that guy in."

"Are you crazy?" I retorted. "Who are you going to turn him in to? The highly efficient Bolivian police force, which will brook no interference with the youngest of the nation's garbage pickers?"

"We have to teach him a lesson," she said. "And you should shave. Because . . ."

She was silent for a few seconds. I didn't know whether she was going to continue on the subject of my beard or was trying to think of a way we could teach Gallardo a lesson and let him know exactly what we thought of him. Finally she said, with something almost heartbroken in her voice, "You're thinking about taking him up on it, aren't you?"

My only response was a smile. She got up off the floor, leaving the wet trace of her ass behind, and before heading off to her own cot, she slapped me with a soft hand that couldn't possibly have done me any harm, though it sounded as if I'd been hit with a heavy black weight. Then she had a change of heart and raised the same hand that had just left a red mark on my cheek to my forehead, as if to see whether my temperature had risen, whether I had a fever I could blame her for having brought on. Without looking at me, she said, "You're very good at bringing out the worst in me."

The words condemned me to insomnia.

The next day I became aware of just how much headway the conversation with Roberto Gallardo was making inside me. We were performing in the northern part of the dump. Our audience consisted of about three dozen kids, the youngest about six, the oldest no more than fifteen. As I juggled three small, brightly colored balls, I thought: OK, now, when I step aside to let Virginia take over, I'm going to have a look; with any luck I'll find the girl he's looking for or another one whose life he can save. Those were the exact words that ran through my head, I swear. The night before I had flung myself on my cot but even though I was drunk I'd had trouble falling asleep. I was thinking about luck: those kids' luck and my own. When all's said and done, I said to myself, you don't really belong here, you're an imposter; you didn't really come here to make anyone else's life more pleasant, you were just looking for a way out for yourself. My nights were often taken up with thoughts like these, though I never reproached myself for my charade; I accepted that ultimately the important thing is always the act itself, and not the underlying motive. It was true that Virginia, Pablo, Raul, and Mercedes all had reasons for being there that were much purer than mine; each of them had been led to the garbage dump by some deep inner conviction that I never managed to muster. For example, to them, the constant stench only served to strengthen their sense of mission, while for me it was one more unbearable proof that I wasn't cut out for this kind of thing. I was the only one who covered my face with handkerchiefs doused in cologne. The others bore the stench as a badge of heroism. To me, it was simply the most hateful and maddening element of this hell I'd gotten myself into without knowing why. Moreover, I was the only one who continually criticized our work, though this was more out of a feeling that I was wasting my time than from the sense of futility brought on by registering, day after day, that no matter how we got the children to like us, no matter how many smiles we managed to win from the terrible slavery of their days, we were essentially doing nothing more than collaborating with all the shit we were supposedly rebelling against.

The moment I stepped out of the chalk circle where I'd been playing with my little balls to make way for Virginia's number, I knew I'd started working for Gallardo's organization. I took a long, slow look at the face of each kid in the audience, eager to find one who would give me the full experience of beauty, in Gallardo's simple definition. I was out of luck, but the mere fact of having made this patient, detailed inspection—I even rated each child's body on a scale of one to ten; the highest rating, a six, was obviously not a life-saving score—gave me a strange feeling which seemed funny at first but then made me so uneasy that I ordered myself to stop playing with fire. Nonetheless I continued to play with fire that whole day; it was thrilling to play with fire.

I swear I wasn't thinking about the money I'd make if I found the girl Gallardo was looking for, or any other child who stood a chance of meeting his criteria. I was only playing a role—a foolish way I had of entertaining myself at that point in my life. In a given situation, I would cast myself in a given role. For example, if the bus I was riding on broke down and we had to sit for hours in a ditch, instead of being the traveler who loses his temper and joins the chorus of loud protests, I would resolve to be a kind of yogi, who knows that one can easily rise above even the worst circumstances by training one's will to accept the will of destiny with resignation and expect nothing more. I admit I wasn't always the best yogi, and since it was rather common, in the part of the world I was circulating in, for buses to leave you stranded in the middle of the highway, I had many opportunities to fail. At most I could hold out for twenty minutes, silently chanting "om namah shivaya." Then I'd give a hard punch to the back of the empty seat in front of me, scream out my desire to shit on the motherfucking bus company, and get off the bus to unite my wrath with that of my fellow travelers who were vociferating at the side of the road.

That day I didn't run across a single child of exceptional beauty in that apocalyptic landscape of endless mounds of garbage. Several families had settled at the foot of each hill and often had to defend their land from those who disputed their claim. Fights were not unusual, nor was it at all unheard of for a knife to flash in the shadows and for blood to flow and for screams to ring through the dump's rank air. When the time came for the trucks loaded with the day's garbage to arrive, a crowd would gather at the dumping spot and a ferocious struggle would ensue over broken trophies, stained clothing, various sorts of scrap metal—anything that could be sold at the market the next day. There was little point in hoping for food; whatever boxes restaurants and supermarkets tossed into the dumpsters disappeared immediately, fought over by people in the city who'd learned those establishments' daily schedules and kept close tabs on them. Even so, the remains of some banquet always emerged, a cluster of spoiled grapes, a box of yogurts, their expiration date long past. I took pictures of all of it. I knew very well that the only benefit

I could hope to derive from this experience—which I'd signed on for without asking myself what on earth I was looking for or what I could possibly expect to find in such a hellish place—was a collection of photographs I might be able to persuade some magazine to publish when I got back to Spain. But on that day I stopped taking shots of the wretched squabbling, the children endlessly tunneling into mountains of garbage, and instead began to look for bodies that deserved to be photographed. I asked a few of the boys and girls to pose for me, and shot some close-ups, but even as I pressed the shutter button I knew that my subject—anxiously waiting for me to produce the image immediately, and disappointed to learn it would be some time before I developed the picture—was not going to interest Gallardo or his organization.

Little by little I was becoming . . . if not actually Gallardo's friend then at least his drinking buddy. He was a man who suffered a great deal from his own ambitions. He felt like a failure; he'd spent five years scouting for the organization and hadn't yet been considered for a position as a branch director in charge of a given region—a position that would give him an office of his own. Whenever I tried to find out about his past, Gallardo barred my way; he didn't want to tell to me how he had gotten started in the business, and even the information he gave me about the Club was always insufficient, facts I could more or less have guessed on my own: that it was headquartered in Paris and the Spanish branch was in Barcelona, that the Club's boys and girls would travel anywhere to take care of a client, that naturally the Club also functioned as an agency, loaning out its personnel for porn films and millionaire bachelor parties, or to serve as companions or pets: I also learned that the richest regions, where scouts were sent as a reward, were Thailand and the Caribbean, but that the youngest and most adventurous scouts preferred more complicated destinations, countries that had just gone through a war or an economic collapse. Once the war correspondents decamped, the Club's scouts were always next on the scene. Gallardo wasn't even willing to tell me how many lives he'd saved, whether he'd fallen in love with any of the pieces he'd scouted, or whether his trip to the La Paz garbage dump was his idea or the organization's. He wouldn't talk about money, either; all he'd say was that there was lots of it involved. Of course the clients' identities were kept secret; they were important people; he didn't know and didn't want to know who they were, and if he ever heard a rumor about a client's name, he tried to forget it immediately. The one thing he did tell me was: "When you become part of the Club, it's best not to say much and not to hear much; just go, scout, turn in what you find, and collect your money." He also told me that his biggest success story had nothing to do with any piece he'd discovered in some repellent spot. What he'd found was a scout: a woman in her thirties he had met under circumstances similar to those we were in now, and who emerged within just a couple of seasons as the Club's top scout. That woman was now director of the Barcelona branch, and she was the one who would interview me if I wanted to join the Club Olympus as a talent scout.

I held out for two months in the garbage dump. I had made a commitment to stay for six months before going home and being reassigned to another area. You get yourself into these things because you want to travel. There's all that stuff about helping others and doing useful things, making some gesture that will save the world, but traveling and learning geography up close and personal is the main thing. Otherwise you might as well just stay home and pay a daily visit to your own city's slums, the long grim alleys where children chase the rats off a small patch of ground so they'll have a place to play soccer with the ragged remains of a ball they found in a dumpster. The plan I'd signed up for specified that our mission was to entertain the kids, help them escape for a little while each day from the nightmare they were drowning in, and also try to teach them things like reading or writing. We'd brought a stack of reproductions of famous paintings with us, in imitation of the Pedagogical Missions the Spanish Republicans sent out around the time of the Spanish Civil War; the idea was that we were going to help the children appreciate the beauty of paintings by Hieronymus Bosch or Vincent van Gogh. I considered this aspect of our work hilarious and was constantly making sarcastic remarks about it, to the displeasure of the other members of my group, who were finding me harder and harder to take. Occasionally they'd ask, "What the hell are you here for, anyway?" And I'd shrug; any answer would have required a series of rhetorical gymnastics not worth wasting my energy on. And then, two months after my arrival, I quit. I said, "I can't do this anymore." I paid Virginia the fifty dollars I'd bet her that I would be able to hold out to the end and boarded a plane back to Spain, a few kilos lighter than on arrival and with a permanently atrophied sense of smell. Gallardo had left a week before, having finally found the little goddess he'd been after. One night the three of us had dinner together. The girl's face was dizzying: large green eyes, a mouth that cried out to be nibbled, a skinny body that would soon be developing into something more.

"You could fuck her today for a handful of change, muchacho, but a week from now an hour with this girl will be worth two thousand dollars plus expenses. Now that's what I call saving someone's life."

So Club Olympus scouts are lifesavers. I'm repeating the words to myself over and over right now as I talk to Nadim, who comes from Mauritania, has landed on this beach near Cádiz, and doesn't know what will become of her or whether to trust me; she wonders if she did the right thing by abandoning her group at the Guardia Civil station. She clutches the cup of coffee she's just been served, trying to warm her hands. She knows some English, so I don't need an interpreter. I give her a smile, but her face registers no response until I say, "And now?" I ask her whether she knows anyone in Spain, what her plans are— you know, a few preliminary questions just to pave the way. This was always the part I was worst at. I liked catching a piece; my adrenaline surged, and my heart pounded. But once the piece was in front of me and it was time to move on to the second phase of the capture, I would start to lose interest. Sometimes it was because what I really wanted was to keep the piece for

myself; other times I worried I wasn't going to be able to prove
that what I was doing was saving her life. And of course sometimes I resorted to pure fiction and brought the piece I'd captured
all the way back to the Club's branch office without giving her
the slightest notion of what kind of business she was getting
involved with. I once had to convince the young, chronically
unlucky mother of a skinny and adorable little Romanian boy I
found in a shantytown on the outskirts of Madrid that I was a
representative of the Barcelona soccer team and wanted to take
her son away with me to try out for the second string. I overcame
her qualms with a solid wad of euros, of course. "He doesn't
know how to play soccer, but they can always make him the
goalie," she said, as if inviting me to invent some other, more
convincing story; not that she was thinking of raising any objec-
tions to the sale of her son, but she felt obliged to demand a minimum of verisimilitude to help her deceive herself with some
semblance of credibility.

I took one of Nadim's hands, drawing it away from the coffee
cup. She let me. I gazed into her eyes. I said: "I'm here to help you.
I can help you. I have an offer to make you, and it's up to you to
decide whether or not to accept. If you accept, you'll come with
me and I'll arrange all the paperwork you'll need to stay here. If
not, I'll have to take you back to join the others, the Guardia Civil
will send you all back to your country, and you'll have to cross the
sea another time, hopefully with better luck than today."

As if to reprove me for having chosen this approach, my cell
phone rang. On the little illuminated screen appeared the word
Her. In my address book, that's the name for Carmen Thevenet,
aka the Doctor, aka the Big Boss Lady or the Thousand Eyes
That Never Blink.

"You're meeting me at the Hotel Reina Mercedes in Madrid
tomorrow at nine a.m.," she barked.

"Good evening," I answered.

"Drop whatever you're doing wherever you are and get started. This is a red alert, a very, very, very big deal."

"But I've just made a capture."

"Leave it where you found it. What is it this time, another shipwrecked girl? You're starting to get boring; you're slacking off. You're not going to get anywhere that way. On a scale of one to ten, how does your latest catch rate? Anything but a nine or a ten automatically fails."

I took a look at Nadim. Her eyes were lost on the motionless surface of her coffee which reflected a fragment of her face. No, she wasn't a ten or even a nine. Judging her by such exacting criteria, it could be that I'd chosen her because she was the most beautiful member of her group of shipwrecked refugees, but now that she was out of that context—though I'd have no problem selling her to the Club—she wasn't going to fetch the kind of astronomical prices that were paid to the Club's biggest stars. Only a little while earlier, I'd been thinking that Nadim was going to be one of my best and most celebrated catches. Now that conviction slowly deflated. I tried to imagine her in a sexy dress and could only see her as a degraded caricature, more like one of the whores who throng along Madrid's Paseo de la Castellana or the Alameda de Hércules in Seville than like a delicious, glittering star of the Club's firmament. I could almost hear the Doctor's voice upbraiding me for bringing her such a piece, scolding me for lowering the Club's standards of excellence, delivering one of her characteristic aphorisms such as, "The greatest scouts aren't the ones who bring in lots of vulgar pieces but the ones who extract only diamonds from the mud," or, "I'd rather have one diamond than a thousand tiny chips of gold that I'll never be able to melt into a single piece." However, I knew the Club's beauty experts were capable of transforming an apparently vulgar piece into a more than respectable imitation of a diamond. And Nadim wasn't vulgar; she was tall, her face was somewhat angular, she had large eyes and an intense gaze— which, however, inspired more tenderness than desire; the worst thing that can be said of the eyes of someone who wants to get into the Club is that they inspire tenderness. She might be a little too thin and would need to have some breast enhancement work done, but there was definitely a lot of potential. Finally I took a chance and said, "An eight and a half, but that's natural. I just took her off the beach; she's just been separated from the group she was shipwrecked with, and she must have had a boyfriend or a brother among them; she doesn't know where she is. She'll be a nine in a few days and a ten once you've taken charge of her."

"You're exaggerating," the Doctor said. "I'm sure you're exaggerating. With a heart as soft as yours, you'll never amount to anything. Are you sure she's not pregnant?"

"No. If she is, it doesn't show, so . . ."

"Right—we'll have to pay for an abortion on top of all the other fixing up she's going to need. Have you looked at her teeth?"

"Carmen, I only just sat down to have a coffee with her."

"Fine, then. Nine a.m. at the Reina Mercedes. If you want, you can bring her along, and if not, you can leave her where you found her. But get in the car right now and start driving."

I knew that if I took her to Madrid and the Doctor rejected her at first sight, I could still help Nadim out by taking her to the alternate club where I sent pieces I had scouted who couldn't stand up to the Club's severe examination. After the Doctor took over as head of the Club's Spanish branch, the requirements for approval rose considerably. Carmen Thevenet was a woman who brushed her teeth every night until her gums bled. Sometimes she'd stand there brushing for half an hour until she managed to extract a thread of blood. If a single detail can evoke the entire geography of a soul, that detail had, for me, come to represent the whole of the Doctor's soul. She also collected old books with uncut edges. When I discovered this, I found it highly implausible. I imagined that she bought books with uncut edges so she could enjoy the pleasure of slicing the pages apart with a knife; there are people who enjoy even stranger forms of relaxation. But not only did she collect books with uncut edges—the only collection of such books in the entire world, she liked to brag—she also read them without cutting the pages apart. Once, in a good mood, she explained how she did it. Every book consists of signatures of sixteen pages each. In a book with uncut edges, the only pages you can read are the first, last, and two middle pages of each signature: four out of sixteen. Those were the pages she would read. That is, in a 320-page book, the Doctor would read eighty pages. She would just invent whatever lay between—i.e., whatever was obscured from view by the joined edges of the pages. But, she explained, it was nothing at all like skipping pages just to get ahead. If she read a page where a man was cheating on his wife with the woman next door and then, after the inevitable skipping over of the uncut pages, the neighbor disappeared, Carmen would simply make up what happened in between; she would decide that the wife had killed the neighbor or that the neighbor had gone to India to spend the rest of her life caring for lepers.

The most curious and excellent part of this was that in other aspects of life, as well, Carmen continued to behave like a reader of books with uncut edges: she only wanted to read part of every story, preferring to invent the rest for herself, letting her imagination weave the links between the isolated facts she was given. She hated knowing everything; she always needed to be the coauthor. Though she was a little engine that could never stop churning out speech, she never said much about herself, or rather about her feelings, and she almost never talked about her years as a scout and her rapid rise up the Club's ladder before taking over as director of the Spanish branch. Nor did her ambitions end there, of course. She was pushing for a transfer to New York; Europe was too small for her. She had wild illusions for the future that seemed to come straight from the realm of science fiction. For example, she dreamed of a time when those who evoke desire in others might live off their royalties. That is, if you happen to masturbate while thinking about someone—a dancer, someone who walked past you in the street, a waitress in a nightclub, your teenage neighbor—that person would be paid for having lent his or her image to your desires, for having been used. How to go about collecting money for this didn't strike her as much of a problem; she argued that composers' royalties aren't paid out on a case-by-case basis but by more general criteria. I didn't understand her reasoning very well, but that was probably because I didn't care and the whole thing seemed so outlandish it wasn't worth discussing. In any case, this fantasy of hers about royalties for the objects of desire—"Just think!" she'd say. "You might get a nice little surprise at the end of the year. There you were thinking no one felt the slightest desire for you, and suddenly you get a statement detailing precisely how many people have jerked off thinking about you, for which you're entitled to such-and-such an amount of money. Wouldn't it be fantastic?"—was given concrete expression when she increased the price of the Club's models. She said that 70 percent of the price the Club charged was for the services that were actually rendered, and 30 percent was for the future desires those services would arouse. Because obviously, if someone hired one of the club's stars for an hour, he wasn't only going to spend one unforgettable, magnificent hour with that individual; his mental images of that session in the future, when he was alone, stroking himself with closed eyes, trying to recapture the sequence of burning movements that had driven him wild during the session. Those echoes or afterimages of that one, pricey session were covered by 30 percent of the set price for the piece he hired. "Image rights," she called this.

Sometimes she'd surprise you with a sharp turn of phrase, and you weren't sure whether she'd gotten it out of one of her uncut books or was actually trying to express, with her usual self-assurance, the vestige of some former bitterness she had long since laughed off. "I not only came to my marriage a virgin," she told me once, "but to my first experience of adultery, as well." And: "In a marriage, sex ends up being a legal form of incest, doesn't it? You start realizing that going to bed with your husband is like going to bed with your brother." And also: "For most men, copulation is just a more sophisticated form of masturbation." I never discussed any of these lines with her but smiled indulgently when she delivered them. The greatest gem of them all, the one I liked so much that I noted it down in a little book I used to carry around with me to jot my thoughts in—or rather, I began by jotting my thoughts in it and ended up using it to write down phone numbers and e-mail addresses—was: "Growing older consists of ceasing to fantasize about the future and resigning yourself to fantasizing about the past." She said this as a way of letting me know that was how she felt, and warning me to be on the lookout for the moment when my own decline would begin.

When I returned from Bolivia, still unsure what I was going to do—while keeping in mind that whenever I decided to I could use Gallardo's name to pay a visit to the Doctor and learn more about the Club Olympus—I didn't know if I was capable of putting together a photojournalism feature that some magazine might buy; nevertheless, I tried to find a publisher for my experiences as a volunteer in Bolivia. Among the many photos I brought back were a dozen fairly decent, publishable ones which I sent off to a number of magazines, accompanied by a lousy text about life, if you can call it that, on the garbage dump of La Paz. I was not at all confident that the article would be accepted anywhere, so I leaped for joy when I got a call from a weekly magazine that was thinking of publishing my work if I didn't want some ridiculous amount of money for it. For a few days, before falling asleep, I granted interviews as a legendary reporter, and when, over breakfast, my mother asked what I was thinking of doing with myself next, I told her I was planning another journey in search of a subject for a new photo essay.

I spent hours staring at my photographs printed in the pages of that magazine. I read and reread the pathetically inadequate text which the editors had barely altered. I relived vivid scenes on the La Paz garbage dump and set new challenges for myself; I tried to pay attention to what was going on in the world in the hope of discovering some geopolitical hotspot where I could take my camera for a visit. It was a strange period of my life, during which I considered myself capable of any feat, no matter how daring, as long as it would consume all my time for the next few months. The dark hours of my experience in Bolivia were entirely erased; all that was left were a few fragments of the story, the parts I could use to make the narrative seem heroic. I'd wrung those bits of narrative dry to make my fictions all the juicier, and now experienced them only as necessary and good; they caused me no pain at all—on the contrary, they nourished my vanity.

But the weeks went by and left me with nothing. I couldn't go on swinging through empty space pretending I was still savoring the sweet taste of one small and entirely forgettable success. The story about the Bolivian garbage dump had no echo anywhere, and if at certain moments between sleeping and waking I managed to convince myself that my phone would soon be ringing off the hook with pleas that I bring back news stories from exotic locales, the slow course of real life, the onerous burden of the present moment, and the stubborn muteness of my telephone persistently put the lie to my exalted desires. No one at the other end of the line wanted anything from me.

The situation was a gold mine for my brother. "Our tireless foreign correspondent," he'd say when he saw me sprawled on the couch exhausted, toying with the remote control. My mother didn't pressure me but went on tackling her "little thing" as usual, at that point through a combination of working out and going to church. According to my brother, she was seeing someone; he wasn't sure if it was her personal trainer or the priest. He hoped it was the priest; an affair with a personal trainer would have been so tacky, so entirely in keeping with the most codified traditions of pornography. Whereas a priest seemed much grander, like the plot of a novel by Eça de Queiroz—something to make us proud of her. My father remained exclusively concerned with his team's standing in the play-offs and his efforts to prevent the economic crisis from affecting his company's profitability. He had long since made a rule (which he did not always keep) of avoiding any kind of dispute with my mother, but sometimes, when she insisted he do something to help his sons find work, even if it was only a job as an errand boy for the company he ran, he would lose his temper and serve us up a lovely fairy tale, its main character a boy whom no one ever helped and who always had to make do for himself (my brother and I were delighted with the expression "to make do for oneself"; "I'm going to make do for myself," my brother would announce every time he headed for the bathroom), a boy who owed no thanks to anyone for anything. And that's what was going on in my life when I met Luzmila.

There I was, driving at night with soft music on and a beautiful woman stretched out on the backseat trying to sleep, her memory thronging with images like wounded soldiers who know they're about to die and whose only desire is to kill before sacrificing themselves. Engulfed in a darkness that adhered to the car's windows like a giant decal, Nadim and I proceeded toward Madrid, following the stubby beams of the headlights that seemed to invent the road as they went along. She climbed into the car as if she were entering a cell she knew she wouldn't be able to leave until she'd lived through many a nightmare and made many a scratch on the damp wall to mark the death of yet another day. I had already come to know the anguished sadness of that gaze very well; I looked for it in the faces that posed for me, I loved to photograph it, and when I saw it gleaming in the darkroom's shadows, my heart would beat faster and I'd take it out of the tray and hang it up with a clothespin to dry and stand there hypnotized by that beautiful, poignant sadness, all races and ages united in the brotherhood of its glitter. I drove along without wondering why the hell the Doctor wanted me so urgently, simply enjoying the soothing music; whenever I got tired of its melancholy rhythm I'd give the radio a try, the airwaves filled with the late-night confessions of lonely hearts, retired old men no one ever visited, teenagers whispering into the receiver so as not to wake up their parents, people with problems who'd been waiting all day to make this call, waiting all day for the microphones to open so they could finally talk about a pain that was gnawing at their soul, an experience they could no longer keep buried in the deep, dark cellar where we all hide the stories we cannot bear.

I wasn't worried about what would happen to Nadim; as far as I was concerned, she was saved and I had saved her. Even if all I'd been able to do in the end was abandon her to her fate on the streets of Madrid, I would have left her better off than I'd found her, and consequently would have served as her bridge toward that better place to which we all aspire. As the car's headlights went on swallowing up the kilometers, I sometimes found myself trying to imagine Nadim's story. Every piece I've ever scouted, including the ones who got away, are the bearers of monumental stories. Sometimes the air in those stories is fetid and sickening; at other times there are epic feats that are hard to speak of without waxing grandiloquent or implausible, but there's always a sadness in their ascending stairways, a sadness that pervades everything. There is always despair on those playgrounds, be they minefields or rat-infested garbage dumps or vast beaches where the slap of the waves is like a torturer's chuckle.

Someone on the radio was telling a story that was as sensational as it was engrossing—something about a man and a woman who were lovers when they were both twenty, then stopped seeing each other, and then, a long, long while later, were both killed in the same car accident, a headlong collision with each other. I thought about that story, trying to envision the characters' faces, trying to imagine what the two lovers had told themselves in the seconds before they crashed into each other. And I remembered that after my brother picked up the expression *omniscient narrator* from somewhere, probably from my mother—every time she acquired some new bit of knowledge, she tried to transplant it into her daily life to keep it alive in her mind—whenever anyone asked him what he wanted to be when he grew up, he would always reply, "An omniscient narrator." That was what I wanted to be: an omniscient narrator. I wanted to slip into the story Nadim was telling herself and copy it down here. It was a futile aspiration, of course, and yet somehow legitimate; maybe I simply wanted to vindicate my actions or was still trying to prove to myself that what I was doing was more than a terse slogan and indeed, nothing less than an irrevocable command: after all, my job is to save lives.

I made the decision eight or nine months after I came back from Bolivia. It had nothing to do with my personal salvation or some need to show that I did indeed possess the calculating mind, cold blood, and lack of all feelings and scruples that my brother celebrated in me, my mother reproached me for, and my father viewed as convincing proof that it was unlikely I was any son of his. After publishing my story on the La Paz garbage dump, I tried to come up with a few others; the good thing about journalism is that anyone who has figured out how to disguise his own inadequacies can do it. It's the same in art: the fact that you don't know how to paint doesn't mean you can't earn a living as a painter. But my inadequacy was that I was too imaginative. I thought, as I walked through the city—which was what I did with my time, mostly—that I could put together a nice little photo essay about war without ever leaving Seville. Without ever leaving my native city, I could disguise myself as a war correspondent and take pictures of places that looked as if they'd been bombed, people who appeared to have been cast into total poverty after airplanes had dumped their shit onto them. Tramps with empty gazes, facades hiding vast fields of rubble where junkies pretended to be alive, forsaken old women with a raging fire stuck to the palms of their hands, people come from real wars to exchange their university degrees for a piece of cardboard hanging around their necks that asked for help in broken Spanish. I spent the last money I had developing a hundred shots of chilling places I'd found in the center of the city. The overall impact was devastating: there was a war going on, these peoples' eyes spoke of it, the conditions they were living in proved it; all you needed was a fake caption, all you had to do was write Grozny where truth dictated you should put Seville. I was particularly struck by one of the girls whose picture I took; she was speaking to the customers of an outdoor café with an angry look on her face, as if she were demanding they give her money for food. When I got a little closer, I realized that her face was incalculably beautiful. Her accent sounded vaguely Italian, but Italy is not a country that currently vomits its poor out across the earth so I guessed she was Romanian. I was mistaken. She was Albanian. Her name was Luzmila. I swear that at that moment, when I offered her twenty euros if she'd let me take her picture against the battered walls of a building falling to ruin, the thought of Gallardo and the Club Olympus never crossed my mind. For once I was too concerned with sticking to a plan to muddle my head with enthusiasm for other possibilities.

I mean that I had made it very clear to everyone at home what I wanted to be, what I was going to do with my life, what I was going to put my energies into. I was twenty-four years old, and the time had come to make a decision. I made several. I decided to start living with Paola, a girl who'd been coming on to me since before I went to the garbage dump and who made a living teaching English at a language school. I wasn't sure whether things would work out with her or not, but I knew for a fact I'd be better off with Paola than with my parents. When the photo essay on the fake city at war was ready, I showed it to several editors,

and for once they were all in splendid unanimity: they rejected
the story and accused me of fraud. A few of them recognized one
or another of the beggars; another lived right next to one of the
buildings I'd photographed; another tried to convince me he was
impressed with my bravery but then claimed to have published
something about Grozny only recently; he hadn't understood the
point of the piece. All right, I told myself, there's no reason to
lose heart. And Paola told me, all right, don't lose heart; they're
looking for someone in the neighborhood to coach a junior soccer team; there's not much money in it, but it isn't a lot of work,
either. My father was sure to be delighted when he learned how I
intended to make a living. At first he'd say nothing at all, limit-
ing himself to the almost imperceptible twitch of the lips that was
as close to a smile as he ever came. Then, a while later, out of the
blue, as he was peeling an orange or scratching his head or filling
his pipe with tobacco, he'd come out with it: "All coaches of junior and children's leagues are pedophiles, and they all end up in
trouble for abusing some child."

One thing was certain: I was starting to resign myself to my
fate and get over the fact that my catalog of heroic deeds
recorded no experience worth recounting besides those months
spent on the garbage dump as a saintly artist without borders
trying to coax a smile out of some poor child. If it occurred to
anyone to ask me why the hell I'd wasted my time studying theater arts, I'd reply that my initial aim was to become a politician,
a mayor, an arts manager, or something like that, for which you
had to know more about theatrics than about political science. I
never went to auditions or anything like that. I went on taking
pictures, but they were all of junior soccer matches—and I swear
I never snapped a single shot in the locker room. But in the end
it all came crashing down around me, all of a sudden, on a single
afternoon.

For the moment, however, I'm starting to feel drowsy. Madrid is still a long way off, and I've decided to stop somewhere and get some sleep. I'm in luck. I pull off the motorway at the next town and soon find a cheap place to stay. I leave Nadim stretched out in the backseat to give her an opportunity: if she wakes up and decides to escape, she can go ahead and do it; it will be easy. All she has to do is open the door, get out of the car, and walk off into the streets of this town on a solitary adventure that will take her through a labyrinth of inglorious scenes to some police station or into the tentacles of some mafia that will ultimately deposit her in the Casa de Campo park in Madrid, wearing nothing but a pair of tanga panties accessorized with a cheap little purse to conceal the switchblade she plans on using to defend herself against any hypothetical assailant. The room smells of disinfectant, and the bed receives me with a groan of its ancient springs. I know I'm not going to get much sleep. For some time now I've been suffering from a psychological breakdown that has chosen to reveal itself in a very comical way: itching. As soon as I lie down, my testicles start to itch. Go ahead and laugh; you have every reason to. It's a tragic situation that no dermatologist has been able to do anything for. They prescribe painkillers, tranquilizers, creams, but nothing helps. The itching starts up no matter what. I've started to call it "my little thing"; I have no other name to give it. I've accepted the fact that it's a punishment, that I'm being punished, and of course it could hardly be more significant that my guilt has chosen to manifest itself down there.

Whenever I'm running late or have no idea where I'm going, I apply a strategy that yields excellent results. I imagine it's the same one almost everybody resorts to in those situations, though I've never heard anyone else own up to it, perhaps because some might consider it childish or absurd. Here it is: I begin by choosing a random pedestrian who happens to be walking a hundred meters or so ahead of me and transform him or her into a runner who's that far in the lead in the last leg of an Olympic track event. I then do my best to get ahead of my opponent before reaching a point I've designated as the finish line before starting the race. Should my fellow pedestrian veer off the established course, rather than proclaiming myself the winner I simply choose another opponent and a different finish line.

On the afternoon that brought my tidy little life as Paola's consort to an end, I needed to calm down a bit and couldn't think of anything better than an Olympic finale to cool down the anguish that was scalding my chest. I chose a blue spot in the distance and decided its nationality was German, I'm not sure why. I clenched my teeth, selected the end of Avenida Menéndez Pelayo, about eight hundred meters away, as the finish line, and quickened my pace. To give you a clearer notion of my innocent pastime, I should confess that while I'm pursuing this fellow pedestrian, rising to meet my own challenge and fully intent on

wresting the gold medal in the fifteen-hundred-meter race from
my opponent, I entertain myself and safeguard my mind from
injurious thoughts by taking on a heroic identity—my country's
last hope of winning the lone medal that will salvage the honor
of our national team. An inner voice broadcasts the race, spurring
on the runner: me. Of course another part of the spectacle is the
wild cheering of the crowd, waving my nation's flag and rooting
for me like mad.

The girl I needed to pass had short hair and was wearing sneak-
ers and beat-up jeans. At that point I was only sixty-five meters
away from her but hadn't yet noticed that she was Luzmila. I still
had more than five hundred meters to go before reaching the stoplight that marks the end of Menéndez Pelayo, one of Seville's main
thoroughfares, which is lined with two rows of trees that yield at
the avenue's end to the sudden greenness of the Murillo gardens.
There I was, swiftly overtaking other pedestrians who were stroll-
ing along with annoying calm as if they weren't even in a race,
forgetting all my troubles, no longer lost in treacherous illusions,
fully concentrated on the race, absorbed in the announcer's empha-
tic second-by-second commentary and the spectators' cheers. Every
time I passed another person my feat was jubilantly celebrated by
the inner voice that had exclusive broadcasting rights, and the fans
would go through the roof, ceaselessly urging me on, applauding
louder and louder, chanting my name.

The gap between me and the German was closing. Soon she
was only about thirty meters ahead. That was when I realized
who it was I was pursuing. Then something happened that made
everything much more difficult. Luzmila looked around and
noticed me among all the people on the street, and suddenly she
seemed to remember that she was late for wherever she was
going, and began walking faster, which the voice broadcasting
the race took as evidence that our opponent had noticed her

victory was jeopardized by my breakneck rush forward. The change of pace and the fact that the girl had spotted me forced me to speed up even more. Of course I also wondered: she recognized me, so why is she running away? Perhaps she thought the photos I'd shot of her hadn't come out as well as I had hoped and I was chasing her to request another session or make her give back the money I'd paid her. Despite her stepped-up speed, I managed to get right behind her, so that I could easily have stretched out my arm, touched her, and said, "Hey, don't you remember me?" The stoplight was still two hundred meters away.

Just as I was about to pass her, with the crowd roaring my name and the medal's welcoming sparkle winking at me from the platform next to the finish line, just as I was about to pull up alongside her on the left and sprint forward to an easy victory, she surprised me by speeding up even more and keeping me from closing in. I didn't say a word; I wasn't even looking at her now. She didn't look at me, either. She was going to make me pay dearly for my victory; she seemed to want to make things hard for me, as if she somehow knew we were fighting for a gold medal and the top position on the platform and the honor of listening to your own national anthem with your hand on your chest as the flags rise during the ceremony.

The inner broadcaster was now practically strangling as he shouted me on, urging me not to give up, not to let our nation's only chance at a gold medal slip through my fingers, not to let the Albanian—but wasn't she German? Someone asked the announcer, and he explained, "No, there was a mix-up; she's Albanian, Albanian"—win, and the crowd was on fire, screaming and clamoring, the whole stadium on its feet, though I was no longer sure whether they were celebrating the fact that I was neck and neck with Luzmila or that Luzmila had reacted and was going to make it hard for me and not let herself get beaten. After all, Albania had yet to win an Olympic medal, either.

We covered a long stretch of ground side by side, like two impeccably trained soldiers on parade. The Albanian girl was watching me, and I was watching her; we were gauging each other's strength, each keeping an eye on the other without losing sight of the stoplight that marked the finish line. I was on the verge of stopping her, telling her everything, and having a good laugh with her about my whole Olympic nonsense, but how would she react to a story as lame as that, and in any case, what could I possibly say? That utter ruin had just befallen me? That only a short while earlier I had discovered that my girlfriend had a handsome lover and that my favorite TV series, *Frasier*, had just been canceled? And that in order to drive this avalanche of misfortunes from my mind, I had invented a race and happened to make her my opponent, and hadn't been able to stop trying to beat her even after I realized I knew her, and her pictures had come out beautifully and I'd like to show them to her and give her a couple to keep?

Please don't imagine that there was any connection between the three factors that were playing a role in my distress. Setting aside *Frasier*, which was nothing more than the straw that broke the camel's back, the truth is that if utter ruin had befallen me, it was because Paola was getting it on with the former coach of the junior soccer team. I had no idea how long they'd been seeing each other—possibly even since before I moved in with her. I'd often had a beer with her lover in the bar where I used to wait for Paola in the evening after her classes. He was forty-something and sold cars, though he acted as if he were about to buy the Volkswagen corporation itself with a little ready cash he happened to have. Despite the hair gel, the smile straight out of an ad for unbreakable dentures, the many hours spent in the gym buffing his abdominals, and the cosmopolitan charm of his lengthy digressions—about the Amsterdam house pulleys that are used for lowering coffins; the loudspeakers on the cars in Palermo that are constantly blaring because a red light in that city is not so much a command as a suggestion; the Cuban women who perform the *centrifugado,* a wildly exotic sexual practice requiring extremely fast hips; the hundred thousand palm trees of Tozeur; and many other things he'd learned firsthand and not during a prolonged perusal of travel magazines—I liked him just fine. Anyway, I gave this master of the universe wannabe an uppercut that dislocated his jaw; I guess his teeth weren't that indestructible after all. Paola jumped and then must have felt that the roof was caving in over her head because she covered her face and leaned forward as if the building were collapsing. "It's not what you're thinking," he murmured before I knocked him out. But obviously I wasn't thinking. "Calm down, don't be an idiot," she urged just before the sound of my fist cracking against her lover's face made her jump. My eviction was guaranteed, as was the coming hospital bill and the fine I'd be forced to pay by a verdict I'd have a tough time beating. The announcer's voice and the fervor of the spectators shaking the stadium bleachers inside me with their flags and their applause gave me renewed strength, driving me not to disappoint them, to go on. I'd convinced myself that the Albanian girl was my only enemy, the only being on the planet who stood between me and the thrill of victory. She was my disease, and I had to fight her, beat her. To lose would be to give in to death. I couldn't allow myself to be defeated; I'd already lost too many things: Paola, a place to live, my favorite TV show. The stoplight was only a hundred meters away.

As a boy I occasionally indulged in certain trivial superstitions. Before an English exam, for example, I'd look at one of the shelves in the living room and make myself a dare: if you can guess the number of books on this shelf, it means you'll pass the exam. And I would guess a number, and if I was right, I was convinced there was no longer any need to study until the wee hours. I couldn't possibly have hit on the exact number of books by pure chance. My correct guess was a sign from God that any further rubbing of my elbows against my desk would be a waste of time; the exam was in the bag already, even before I took it, and this was guaranteed by the books on the shelf, whose number I had precisely determined. I don't know why I remembered those youthful superstitions as I pressed on, determined to get ahead of the Albanian girl, who was doing all she could to make sure I didn't. And of course I knew it was extremely stupid of me to succumb to the notion that if I did manage to win the gold medal in the end, it would mean I'd soon find a job that paid much more than working as a junior soccer coach; Paola would leave her lover and give me some acceptable explanation for what happened; and they'd start running *Frasier* once again.

I was blinded by the absurd certainty that what the Albanian girl really wanted—as if she were fully aware of all that was going on inside me—was not to let me get ahead, not to let me win, not to give me the pleasure of taking my revenge on all the things that were turning out so badly. She knew I'd been betrayed, that I was going to have to face criminal charges, perhaps she even knew my girlfriend's lover, and in any case she was clearly overjoyed that they'd taken *Frasier* off the air. She knew I'd said to myself, as before that English exam, OK, here goes: if you can win this race, you'll melt the pain that's freezing your chest, you'll find another job where they'll pay you much more money, Paola is replaceable—in fact you've never loved her, and there's no reason to be hurt that she deceived you; she'll beg your forgiveness, and you'll tell her to go to hell because you're going to meet someone else, someone much better, someone who will never deceive you—and *Frasier* will soon return to your television screen.

How was that possible? I don't know. There are times when your mind is cluttered with too many things, your head is a storehouse of ridiculous ideas—mirrors reflecting other mirrors—and the commotion of your thoughts keeps you from isolating any one of them; they're all enveloped by a sticky plastic substance that transforms them into a single viscous mass. I thought of Paola's body convulsed with pleasure beneath her lover, maybe in the same bed I'd been sleeping in for the last several months, or in improvised love nests to make their passion all the more adventurous: café restrooms, hotel phone booths, dimly lit garages. I also thought about my résumé, carefully sealed in a padded envelope and sent off to the human resources directors of many companies. And I thought about how wonderful it used to be when ten p.m. finally rolled around, and after a frugal dinner in the kitchen, Paola and I would plop down in front of the TV and wait for the next episode of *Frasier* to begin. And I thought about how ridiculous this whole situation was and why the Albanian girl wasn't letting me pass her and all the factors that were driving me to beat her in that race. And I thought about the invisible audience jammed into the stadium inside me, and the announcer who never stopped exhorting me as he relayed every moment of the race. And I thought about how certain pedestrians are superstitious, and if they notice that someone's about to pass them, they walk faster to keep anyone from getting ahead of them; for people like this, having someone get ahead of them on the street is like having a black cat cross in front of them or spilling salt on the table. There are some pedestrians who are always ready to start a race and who will give their all before they let some stranger outwalk them. Maybe the Albanian girl belonged to that breed, maybe her zeal had nothing to do with reaching any given point before I did, catching up to some other pedestrian she'd selected as her own opponent, or even beating me to make it very clear that I wasn't going to find a better job than the one I'd just been fired from, that Paola had left me for good, and that I could kiss *Frasier* good-bye forever. Maybe all she wanted was not to feel that anyone had gotten ahead of her.

Then suddenly, we both passed an old man who wasn't exactly hobbling along himself—I on the left, Luzmila on the right—and she slowed down and finally let me get ahead, just twenty meters from the finish line. It took me a moment to notice my privileged position because I'd decided to go into the home stretch of the race with my head down to isolate myself from everything except the uproar of the crowd clamoring for my victory. As soon as I noticed I'd pulled ahead, I was completely dumbfounded. I felt like stopping, waiting for her, and asking her why the hell she'd made me sweat by refusing to let me get ahead of her for so long, only to let me pass her just a few meters from the finish. Despite my imminent triumph, which was already being cheered in the stands and trumpeted by the announcer, I wasn't happy. As the crowd chanted my name and waved their flags, I took a backward glance and immediately understood everything.

Luzmila's face, as she pulled ahead of the elderly man, bore the unmistakable expression of one who has accomplished what she set out to do: pass the old man who was trying not to let her. He was her competitor, and the finish line selected by my Albanian acquaintance—who may not have been representing Albania in her race against the old man; perhaps she, too, was representing Spain, and this was her way of feeling as if she belonged here, welcomed, with all her papers in order, a star athlete, and perhaps she, too, was cheered on by thousands of spectral voices inside her head and by an energetic and supportive announcer—may have been the striped awning of the candy store we'd just passed, since that was where she slowed down, changed her rhythm, shortened her strides, and let me get ahead.

I kept going until I reached the stoplight, but no longer with any competitive urgency. I took another look behind me. Luzmila was walking along without looking at me. But between her and the old man a space of a few meters had opened up, into which, suddenly, as if from nowhere, a heavyset bearded man in a lumberjack shirt had appeared and was vaulting into a maneuver that would put him in the lead and leave her behind. I couldn't help it—of its own volition a cry erupted from me: "Watch out! Run, run!"

She gave me a look of fear, then turned around and saw the lumberjack gaining on her, his jaws clenched, his face contracted, his eyes squeezed almost shut. She started to run. The bearded guy was completely bewildered. She crossed against the light, was almost run over by a car, and had to dodge two motorbikes that braked noisily to keep from plowing into her. This brought on a whole musical interlude of protesting honks. But she reached the other side safe and sound and from there turned around again to look at us, at the bearded guy and me, standing next to each other now, waiting for the light so we could cross. Then she started running again. The beard wanted to know what in Christ's name was going on, *coño,* so I told him. I told him it was nothing, that I'd been fired for beating up a coworker and breaking his jaw and that the coworker I beat up was fucking Paola and that on top of everything else the TV had stopped running *Frasier.* He didn't say a word. Another crackpot, he thought. The old man was about to reach the stoplight, too. When it turned green, the beard, still keeping a corner of his eye on me, whether out of compassion or suspicion I don't know, went on with his walk, quickening his rhythm. There were a lot of people on the street, and he wasn't going to have the slightest trouble finding some opponent in the distance to compete against in his own Olympic finale.

I didn't cross. I walked up to Carlos Quinto and dropped into the Café Oriza to display my shiny gold medal to a couple of gin and tonics, a gold medal that meant nothing, that couldn't possibly mean I would find another job, or that Paola would decide not to leave me just when I needed her more than ever, or, of course, that a new episode of *Frasier* would be televised that night. No, it didn't mean any of those things, and correctly guessing how many books were lined up on a shelf in the living room never meant that I didn't need to study in order to pass an exam either; whenever I let myself get carried away by one of those idiotic certainties and put it to the test to confirm or refute the invisible and secret relationship between correctly ascertaining the number of books on a shelf and passing an exam I hadn't studied for—I failed the exam.

But that black afternoon held a breath of fresh air in store for me, a bit of relief, a small but adequate ray of light: Luzmila. I was sitting in the café window feeling like a vintage toy on display in the window of an antique shop, occasionally noticed by passers-by in the street, some of whom would stop and have a look at the price tag hanging around my neck, then gesture that the price was too high and continue on their way. No one was going to buy me. Suddenly a shadow fell across my face. The Albanian girl was standing in front of me like a waitress impatient for me to give her my order and stop looking at a menu I wasn't going to choose anything from.

She said: "Coca-Cola. You buy me."

I grinned. A slight dilation of my pupils must have expressed my surprise at seeing Luzmila there before me with her green eyes and her smile, which looked as if she were wearing it for the first time, and her hands with their long fingers and dirty nails, and the little tattoo that illustrated her shoulder with a boat floating atop a wave that was no more than a scribble of green ink. We had absolutely nothing to say to each other, but our conversation lasted into the early hours of the morning. First in the café, then in a plaza where elderly men were feeding pigeons and a cat lurked behind a tree waiting for a pigeon to stray his way so that he could have some dinner too, then at the back door of a hotel while we hung around waiting for the containers with the day's leftover food to come out—which was how Luzmila managed to get something to eat every night. A crowd of undocumented immigrants, old men living on tiny pensions, and beggars would gather to squabble over a few stale croissants or some cold cuts, or a bag of bruised apples or peaches on the verge of spoiling. After Luzmila had treated me to dinner—we managed to get our hands on some slices of sausage and a few rolls—we headed off to a different plaza, where the noisy fountain was shut off at the stroke of midnight. In her Spanish full of mistakes and Italian words, she was filling me in on brief episodes of a shadowy story: a violent father, total poverty, violent brothers, a mother who hung herself, violent neighbors, impregnable mountain landscapes. "Am sure someone made movie about it," she said to sum up her tragedy and merge it with that of the thousands of her compatriots who'd started walking one day to see if they could reach a port where they could hide out on a ship that would take them anywhere away from there. And yes, that movie had been made; I saw it a few days later, once I was reinstalled in my parents' house—"There's only one thing worse than a junior soccer coach," the old man told me, "and that's a junior soccer coach who's living with his parents." When they found the corpse in the packed truck that was carrying the Albanians like so many cattle to a port where there was some hope of a ship bound for Italy, I broke down again and started in with the sobbing, but this time not even my mother showed any concern; she didn't even toss me a blanket to help me get warm. "That boy's coming to a bad end," my brother opined. "I'm warning you now so you can buy yourselves something nice for the funeral."

That night, in an unlit park where the city's heavy breathing sounded like a monster fallen asleep after a hard day, Luzmila said, "For hundred euros I let you fuck me. For fifty, I suck you. Sodomy, no."

The words, of course, stunned me, even if only because after using no euphemisms to say what she meant, she suddenly used a proper word instead of the expression that fit the tone of the rest of the phrase. She didn't say "in the ass"; she said "sodomy." Luzmila was demonstrating her enviable capacity for mastering a language and speaking it as if it were her own natural tongue; in a very short time she went from broken Spanish full of mistakes and words on loan from Italian to fluent, crystalline Spanish, all too sharp and clear, in which she was even capable of coining unexpected puns. I smiled and asked if she often had sex for money or if this was a special gift she was giving me because of the time we'd spent together. And it was my obviously stupid question that made me remember Gallardo and the Club Olympus, and gave me the idea that if I took Luzmila to see them, two lives could be improved at one fell swoop: hers and mine. Hers, because, after all, if she was turning the occasional trick anyway, there was nowhere else her beauty would earn as much for her as in the Club, and it was sheer waste for her to sell herself cheap on the Alameda de Hércules to be had by nobodies with no funds whatsoever invested in the stock market; and mine, because I was giving myself a splendid opportunity to harmonize two vital impulses: that of helping others and that of saving myself, or rather, that of saving others and that of helping myself. I accept and admit that this rationale was no more than a passing and none too convincing way of placating my own churning stomach, but deluding yourself in order to move forward is a strategy the heroes of every age have always practiced, with little heed for the fact that the lie they take as their mandate only conceals the extent of their own powerlessness, emptiness, and dissatisfaction; the pole you use to make this vault is the least of it.

In the small hours of the morning after my nocturnal outing with Luzmila, I fell asleep in the doorway of my parents' apartment building. I could have gone inside—keeping the key to your parents' house is a transparent sign that you don't want to separate entirely, because of what might happen, and from the time I was a boy to the present, even today, the first thing I say when I wake up in the morning is my name, my age, and my parents' address, an apartment where no one I know now lives—but I decided I'd rather stay at the foot of the stairs. If some early rising neighbor found me there, I'd tell him I'd forgotten the keys and didn't want to wake anyone up. The bad thing was that the first early rising neighbor was my father, who said nothing but "Ah, the return of the idiot son. If you'd joined the military, your life would have gone better." I never thought of asking him what the hell he meant by that; I just climbed the stairs and collapsed onto the living room sofa.

Later, at noon, having eaten breakfast across the table from my mother, who observed me without saying a word but sighed from time to time and looked away whenever I tried to meet her eye, I phoned Paola to make note on her answering machine of the fact that I'd stop by to pick up my things later that afternoon. My things were a few books, a few CDs, my camera, and a few framed photos. I asked my mother if I could borrow her car.

"What about your car?" she said.

"It wasn't my car; it was Paola's."

During that period my mother had enrolled in a bookbinding class at the Women's Center. She went to class three times a week, primarily to chat with other women who, like her, were less interested in bookbinding than in meeting women who would listen to them talk in exchange for being listened to themselves. My mother had come up with the idea of using clothes she no longer wore to bind books she was no longer going to read.

She converted an old blouse she didn't want to throw away—because it brought back the scent of who knows what afternoon or what solitary, nocturnal stroll through some city while my father slept in a hotel room that was obviously far too grand for the two of them—into the jacket that covered the life and death of Madame Bovary. The checked fabric of a skirt that was way out of style and that she wouldn't have been able to wear anyway without some liposuction to shrink her hips was used as a binding for *Jane Eyre*. Between the books my mother dressed in her most cherished clothes and my father's collection of biographies of the widows of legendary men—this was his obsession: curiosity about the lives of the women whom History's great men chose to marry—the bookshelves in our home were becoming eccentric enough to warrant nomination for that anthology of human idiocy, that Sacred Book of our time, the *Guinness Book of World Records*.

"If I were you, I'd keep it. I'd leave the books there, and the CDs and of course the photos, too, along with those clothes you shouldn't be wearing anyway, and that murderous dog of yours, and I'd keep the car. That's what I'd do. With that car you can start over again from scratch anywhere you want to, but with that dog and those pictures you take, *hijo*, there's no way to get ahead; there just isn't."

The dog wasn't mine either. It was a rottweiler that Paola called Paolo and I called Omniscient Narrator. I imagined our story as narrated by that animal which in just a few months had gone from a sweet little puppy into a monster whose blazing eyes sent you recoiling against the ropes. Of course Paola must have listened to my message and given Omniscient Narrator strict orders not to let me take anything from the house. She hadn't had time to change the lock, but with that beast prowling around on guard she didn't need to. The moment I stuck my key in, a growl warned me I wasn't welcome. I spoke a warm word or two by way of greeting, but the dog's gaze reached an immediate verdict that launched his entire body at me, his jaws stretched wide in the attack position. I barely had time to hide in the bedroom to the right of the hallway, where, in fact, almost all the things I was going to rescue, the camera and a few photos, were to be found. Paola could keep the books in the living room and the CDs in the den. The problem was how to get out of the bedroom while evading Omniscient Narrator. Jumping out the window was a little risky; not only was the apartment on the seventh floor, but there was a small park down below where the youngest children in the neighborhood played on the swings, fought with each other, or simply got themselves dirty in order to give meaning to their mothers' lives. From the other side of the door came the sound of Omniscient Narrator's vigilant breathing; I could practically feel his eyes boring through the wood to meet mine. And then I remembered that the bar and weights Paola used for her morning workout were under the bed. Lying on her back, she would do a hundred thirty-kilo lifts, then fifty sit-ups, then another fifty push-ups, then she'd hop into the shower. I squatted to feel around for the bar, which I thought would be more than sufficient to keep the dog away from me on my way out the front door. I wondered if I should use one of the weights as well, one of the ten-kilo weights, and maybe throw it at his head if he didn't get the message while I was using the bar to keep him at a safe distance. But it turned out to be hard to carry so much stuff: my camera, the pictures, the bar, and the weight. I decided to put my plan to the test, step out the door with just the bar, and see what happened. If I managed to intimidate the dog and force him back until I could shut him in the bathroom or the kitchen or wherever, then I could calmly return and collect my things. But no sooner did the door open than Omniscient Narrator had his muzzle inside and was growling—conclusive evidence that things were going to turn violent however hard I tried to keep us on the path of dialogue. I spoke to him through the door and received only silence for an answer. He didn't even growl; the dumb beast was trying to make me think he'd left his post. It was clearer than water that Omniscient Narrator was capable of chewing up that steel bar as an appetizer before proceeding to devour one of my legs. If my reflexes were quick, the best I could hope for was to grab the doorknob and start screaming through the keyhole so the neighbors would at least take note of my death and could then say a few words about the sinister event when the TV reporters showed up in quest of a touch of vivid yellow to cap off the nightly news. OK, I was going to risk it with the weight. Not the ten-kilo; the most I could hope for with that one was to raise a little bump on the dog's monstrous head. It would have to be the twenty-kilo. With luck, if I managed to hit him on some funny bone that would addle his brain for an instant and render it incapable of issuing orders, I'd reach the doorway to salvation with my camera—my interest in recovering the framed photos was gone. Brandishing the round twenty-kilo weight, I opened the door a crack, keeping my foot pressed against it as a brake against the dog's onslaught, which came without delay. Around came the muzzle, the wide-open snout displaying the lacerating edges of the teeth. I told myself: no, it's too soon, it's too soon. I moved my foot a few *millimeters* away from the door, and now Omnisicient Narrator's enormous head appeared. I think there was one instant when I knew he was going to kill me and I shouted to myself over an interior loudspeaker that set every cell in my body on fire: YOU'RE AN IMBECILE. As I was passing that judgment, I dropped the twenty-kilo weight on the dog's head. It knocked him out immediately. To tell the truth, I was a little disappointed. I didn't count to ten. As soon as I'd verified that his belly was still rising and falling, I picked up the twenty-kilo weight again and finished the job, mouthing a couple of insults at Omniscient Narrator in the bargain. This really was the way to begin a new life: leaving a dead dog behind you. Back in the car, after having gathered up all of my things—camera, photos, albums of negatives, books, CDs and videos, as well as a few clothes—I thought: the day you decided to start a new life, you were brutally attacked by your own dog.

Of course there was no way to fall asleep or resist the temptation to scratch. I tried to interview myself as a way of escaping from that cheap hotel room whose walls seemed to be moving in the darkness, as if seeking to bend down and give me a kiss that would pulverize my bones. Let's see, I said to myself, you're the first man to prove the existence of life beyond planet Earth, the interviewer is a stunning blonde, all smiles, who wants to know everything about your childhood and adolescence and how you managed to strike up a friendship with beings from the Dark Beyond, a stunning blonde who will gaze at you in bewilderment when the interview is over, for by then you'll no longer be the first man who's provided credible proof of intelligent life on other planets, but a mirror that distorts her features and shows her herself at her very worst, as she never wants to see herself again, as she feels herself to be on her very worst days when the world is a parade of senselessness where nothing is right and nothing is worth the trouble. Nothing.

The bad thing about these bedtime interviews is that the pretexts start deteriorating as you get older, along with the principle of plausibility, to which, like it or not, you have to render a minimum of respect, however free a rein you give your imagination. If you're fourteen years old and tell yourself you're an astronaut, well, OK; who's to say whether you just might not be the first man to set foot on Saturn? But if you give yourself an interview at twenty-five pretending to be the best goalie in the league, that's already a little flimsy and you have to work some sleight-of-hand to reconfigure your past so as to allow yourself to dream that you really did make it into the First Division. As you start closing in on thirty, your ability to grant an interview and project your highest hopes onto the future without correcting your past is already pretty limited, especially in my case. I can't even fantasize about becoming prime minister of Spain—how are you going to be prime minister of Spain when you've spent your life recruiting prostitutes? But despair makes your imagination more indulgent; after all, if a pair of extraterrestrials shows up and chooses you as the only human being to whom they will give convincing proof that not only do they in fact exist but they also spend all their time fucking like porn stars—such a thing could happen to anyone, at any age: fifteen, twenty, or fifty. But, as I said: nothing.

There it was, concentrated on the left side of my groin, the itching, which showed up like clockwork thirty seconds after I stretched out in bed at night—strangely enough, when I lay down for an afternoon siesta I never had any problem—an infallible reminder that something had gone wrong in my psyche and that I wasn't going to be able to repair the breakdown with one Atarax or even two. I got up and cursed my fate. I couldn't even wait for morning in the hope of eventually losing consciousness; by dawn I would already have been on the road for an hour on my way to Madrid. At least when I stood up the itching grew more bearable and the walls stopped moving. I looked out the window. The lightbulb above the entrance to the hotel glinted off the chassis of my car. I was so tired I thought I might be able to fall asleep with my forehead pressed against the window's dirty glass. The itching was better now, but I knew if I lay down it would start up again with a vengeance. There was no solution. Sometimes I scratched so ferociously that I broke the skin, and then it got even worse, the stinging made me curse my own rage and lack of self-control, and the resulting sores didn't just fuck up my life when I lay down in bed at night like the itching; instead I'd walk around at all hours of the day and night as if I'd been sodomized by Mazinger Z.

When the torture of the nightly itching first began, I would often try to gain some relief by masturbating. The comfort was fleeting, of course, but it allowed me about an hour's pleasant snooze, a temporary flight to some nebulous point from which I was quickly jerked back by the report from some thug's motorcycle, any little sound from the floor above, or a word my own voice spoke aloud from out of my light sleep. But itching is like rats, whose immune systems soon formulate an antidote to any kind of poison. The future of laboratories that create rat poison is assured; they know from the start that they won't be able to come up with a powder that can do away with the rodents for good. All I know is that not long after I started working in earnest for the Club Olympus—and by working in earnest I mean I stopped doing the other things I used to spend my time on and focused all my energy on the Club because it was paying me the kind of money I'd never dreamed of being able to earn without selling my soul for a pistol and holding up a bank—I had my first sexual crisis. To put it poetically, nothing and no one could give me an erection. Of course that did not cut down on my ability to recognize the beauty and distinction of a jewel in the mud; I'd never really adhered to Gallardo's definition of beauty anyway. It did force me to be more demanding, to imagine that if something hadn't malfunctioned in the circuitry of my soul, the piece I was after would arouse my appetite immediately. My statistics in the Club didn't suffer the same cataclysm that I was going through, so I didn't think it was necessary to discuss my problem with anyone there. And on the bright side: my lack of appetite made it certain I wouldn't tamper with the goods between the moment I discovered them and the moment I placed them in the Doctor's hands.

Suddenly the door of my car opened, and Nadim stepped out. Never for a moment did I think she was escaping. I preferred to imagine she was simply going off to pee. But the minutes went by, and she didn't come back. What the hell did she think she was going to do in that shithole of a town? The truth is, I felt wounded. After all, you invest a lot of yourself every time you scout someone whose life you intend to save, and I don't think that deserves to be repaid with a gesture like this, which no matter how you look at it is unfriendly. But after all, it was her life; she knew best. She'd end up working as a whore along the highway and get knifed one night, and no one would even bother trying to identify her corpse, which would be no more than another drop in the mighty ocean of crime against immigrants—an ocean that is ultimately rather convenient to the state, swallowing up as it does some portion of the flood of illegals. I went back to bed with my hand in my Calvin Kleins, pinching myself wherever I located a focal point of the itching, trying not to scratch in order not to inflame the skin, and suddenly, just before resting my head on the pillow, I remembered my Leica R8—value: thirty-two hundred euros—and the state of idiotic somnolence I must have been in when I left it in the glove compartment without a second thought. I pulled my pants on at top speed, then my shoes, forgetting all about the cigarettes on the night table and putting the bad scene of the bedtime itching behind me. A scare is a thousand times more effective than all the dermatological anxiolytics that all the world's laboratories will manufacture for the next thousand years; a scare immediately removes your hand from the afflicted area. Naturally the Leica R8 was no longer in the glove compartment. I'll kill her, I said. I'll kill her. But first I had to find her.

OK, hombre, I told myself as I started the car, let's see: maybe she wasn't planning to rob you at all; maybe she just wants to take a self-portrait and went off to look for a brighter streetlight. The idiot, I'm sure she'll sell it for a handful of change, I told myself, also. You're the idiot, I added: leaving the Leica in the car—God himself could not forgive you for that. When I start up these conversations with myself, I admit I lose much of my charm. In the end two or three turns around the sleeping streets of the town were all it took to prove that Nadim had been swallowed up by the earth, or by a helpful entranceway where she was probably curled up around my Leica at that moment. I stopped at a café that announced its presence with a sickly light over its peeling doors. They were just opening up; it was the typical small-town spot where local workers drank their breakfast anise before heading to the construction site. It struck me as perfectly plausible that the crazy immigrant might have decided to request political asylum in there and exchange my Leica for a coffee with rolls. The girl who waited on me had sleep glued to every curve of her lovely face. The kind of piece I would never have the nerve to try and pick up, I said to myself, the kind of piece that's out of the Club Olympus's range. Certainly if the girl had the kind of intelligence that in many, many people would win out over any scruples or family pressures, she would ultimately see that the future I was offering was a hundred times more dazzling than the one she already knew from memory, but then again I wouldn't be able to tell myself I'd saved her life, because her life was not in any danger and, compared to that of most inhabitants of her town, might really deserve to be called a life. In the end I ordered a coffee, made my inquiries, was answered with a no, loudly cursed all black people, and watched the girl stifle a yawn with her hand. The first customers came in, their voices loud in contrast to the ghostly silence outside. I hadn't stopped thinking about my Leica, and as if my thoughts had found some magical way of influencing reality, I saw it shining in the beefy hand of one of the men coming in. Without a moment's hesitation I said: "That's my camera. A black woman I picked up on the highway stole it from me, and I've been looking . . ."

"For the woman or the camera?"

"I've just found the camera. How much did you give her for it?"

"Ten euros, just what she needed."

I learned that Nadim had managed to reach the train station, where she was waiting for an express to Seville. I told the man we could settle this with or without police involvement; it didn't matter to me; I had all the time in the world and no further interest in the black girl's fate.

"Hey listen, you calling my friend a thief?" asked one of the other guys who was with him, the kind of midget who waxes bold when he knows he's protected by circumstances and two or three bored mountains of human muscle.

"Not for a moment," I said, without losing my calm, and even flashed a smile so he could see that I, too, knew how to be charming when I wanted to be. "Here's the story: I can prove to you that the camera belongs to me, I can prove it was stolen from me, I can prove a lot of things that you guys can't prove, and what I'm saying is that we can resolve this with or without the police, that is, either among ourselves, in which case you'll get your ten euros back, or else with the help of a few men in uniform, in which case you'll have to hand the camera over to me without getting your money back."

"Oh, a wise guy. We've got a wise guy at breakfast this morning," said the midget. The others laughed. I noticed one of them had two gold teeth, which led me to regret the approach I had chosen to take with this group. Customers kept coming into the café. The girl behind the bar didn't say a word, just served up what was ordered—or wasn't even ordered, since she knew in advance what everyone's usual was—and shot me a look from time to time, perhaps feeling sorry for herself.

"Ten euros?" said the man with the camera. "Who told you this cost me ten euros?"

"You did," I answered naively.

"You didn't hear me, hombre. I said a hundred euros. And I bought it thinking I could sell it to El Tito for at least two hundred. It's a good camera, hombre."

I didn't think twice. I said: "Great. One hundred euros, there you go; you've just earned yourself ninety euros in less than a minute, and I'm getting my camera back."

"Look, I'm in a hurry and I want my breakfast, so give me another hundred or leave me alone. You can go down to the police station if you like. Ask for Matías. He's my brother, and he's on duty right now; let's see what he has to say about this. If he tells me you're in the right, then that's fine; I'll take the hundred euros and give you the camera."

There was no arguing with that. Two hundred euros and breakfast for the whole gang, and the Leica was back in my glove compartment. As I was on my way out of that godforsaken town, I said *I'm not leaving it like this* and shifted the car to reverse. I asked a man on his way into the café for breakfast where the train station was, and he told me. And there was Nadim, lying on her back on a green bench where Carlos had engraved a message declaring his love for Raquel, Pedro had sworn that no one had nicer tits than Marta, and another individual who preferred to remain anonymous shat on the king of Spain, the Real Madrid, and a certain Channel 5 newswoman.

Nadim looked at me, and smiled a smile beyond all adjectives, a smile that made her even more beautiful. I took my Leica and captured that smile, which she held to make the task easier when she saw me aim the camera at her. Then she sat up, brought her knees under her chin, and circled them with her forearms. She was adorable, prettier than when I'd picked her up in the Guardia Civil station. I kept on shooting until I'd finished the roll. Then I looked inside my wallet; I had three ten-euro bills left. I gave them to her and wished her luck. And as I was walking away, I whispered, "I bet I'll see you someday in the Casa de Campo or along the Alameda de Hércules, but it will be too late then, far too late." I have one of those shots here, those huge eyes gazing at me from that remote dawn, with an old-fashioned innocence shining in them and that smile I cannot diminish with a single adjective.

The Doctor did not scold me for showing up half an hour late looking awful. She asked after the piece I'd scouted in the latest shipwreck, and since I didn't feel like telling her the whole story, I said the piece wasn't worth it; she was pregnant and missing two important teeth. She didn't believe me, of course, but let it pass. She knew me well, that woman, maybe too well for my own good. I remember the first day I ever sat down in her office, I thought that if I didn't end up kissing the ground beneath her feet, it would only be because she would insist on exempting me from any such display of gratitude. She treated me as if I were her son, a son with whom she wouldn't mind committing incest. She talked for quite a while about Gallardo, which was the magic word I had used to get her to meet with me; she called him a fool, a flatterer, a poor fellow, and a few other fine things such as Argentine, which in this case was a pejorative. No one would ever have guessed there had been a day when Gallardo found a new career for her that became her life's work. She was one of those women who flesh out every conversation with episodes from their lengthy biography. If you were starting to unwind while talking about your experiences on the La Paz garbage dump, she would cut you off immediately so you could relax while listening to an episode of her past. After a bit you'd start wondering: what does all this she's telling me have to do with the garbage dump? But by then it would be too late. What did you study in school? Theater arts? Well, she used to go out with a guy who earned a living working as a model in art classes—as if theater arts had anything to do with fine arts—which made her remember that the same guy ended up going off to Amsterdam, where she, of course, also once lived for a while with the blind brother of a friend who was a seer—or was it the other way around?—with the seer brother of a friend who was blind. Never mind; the main thing is that Amsterdam . . . and here followed two or three paragraphs about that city, a mix of reproaches and tender words, hints that only there will she finally settle down one day, and enumerations of streets and places where any tourist who visits the city must go if he wants to get the real taste and smell of Amsterdam. Once I tried timing how long the Doctor could remain silent while I was talking: thirty-four seconds. And that was when I was speaking very harshly of another scout whom she couldn't stand and wanted to fire as soon as possible.

The fact was that she had a special liking for me. She hadn't been in charge of this branch of the Club for very long, and she was particularly annoyed because New York had requisitioned the services of two of her best pieces. She wanted to find some new blood to strengthen the branch's position; she was certainly not going to resign herself to a permanent fifth place in the Club's profitability rankings (Paris, Tokyo, New York, London, Barcelona). And then I showed up with Luzmila, whom she accepted the moment she saw her. Luzmila, the little dear, said, "You must know, señora, that I won't work for less than a hundred euros."

"*Chiquilla*," the Doctor said soothingly, "at this company we don't pick up the phone for less than three hundred euros."

Then she turned to me: "Do you really want to give it a try?"

"It might be fun," I answered.

That answer was the key that opened the Club's doors to me, more than the discovery of Luzmila or the fact that as soon as she saw me walk through her office door the Doctor started flirting with me and didn't stop until she'd conducted me to the bedroom of her penthouse apartment which was hung with framed portraits of macho men by Tom of Finland.

"That's it; having fun—that's the most important thing. I like that. I like you. I'm going to offer you something, something good, something that's going to make you very happy. Apart from the matter of the Albanian girl, of course. For her, we can give you fifteen hundred euros. She'll need a little domesticating, a little taking in hand, but that's our affair. I imagine Gallardo's warned you about some of the rules. You know already that you're not allowed to play kiddie games, falling in love and all that nonsense. I'm telling you this because it looks as though you have some feelings for the Albanian girl. If that's how it is, we drop the whole thing right now. In order to work as a scout, it's absolutely necessary that you not be afraid of air travel, that you have good, very good relations with the forces of law and order—but I'll take care of that for you—and that you don't fall in love. At least not with someone you've got to hand over to the Club. But it's best not to fall in love with anyone. That says a great deal in the scout's favor. Of course you have to have wide-ranging tastes, as well. You've got to have a hearty appetite. Around here we need men as well as women, and of every conceivable hue in the erotic rainbow, you understand? We need effeminate young men, which we're short on right now because the material they're bringing in from Morocco leaves much to be desired, and little virgin girls. We need flashy working-class types decked out in leather, large impressive Negroes, extraordinary sensual Caribbean women, and delicate Thai flowers. You're going to love the first job I'm giving you, just to break you in; you'll work alone, you'll be far away, and that's good, really, you're going to thank me for it your whole life. You know what's going on in Argentina? One hell of a crisis, an economic collapse that serves our purposes beautifully; there are lots of good-looking people down there. I'm delighted about it, this collapse; the Argentine banks and all the bastards who took their money out of the country have made your work easy for you, easier than easy. Sometimes things like that happen. Take Yugoslavia, for example; that was great for us, they're so fabulous-looking, and of course it isn't always easy to find white people who are willing just like that, but we've got eight Yugoslavs and four Czechs on staff. Every one of them can tell you a whole movie about their life and each movie seems more unbelievable than the last one, but that's only if you make the mistake of asking them who they are, where they come from, and all that. *En fin,* in the three or four years they'll work for us, they'll earn enough money to start their own business or go back to their countries or settle down here and try to live off the interest. But a lot of them don't need to do that, as Gallardo must already have told you. On top of making a fortune with us, most of them, once they're free of us and assuming they decide not to extend the contract, now that they have citizenship—most of them hook up with someone who's fallen in love with them, some capricious client; the same client who paid us hundreds and hundreds of euros, *vaya.*

"Argentina, I was telling you, Argentina's going to be a real treat. One hell of a crisis, and an especially sweet moment for us, people waiting in line for days on end in front of the Spanish Embassy, and you show up, a nice boy with that tactful, under-standing face of yours, and talk to them about a modeling agency in Barcelona, and how you could—and you can—arrange for their papers in less than an hour, with a single phone call. You'll have them slobbering all over you. I need at least three girls and three boys. I'm sure you know, Gallardo must have told you, that there's no rule about trying them out before you bring them in. Trying them out yourself, I mean. Afterward it will be hard to sample the merchandise. And one other thing: not that I don't trust you, but you'll have to stay in touch with me, send me pho-tos of the pieces you think we can use. I don't want to arrange papers for anyone we won't want working for us. Send me as many pictures as you can; use your talents, shine. Does this sound good to you or not? Sounds like fun, no?"

What do you think I was going to say? I couldn't stop smiling. I couldn't stop thinking about my brother and how jealous he was going to be when he found out I was making five times more money than he did. At that point, I didn't even worry about the fact that my mission included scouting for men. Whenever I asked myself why I sometimes felt desire when looking at a beautiful male body, on the beach or in an art gallery—I followed the work of gay photographers like Bruce Weber, Robert Mapplethorpe, Herbert Ritts, George Platt Lynes, with some interest—or on television—once I watched the Mr. Spain competition all the way through to the end and was genuinely upset when Mr. Canary Islands didn't win—I answered myself: you're ethereosexual. I imagine that this meant, or was intended to mean, that I wouldn't dare take my desire for certain men beyond the level of fantasy, I wouldn't take any concrete steps to give it a try, but as with so many other things, I would let circumstances decide for me. If at some point circumstances were propitious, well and good, and if not, I'd resign myself to concealing the desire from other people and establishing its true dimensions only when I closed my eyes to go to sleep. During a certain period of my life, as I was leaving my teenage years behind once and for all, I would hold a daily beauty contest just before falling asleep. I was no longer granting interviews at that point; I'd grown tired of giving them, tired of casting myself in glorious roles. Instead, I would select the most beautiful of all the people I'd seen that day. On four or five occasions the contest was won by a man, and that didn't trouble me in the least. The prize, naturally, was that I would dedicate the moments of autoeroticism that would help me fall asleep to the winner. Among the many winners, I particularly remember a mulatto boy I often saw in the university cafeteria. It was easy to tell that he really liked his own looks: he wore very tight clothes, and long before spring had given any sign of arriving he was already dressed in form-fitting, sleeveless shirts. It's odd that, seeing him so often, I only deigned to give him the prize once. On another occasion an actor who played a bit part in a porn film won; he appeared in only one scene in an early morning movie I watched with one eye on the screen and the other on the hallway to make sure no one was coming in. I remember looking for the actors' names in the credits so I could memorize his. I couldn't find it because I hadn't paid much attention to the name of the character he was playing, a security guard summoned by a blonde whose garter belt was giving her serious problems. As soon as I saw him, I knew my daily beauty contest had its winner, even on a day when I hadn't left the house and the only serious competitor for the crown was a neighbor lady who'd stopped by to borrow a stapler. Here's what I told the

Doctor when she asked whether I thought I'd have a problem scouting males: "I'm ethereosexual."

"Fantastic," she said. "We belong almost to the same group, off by just a couple of letters. As you'll find out, I'm stereosexual: all I'm looking for is someone who can make me scream."

I left for Buenos Aires like someone going to the mountains for the weekend, free of any awareness of what I was getting myself into and without a single exalted qualm about the morality of my mission. I told my family the trip was my second assignment as a nongovernmental artist in support of lost causes. My father could barely hold back a laugh; all he said was "Don't even think about bringing back some Argentine girlfriend if you want to go on occupying a bed around here." My mother was ripping up a black-and-white-striped dress to use as a binding for the two volumes of *War and Peace;* her only reaction was a request that I remember to say my prayers before going to bed (she was favoring the priest over the personal trainer or the psychologist at that point). Spring was beginning to transform the teenagers of Europe into desirable machines, but I was on my way to an autumn oppressed by unemployment, the precipitous fall of the middle classes into the deep pit of poverty, and a currency devaluation that made every tourist a multimillionaire. I hadn't reserved a return ticket, and the only thing plaguing my conscience was a confession the Doctor had made.

She told me she had initially promised the Buenos Aires trip to Gallardo to help him get ahead a little in his career, "because the truth is that man has serious problems, the only thing that really gets him going is little boys, and of course that's *not* the only type we need, you understand, no? So I thought about it and I said, 'Buenos Aires will help improve your statistics, Gallardo,' because that's where he's from, on top of everything else, and if you ask him about his life he'll tell you he had to flee from the *milicos* during the dictatorship, although not even he believes that anymore. But I owed him one, I guess. So I told him, 'Gallardo, you'll go to Buenos Aires, you'll keep your good name, and no voice on the board of directors will speak of the advantages of dispensing with your services.' But the thing is: life is hard. And there he was with all his problems. Did you know that for a while he was thinking of becoming a monk? He actually spent some time in a monastery, *qué tipo,* after all the opportunities I had given him, sending him to Bolivia to get little boys, just what he likes. But I can't give him . . . For Buenos Aires we need new blood, a fresh approach, someone who really wants to prove himself, show that he's right for the job, and that person is you. But I hope you don't make the same mistake as Gallardo, don't start imagining you only need to go for pieces that are to your personal taste; you've got to think about other people's tastes, too, think about the company and the resources we'll be needing, and don't be filling up the house with blonde girls or boys just because that happens to be your type. You must always keep in mind that the person who's going to pay five hundred euros to spend some time with a piece you found in a garbage dump isn't going to be you. Think about rich, drooling old men, men in their forties who are getting tired of the same old thing and are looking for a more powerful experience; think about crazy women who've been hiding in a closet all their lives and need something vigorous and macho to give them a good thrashing, think whatever you want to think, but don't be a pain in the ass like Gallardo. He's a sick man, really; the truth is almost all redheaded men are sick in the head that way, every single one of them."

If at any moment before the plane took off my resolve had weakened enough to allow the plainclothes policeman we all carry around inside us enough time to convince me of how despicable my assignment was, I had a lucky break with my seatmate, who helped me block out any and all discourse aimed at my redemption. He was an antiques dealer going to Argentina to buy furniture, paintings, jewels, anything at all, because the prices of all those things had taken a rude plunge and were now within easy reach of those who could once only have hoped to gaze at them in glossy catalogs. He'd seen on TV that the Argentine economy was going down the tubes, and started planning his trip immediately; he was full of high hopes. "I'm not the only one," he said in his defense; "two of my colleagues are sitting up there, and I saw a couple of rare-book dealers in line at the gate; you can't let an opportunity like this one pass you by." We all knew that, we all had our suspicions about why we were going to Buenos Aires, and the fact that we were traveling there brought an element of squalor into the atmosphere and made us feel slightly dirty, as if there were a thin coat of slime on our skins. We tried to excuse ourselves, thinking: two other guys who are up to the same thing are sitting over there—without wanting to know that those two were also thinking: two other guys who are going down for the same reason are back there.

To while away the hours of the flight, my brother had found me two novels by Roberto Arlt. "If you want to know why Argentina is going through what it's going through, read this," he announced. The novels were written in the 1920s, and according to my brother they had already laid out the Argentine tragedy in full detail. Maybe so and maybe not, I wouldn't know; all I did was enjoy myself tremendously with the exploits of Arlt's far-fetched characters, who not only helped make the time pass more quickly but also placed a polite barrier between myself and the antiquarian's tireless and tiresome monologue. Predators, I told myself; a planeload of predators solicitously rushing off to be present at the collapse of an entire society. I liked that word and dreamed of printing it on a business card beneath my name. Yes, I was going to be a predator, but my mission wasn't simply to gnaw the bones of whatever corpse lay in my path. Instead, I would be pulling the most beautiful specimens—those who truly deserved a different fate than the one their misfortune had in store—out of the deep shit-filled hole they were in. None of the rest of us did anything to earn the principal gift we were born with, which in our case is simply the fact of having been born in a rich country, where there are social services and some political stability and the state has enough money to buy contemporary art. Why was it such a sin to try to offer this gift to beings who certainly deserved it more than we did? For in the end what I really had to offer was nothing more or less than a Spanish passport. In exchange for the loan of their beauty—their gift—the pieces I scouted would have the right to become my compatriots. Once they'd settled their debt to the company, they could fly off wherever they wanted to, across the globe.

Oh, how very touching this whole line of reasoning is, you must be saying, you're going to make us cry; how tender, how insightful. What is good? What is bad? These questions made no sense; their substance had evaporated well before the plane landed at Ezeiza. The only correct moral question for the times we live in is: What will pay off? What will turn a profit? Now you're probably saying, hey, that's some brainwashing they gave this dumb jerk, who actually believes all this garbage and is using it as a pretext for self-adulation, just to keep from branding himself as one of the bad guys already at such a young age. OK, that's possible too, but I'm trying to get us back to the youngish man with the Roberto Arlt novel resting on the tray in front of him, to the mental flagellations that were heightening his doubts about the morality of what he was about to do, assailing his conscience with a series of questions meant to unnerve him. He was not unnerved. In order to end the assault on his conscience, he chose what was, under the circumstances, the most profitable solution: to obliterate his conscience. Voilà.

I landed in Buenos Aires very, very much in the mood to go looking for delectable creatures whose lives I could save. And I got lucky. Of course—how could I not get lucky? I had an idea which at first I considered a stroke of genius, then a completely idiotic notion, and finally an emergency plan to fall back on if things didn't work out as well as I'd hoped. I argued to myself that under the current circumstances of economic collapse, social rage, and the fall of the middle classes into dire poverty, any beautiful creature who used to spend her time, shall we say, ringing up groceries in a supermarket, would certainly pay close attention to the proposal of an indecent Spaniard who told her about a modeling agency across the ocean where she could take refuge—without, of course, failing to mention the word *prostitution*—and would therefore have little trouble deciding whether it suited her better to remain in chaotic Argentina or flee far away. If this were true of a decent girl like that, then the whores and rent boys of Buenos Aires, for whom calamitous times had also arrived, would certainly be more than delighted to go abroad and practice what was already their profession in a place where they'd be treated much better, would be guaranteed astonishing salaries, and would even have an opportunity to abandon their profession as soon as they were able to save enough money or hook up with a client who would rescue them from perdition. I had no doubt that among those whores and rent boys there had to be a few exceptionally beautiful creatures who fully deserved to be saved. What a naive little pretension this was, or what pretentious naïveté. It had been months since reality had far surpassed my desires, and people who'd never imagined for a second that they'd someday have to sell their bodies in order to eat hot food or pay the rent had long since been forced onto the streets or into parks where more and more succulent flesh with no prior experience was on offer each day. There the well-informed tourist could find a wide array of secretaries, students, butane distributors, waitresses, waiters, and unemployed housekeepers ready to satisfy any client's desires in exchange for a few dollars that would help them make it to the next day. All I needed to do to carry out my mission was have a look around those parks—it was that simple. Luck had decided to act as my personal servant: things had gotten worse, there was a warlike atmosphere in the streets; supermarkets and delicatessens were looted at night, and in the morning the lines in front of the embassies curved around interminable blocks, though no embassy was giving out applications for entry visas and even the Argentine employees of those embassies were turning up in the parks in the early mornings trying to earn some small additional income to ease their distress. If I confessed to the Doctor that her mission had been a literal walk in the park for me, I would risk having her undervalue my incipient virtues as a scout, though it seemed clear that some clever foreign correspondent would soon write a highly disturbing account of how young Argentines, following the Cuban example, had no other solution but to sell the only thing they had left—their almost invariably beautiful youth—in order to get ahead.

Since I was intent on proving to myself how trifling my own scruples were, I decided that the first piece I would scout would be a male, and once again luck rushed forward to attend to my needs, bearing on a tray the perfectly formed ass of Emilio, a former employee of a messenger company who was as handsome as the movie stars whose pictures illustrate the notebooks of teenage girls: a little dimple on his chin, gray eyes, chiseled features, well-honed muscles, perfect teeth, long, straight hair, as easily imaginable in the role of an executive as in that of a rebel without a pause. He was free with words and used expressions that underscored the musical charm of the Buenos Aires accent. When he climbed into the passenger seat of my rental car, he mentioned that the autumn temperature was already beginning to make warm clothing necessary. Nevertheless, he was wearing a tight, sleeveless shirt and a pair of brown leather pants that clung to the perfect lines of his ass. I had a hard time explaining why I'd blinked my headlights at him to get him to walk over. The car was already rolling down an avenue where the streetlights gave off a tired light and the puddles reflected buildings crowned with the neon emblems of companies either about to go under or already bust. I thought the best thing would be to take him to a bar, I'm not sure why; in case things didn't turn out the way I wanted, I guess. I warned myself not to take him to the hotel where I was staying. Finally I opted for a compromise: we went to the bar at my hotel. I was nervous, not knowing how to react to his flattery—"a young, handsome client; this is my lucky night!"—and not daring to come right out and invite him to become part of Club Olympus's select catalog of beauties. I told him I was a photographer and didn't want sex.

"As long as you've got money," he said, disappointed.

"No need to worry about that. That's precisely what I want us to talk about before the photo session: money."

And then I came out with a hasty speech about the humiliating situation that young people as handsome as he was were having to live through. I had traveled to Argentina precisely in order to rescue a few unfortunates from that situation and offer them a chance to restore their lost dignity.

"We lost our money, not our dignity," he said. I had to correct myself. Then I went on with my halting speech. I believe he was thinking: he's pulling my leg; this idiot is trying to put one over on me; wasting my time telling me a fairy tale as if I were an idiot. Emilio was losing patience. He'd barely touched the orange soda he'd ordered. Suddenly we were upstairs in my room, and having tucked the dollars I gave him into a pocket of his leather pants, he took off his clothes and leaned against a wall, while I adjusted the ceiling lights and floor lamps to improve the lighting. Not that I was trying to make it an artistic session, but I like for things to come out as well as possible. I imagine Emilio must have had a hard time believing what was happening, saying to himself: when I tell them about this, they're going to think I've been smoking dope again. I started shooting. I hadn't bought the Leica yet; at that point I still had a Minolta 404 automatic that could correct my mistakes. Seen from behind, Emilio was a perfect Greek statue; from the front, his beauty was a little marred by the discrepancy between the classic form of his biceps and his underdeveloped abdomen, which showed no sign of muscle, only a tanned smoothness interrupted by the line of hairs connecting the groin with the navel. I shot a few close-ups of his face, head-on, gazing at the camera, and in profile, with his eyes lost on the ground or fixed on the ceiling. During one of those shots, Emilio smiled mockingly and said, "You're starting to get aroused." It had quite an effect on me, because all I saw were a pair of lips speaking the words, as if those lips didn't belong to Emilio but were an independent creature living inside my camera's viewfinder, as if the voice of my consciousness had somehow been transplanted into the external world and was capable of saying out loud things only I could hear in the deep abyss of silence where we're always telling ourselves everything and the narration of our lives goes on incessantly. It was true: I had an erection, and he had noticed. I put the camera down and walked over to him. His smooth, rock-hard ass was the first thing that my hands, tired of the ceremonies that had postponed the moment of truth, got busy with, as if magnetically drawn by an irresistible desire. He started giving me little bites on the neck. Soon we were lying down without wasting another word, though first he warned me—"The dollars from before won't cover what I'm going to do to you now; you'll have to give me more"—and I nodded and pushed his head down toward my belly. My first homosexual—and stereosexual—experience left my body tired and my soul purring with pleasure. I slept straight through until very late the next morning. Before he left, I told Emilio that what I'd said about the Spanish company needing models was true and that we could meet the next day at the hotel bar and continue our negotiation. That would give me time to develop the photos, scan them, and send them to the Doctor, so she could give me her opinion. I didn't have to wait long: "You're off to a good start, muchacho, I knew we could trust you." She included a number at the Spanish embassy that I'd have to call in order to arrange for Emilio's papers, and another number for a travel agency where the Club Olympus's newest piece could stop by to pick up the ticket to salvation I was about to grant him.

When I met up with Emilio again bearing good news, a light came on in his face that I would have liked to capture on film—a light of joy, perhaps with a dose of incredulity, as if he couldn't believe it were possible that the nightmare into which he and the whole country had sunk was finally about to be over for him. When I told him he could stop by the travel agency the next morning to pick up his ticket while I went to the embassy to do the paperwork for his identity card, it was as if I had stunned him; he kept looking at himself in one of the bar's mirrors as if he wanted help or needed someone to pinch him. Then he said, "Let's go up to your room. My treat."

After we'd messed up the sheets a little and I told him that in a couple of weeks my entire savings account wouldn't be enough to pay for what he'd just done to me, Emilio seemed melancholy, as if he'd flown off to a point in his mind so distant that he would never be able to tell anyone what he had imagined there. I asked him, "Where are you right now?" and he asked if I needed more people for this modeling agency of mine. I told him I did, in the hope that he'd make my path to success on this first scouting trip even smoother. He told me about a cousin of his who'd also been forced to turn tricks after the radio station where she'd worked as a sound technician had fired more than half the staff and sharply cut back on its programming. I told him we could go right over and see her that moment, and we did. The girl turned out to be a disappointment though. She was pretty, but we were looking for exceptional beauty and she wasn't in the same class as the other candidates who were hoping to win one of the joy-inducing lifebuoys I was carrying in my wallet. Trying not to offend Emilio, I went through the whole routine to prove I was seriously considering his "cousin," who it turned out was not at all related to him, but simply a friend or neighbor or lover. I took some nude photos of her in my hotel room, but when Emilio asked her to give me a blow job I said there was no need; I was sated and wouldn't be able to respond appropriately to the favors she was eager to lavish on me. Even though I knew full well there was nothing to be done, I did run my fingertips over the most attractive parts of her anatomy—a pair of perfect, prodigious tits, no surgery at all, she said, nature in its purest state. After his friend, neighbor, or lover had gotten into a taxi and left us alone in the mirrored bar, I spoke frankly with Emilio.

"She's not what we're looking for." He asked if I could use my influence as a special favor so the girl could go with him to Spain. At that point I decided I had to be firm.

"That wouldn't help you, Emilio. Listen, I'm offering you a golden opportunity and you're the first one I've offered it to, but this opportunity requires some sacrifices; this is only an individual salvation, that's just how it is, but you'll soon see it's better this way. Later on you'll be able to decide for yourself; if you want to bring someone to Spain, you'll have the money, you'll have no problem doing it, and you'll decide for yourself. But at the moment that won't help you, and besides there's nothing I can do to get her a ticket or work anything out at the embassy."

He insisted and went so far as to deliver an ultimatum: "Well, the two of us go as a pair, and if she doesn't go, I'm staying"— which forced me to get a little sharp with him. A few moments of distrust sprang up between us, and I was already seeing myself canceling my appointment at the Spanish embassy and calling the Doctor to tell her I'd blown it—because who else was there to blame? Fortunately I realized in time that this was no more than a desperate final gambit Emilio was playing in order to force me to yield. But I couldn't possibly give in; there was no negotiating. He had to know what he was doing; he was old enough to understand when it makes sense to sacrifice yourself for others and when the privilege you're offered has to take priority over the sentimentality that makes you weak. We said goodbye to each other with the morning already well advanced, having gone back to the room to tangle up on the bed again. He wanted to fuck me, but I wouldn't let him. He pushed my head down his torso, and my moment to prove myself on the male member arrived; I didn't do badly at all, though Emilio got a little violent with me to make me pay for my obstinate indifference to his woman. After we were through, while we were looking at each other in the bathroom mirror as I brushed my teeth to get rid of the slightly bitter taste of his come, he wet his hair, combed his fingers through it, and said: "You owe me fifty dollars. This time you pay."

I did. It seemed fair enough. I paid for the service. It was still cheap enough, at that point, for me to indulge myself. Two days later he took off for Barcelona and his new life at five hundred euros per session. By then I'd already collected two new pieces, both women; I didn't want to risk losing my taste for women after the good times with Emilio. And I went on finding what I was looking for here and there, in parks long after dark, at modeling agencies, gyms, and even without leaving the hotel, where, as luck would have it, I ran across a very beautiful girl whose job it was to clean the rooms. I flirted with her a little, and after she had changed out of her uniform and accompanied me to dinner I suggested she join the Club Olympus. Unfortunately I hurt her feelings, she told me. "Let's forget about it then," I said. But she'd already put her pack of cigarettes and lighter back into her purse and asked for the check; she insisted on paying for her share, not for anything in the world would she allow me to cover the bill for her salad, steak, and glass of white wine. I gave in and didn't even leave the restaurant with her, having decided I'd rather stay and have dessert. The next day she left a note in my room. She'd given it some thought and would like go to Spain after all and try out her luck with the modeling agency I had told her about. She was the only one of the pieces I scouted on that excursion whom I didn't sample before sending on to the Doctor.

I'd been in Buenos Aires for twenty-two days when I decided my search was over. Six girls and three boys. The Doctor was delighted with my efficiency. Some strange things had happened, and I'd met many likable people (though I couldn't save them all—some were likable but not exceptionally beautiful; those were the ones I had to leave behind in the crowds fighting over the leftover food when the hotels took out their garbage). Among the strange things I remember was one night when, after spending the afternoon buying clothes, including, on a whim, a pair of black tanga underwear, I looked at myself in the mirror and found myself so desirable I got hard; that's all you needed, I told myself—to get an erection looking at yourself in the mirror. I flew back to Spain with a suitcase full of photographs, the tremulous happiness of having discovered how to have a good time in bed with a man, and the utter certainty blazing at the back of my mind: congratulations, muchacho, you were born for this; at last you've found a job that's suited to your talents.

The Doctor was radiant, and I was a dishrag. She'd had some reddish highlights put in her hair and wanted to know how I thought it looked. She'd also had work done on her face to get rid of some wrinkles, and the close-fitting dark blue suit that dizzyingly emphasized her curves very proudly announced to all passersby that she had lost weight. On the table, next to her coffee and the Bauhaus ashtray containing the remains of two cigarettes, lay the most recent addition to her collection of books with uncut edges which she was showing off to me: a copy of a romance novel from the 1920s. A piece of bad news was the soundtrack to my cheerful riffle through the new book: she'd found out there was an old man in Havana who also collected books with uncut edges and had amassed nearly five thousand volumes, a number she clearly had no hope of ever matching. For a moment I thought she was going to send me off to Havana to persuade the old guy to give up his collection to her, but just then the conversation turned to the urgent matter that had forced me to spend a good part of the night behind the steering wheel of my car.

The first thing the Doctor did was extract from a file folder several pages torn out of a U.S. magazine. It was a news report from Spain about the immigrants who were thronging into certain cities in Andalusia. Since the United States is one of the few countries whose economy allows for the kind of serious investigative reporting on which a journalist spends several months of work before publishing a text whose every line has been carefully scrutinized by an entire department of fact-checkers, the text was very long. However, it had only a few illustrations, and not particularly good ones. One showed three black men sitting in a park lush with vegetation; the caption identified them as Sudanese in Málaga. The Doctor's lacquered fingertip pointed to one of the three figures.

"Your job is to find that one."

He was a singularly handsome man. Though the photo didn't show much of his body, his muscles were apparent beneath his pale T-shirt. His mouth was almost too sensual, and every other feature of his face suggested wild sex, while a pair of large eyes, two white spots against the severe darkness of his skin, completed his exciting aura of mystery.

"It's absolutely essential that you find him. He's a Nubian. Do you know who the Nuba were or are?"

Not the faintest.

The Doctor explained. An African tribe plagued by Islamic oppression in southern Sudan. Its men and women renowned for their beauty and narcissism. Their occupations: cattle raising, agriculture, and a type of fighting similar to pro wrestling but allowing the use of sharpened stones and wrist straps that were designed to inflict the maximum possible harm. In just under twenty years the Sudanese government had reduced the Nuba to the few hundred individuals who'd been able to flee or hide. Many ended up accepting the government's conditions and joining the very police force whose mission was to annihilate their tribe. Others sought a life for themselves far away. Some managed to reach Spain. A few Nubian villages still remain on the coast of Sudan, thanks to international assistance, having managed to resist the government or force it to respect them. They will become an exceptionally valuable tourist attraction as soon as the region's conflicts die down and photo safaris in search of Nubian warriors or Nubian dancing girls can be arranged. But we didn't have to wait that long. There were Nubians in a park in Málaga. And now the Doctor wanted to track one of them down, a kind of god in peasant clothes who gazes about wondering: what am I doing here?

The Doctor said: "The other day, the director general called me, and his voice sounded urgent. 'I have a very important job for you. Is New York still looking good to you? This is your chance,' he said. 'Take care of this for me, and New York is yours.' Just like that, he said it. I was thinking: you can ask me for the American flag that's planted on the dark side of the moon, and I'll get it for you; you can ask me for the two stones that were struck together for mankind's first fire, and I'll get them for you; you can ask me for the underwear Kennedy was wearing when his head was blown off, and I'll get it for you. When he told me what it was about, immediately I thought of you. Me in New York, and you in Barcelona. No more streets or garbage dumps or beaches full of shipwrecked refugees—an office with a phone, a list of scouts to order around, you'd run the branch, set the prices, all that—I know that sounds good to you; I know that's what you're after. And the best part of all is that they're not asking for that flag or those stones or Kennedy's underwear. All they want is this Nubian. A very, very, very important client of the company saw him—the client or his wife. (Who cares? We're not going to start gossiping about that at this late date.) Anyway, this client was suddenly overcome by an irrepressible, uncontrollable desire and said to himself: there must be someone who can acquire this magnificent animal for you, this creature who belongs to you already because he has induced this desire in you from the moment he showed up in your life even if it was through the vulgar medium of a photo in a magazine. I like to add just a touch of literature to spice up the story, as you can see—I'm sure you'll indulge me. Here's the thing: an important, very important client requests that we find the specimen he has glimpsed in a magazine—an African male who happens to be in Málaga; the director general notifies the director of the Barcelona branch, who in turn calls in her best scout; he gets on the case right away, tracks down the Nubian, recruits him for the Club, and takes him to the director of the Barcelona branch. She in turn sends the new recruit to the director general, who throws a big party to hand over the newly scouted piece to his very, very, very important client. And after all that, in gratitude for her excellent work, the Barcelona director—me—is placed in charge of the New York office, and the highly efficient scout leaves the streets, garbage dumps, and shipwrecks and takes charge of the Barcelona office. Perfect. Simple. Doable. Questions?"

Many. Of course. The first and most basic temptation was to start wondering about the client. Who could possibly come up with the idea of launching a search like this just because he saw a sexy man in a photo—not even a very good photo—in a magazine? But we were strictly forewarned against ever formulating such a question. The Club's clients fascinated me, though I didn't know a single one of them. I used to wonder, during moments of sober reflection, looking at some stranger while sitting in a park or waiting for my appetizer to arrive in a restaurant: Could he be a client of the Club? What kind of services would he ask for? Of course I also wondered about people I knew. By then my brother had landed his position in the Department of Education and Culture, laid in a stock of suits and ties, and gone up ten notches in my father's esteem, but he was still living in the apartment on La Florida and was not known to have any sort of romantic attachment. What sort of services would he request if he became one of the Club's clients? Once in a while we'd talk on the phone, and he'd ask where the hell I was and how I'd gotten there, tossing out barbed questions to needle me and make me lower my guard, but I hadn't had any trouble resisting the temptation to tell him anything about my activities. I imagine he must have suspected something, though I'm not sure what. As for my father, he was far too stingy to waste one drop of his capital—monetary or energetic—on a gorgeous, pillowy-lipped Caribbean beauty or a delicate Asian flower. I spoke to my father once a week, not because either of us wanted to, but just because he always answered the phone when my brother wasn't there. I was calling to check on my mother, to find out how she was and which of her phases she was in. First, however, I had to say hello to my father and tell him something while my mother stopped whatever it was she was doing to come to the phone. He never told me anything about himself, of course, and reserved his commentary on what I said to him for after I'd hung up. I could easily imagine the scene: My mother comes back from the hallway after telling me to take care of myself, my father lifts his eyes for a moment from the television or the magazine or a biography of the wife of a great man, and asks, "What does our masterful artist without borders have to say for himself?" My mother gives him a quick summary of whatever I told her, and then my father states, before plunging back into the life of the great man's wife, the game show, or the business section of the newspaper, "As I've always said, anyone who spends all his time on the move is crying out to the four winds that he's unhappy and immature." And on to the next thing.

With respect to the Club Olympus's clients, certain legends did circulate among the scouts, the modeling staff, and the administration. One of the most disturbing was about a man who fell hopelessly in love with a Cuban boy whose price was far beyond his means. The man visited the Club's office, leafed through the various photo albums—each one designed with irreproachable elegance—pointed out the boy whose services he wanted to hire, and was told what the price was. His only response was a long, helpless sigh. Though it was far too much money for him—two thousand euros, perhaps—he purchased a one-hour session with the delicious creature. It was a terrible mistake. That one hour turned his life into a martyrdom. It turned out that he was a simple bank clerk—or bank manager, according to other versions of the story—who saved up all his money to pay for a one-hour session with the Cuban boy every two or three months. The man soon realized that even if he gave up going to the movies and stopped drinking orange juice with his breakfast, he'd need several months to come up with the two thousand euros, which meant the sessions with his love would be unbearably far apart. So he decided to take out a loan of twenty thousand euros in order to guarantee an adequate degree of continuity for his encounters with the Cuban boy: ten meetings in a single month, one day yes and two days no. After that month, he would never see him again. Presumably he told all this to the Cuban boy himself, who was the one responsible for spreading the story around. Maybe he told him in an attempt to soften the boy's heart. What he achieved was something very different, of course. The Cuban boy told Club management he would no longer perform any services for the bank employee, who'd fallen in love with him, gone crazy. The Club's models have a right to veto. If they sense danger in any client, they can say so and prohibit management from hiring them out to that client. The client phoned the Club in dismay because although he thought he'd made it clear as daylight during his last session that he was to be with the Cuban boy again two days later, the boy hadn't shown up. Management told him that was not the way to hire a model and that private negotiations between model and client were not allowed. No matter what the two of them may have agreed on, the model could not negotiate on his own behalf without being represented by the Club. The client insisted that they send the Cuban boy to him immediately, and management told him that was impossible; the boy was not available, though they could send him another model in the same price range as the boy the bank employee wanted. He answered that he didn't want anyone else, and asked when he could enjoy the Cuban boy's services again. When he was informed that the boy had been transferred to another branch of the Club, the client hung up, whispering in terror, "He can't have done this to me."

Our story ends badly. The client called the Club again to ask for information about the Cuban boy's whereabouts, but the request was denied. He came to the office, claiming he didn't want to cause any trouble but needed to see the darling child and would do whatever he had to do to see him. He was wrestled down, thrown out, and threatened with a lawsuit, but he came back one more time and asked if he could at least have a photograph of the boy. Touching, no? Until one day he couldn't take it anymore and succumbed to despair. There was no further word from him, and everyone who knew the story concluded he must have hung himself or thrown himself out a window.

I once asked the Doctor, "What is a Club Olympus client?"

She answered, "The person whose job it is to take the immigrants you find on the streets or lined up at the back door of a hotel and transform them into machines."

For her the Club's models had to achieve the perfection of a machine; it was that simple.

"No questions," I said finally, still staring at the page of the magazine where an African immigrant was beginning to become a perfect machine.

"That's not good. Didn't they tell you when you were a boy

that it's smart to ask questions? I'm sure you're curious about the client's identity, at the very least. Of course I'm not going to tell you a thing about that, but I am going to give you a piece of bad news which has nothing to do with the client, but is related to your all-important obligation to follow orders."

The Doctor could sometimes be cryptic; her monologues would take strange turns in their attempt to retain the interest of a listener whose legs, inevitably, had begun to fall asleep. I imagine that the look on my face said, "Now what?" She stretched her lips into an understanding smile.

"You're not going to like this at all, I know; I know perfectly well that you're not going to like it, but I'm telling you this is important and at the end of the day she's not going to interfere with my plans to have you take over my position if things go well, I've already got my books boxed up for the move to New York, and in the end, even if she winds up being the one who reels him in, even if you don't work together as a team and each of you goes his own way, and she's the one who ends up with the prize—that won't change my plans."

What was she talking about? My face must have reflected a slight, insolent annoyance; perhaps a white patch broke out on one of my cheeks, or I suddenly changed posture, throwing my body forward and making it clear that I didn't understand a thing she was saying and was growing impatient with her circumlocutions.

"All right, I'm getting there. Luzmila. She'll be your traveling companion on this job. The truth is I'd thought of her as your assistant, but I know you don't need an assistant and I also know she likes to work on her own and isn't the kind of scout who takes orders from anyone. To tell you the truth, given the facts of the case, it's more than likely that she'll be the one to pull the thing off; the person you need to attract is a man, and in the short time she's been working for the Club Luzmila has brought in more men than anyone else. Even so, her statistics aren't so great because she seems incapable of getting women or little girls. Anyway, I thought that in this case you could use some help from her. She'll be taking her orders from you, but I'm not going to pull the wool over your eyes—it's hard to do that anyway, and you'd know I was telling you a lie if I told you she had to obey you—she'll be working on her own; as soon as the two of you get to Málaga, you'll both arrange matters as you see fit. But none of that matters to me; what I need is for you to catch the piece, and I don't care in the least who catches him; the success of the operation, even if you end up having nothing to do with it, will be your success, and you'll be the one who's promoted."

So that was it. Luzmila. Twelve months of work as a sexual machine activated by five hundred euros per session had been enough; she realized she'd rather be doing something else. So she made an appointment with the Doctor, showed up in her office one morning with the stony look she used to give when demanding money from people for a sandwich, forcing them to give her a few coins because she deserved them, and told the Doctor she was sick of going out with drooling idiots, sick of lying on her back under greasy bodies that disgusted her and left her feeling slimy, that she'd started to feel revulsion for the clients who requested her and that she needed to free herself from the contract that yoked her to the Club for three years—a contract which stipulated that should the undersigned not comply scrupulously with the aforesaid conditions and decide to dissociate him- or herself from the company, he or she would have to pay the company the sum of seventy thousand euros in compensation for losses and expenses. It had occurred to her that she might be able to work as a scout, "like the photographer who brought me to you," she said, and added that they could agree to a trial period of a few weeks—the models were entitled to some vacation time and extended leave—which should be enough time for the Doctor to realize that Luzmila would be much more valuable to the Club as a member of the scouting team than as just another model.

The Doctor pondered the pros and cons and added it all up: Luzmila was not one of the more sought-after models, and every client who requested her never asked for her again, which meant that she wasn't doing much to please those who hired her. She hadn't figured out how to transform herself into a machine, though it was still too soon to say that for sure; every model needed time to adjust, in order to complete the metamorphosis from an immigrant sprawled on a street corner into a perfect sexual machine. In the end, the Doctor decided that Luzmila could go ahead and try her hand at scouting. Luzmila passed the test with flying colors and quickly brought several monumental slabs of beefcake onto the modeling team, which the Barcelona office was able to distribute among the Club's other branches, where expensive masculine flesh was always in short supply. And now the Doctor had come up with the idea of reuniting the photographer and the Albanian girl on a special mission, the kind of thing that comes up only once during a directorship, a search for a particularly juicy morsel that had to be acquired in order to satisfy the big bosses and demonstrate to them that proven effectiveness on the part of Club staff members merits recompense.

"Want to go up to my room for a while?" the Doctor asked. "I've been having a lot of luck here in Madrid—I found ten or twelve books with uncut edges when I took a walk along the Cuesta de Moyano yesterday."

"Where is she?" I asked.

"She's here in Madrid. We're having lunch with her. You'll both be boarding the four-thirty plane. You each have a room reserved in the Hotel Málaga-Palacio. Ideally, you should get me some news on the piece you're scouting within the next couple of days, the way I figure it. That will allow me to send an initial report to New York to let them know we're already about to catch the Nubian. Of course, I can't say for sure if he's really a Nubian or not, but you know how I like to give the pieces flashy new names. The Nubian Prince. Sounds magnificent. Even if he's not Nubian, that's how we'll sell him, I like it—don't you?—it's got a powerful sexual charge. It's already putting me in the mood just thinking about it. He's definitely one of the ones who should charge more for image rights than for the actual session, don't you think?—those are always the best: bodies that don't need to do anything to excite you, like a sculpture, they show up and you get excited without their so much as lifting a finger, they leave and you've got them in your head forever, or for weeks, so that you go to the bathroom or to bed thinking about the things they didn't do to you but could have—and there should be a charge for that, shouldn't there? I'm very clear on this; if it were up to me, I'd put his price at one thousand euros, three hundred for the session and seven hundred for image rights. I already have him lodged in my mind, just about, and all I've seen is his picture; that's how image rights are, of course. How many women, lying under some boring man, are imagining they're being possessed by a supermacho, the guy from the corner store or the actor they adore, and if the men who are on top knew where their women's imaginations were sailing, well, you tell me what would happen. But I know none of that matters to you; you're made of different stuff—in fact I'm sure it would even excite you a little if I were to promise you that if I were lying under you today, I wouldn't be able to get the Nubian out of my head. Shall we go up to my room for a while?"

TWO ▌▌▌▌

At this point at least one of you out there must be saying to yourself: there you have it, it's clear as day; this is the story the guy wanted to tell, and he's just given away the plot. He's being sent off to hunt an exceptionally sensual piece, and pretty soon he's going to fall in love; he won't want the magnificent immigrant to be transformed into a machine that switches on whenever a bill is inserted, and there we have the conflict. When you put it that way, it sounds like the plot of a romance novel decked out with a little redeeming social conscience. But I'm afraid I'm going to have to disappoint those of you who are hoping for that kind of plot. Though I admit that it is a possibility and confess that I am sometimes tempted to veer away from what really happened onto the path of fiction, transforming the scenes I carry in my memory into others in which imagination successfully revises reality.

I went up to the Doctor's room and we fucked, though my rather moderate level of desire made it hard for me to satisfy the demands of my *partenaire,* which didn't much matter, luckily, since she'd entered an alternate dimension of the space-time continuum in which the person on top of her was the Nubian, so she was perfectly happy—the power of the imagination is therapeutic; we ourselves are all we need to correct the perpetual mediocrity of reality—while I remained peacefully anesthetized. I heard her get up, take a shower, and then come back over to the bed.

Depositing a kiss in the palm of my left hand, which was floating beyond the edge of the mattress, she whispered, "I'm going shopping." I don't know how much more time went by until the phone rang, dragging me back into the world from the blissful unconsciousness into which I'd managed to sink.

Whenever I spent a night with the Doctor in her Barcelona apartment, I would wait for her to fall asleep—a salvo of snores gave ample evidence that she'd abandoned consciousness—then get up and wreak a subtle revenge. I don't know for sure whether I was trying to screw the Doctor in yet another way or was simply amusing myself with a childish prank meant to prove I felt not the slightest regard for the woman. My vengeance consisted in making her pay in some way for the services I'd just provided, since I felt as if I were being used as a machine every time I ended up between her sheets. And the payment I demanded was the sacrifice of a few of her books with uncut edges. Armed with a kitchen knife, I'd go to the shelves that displayed the Doctor's stupid collection and choose five books, almost always the slimmer volumes. Sitting on the living room sofa, I'd cut open the books' pages, thus causing deplorable harm to the stupid collection. If she ever noticed what I was doing, she never said a word. I must have visited that apartment half a dozen times, which means I reduced the number of her collection of books with uncut edges by about thirty copies—a satisfying percentage. I remember that prior to one of the occasions when I inflicted this punishment on the Doctor—she had taken me to dinner and invited me back to her apartment—I talked myself into accepting by silently saying: ok, let's do it, but it will cost you another five books. My dream, of course, was to reduce her collection to zero, but if I proceeded at five copies per visit, it would take far too long—and would require far too many evenings with the Doctor. So I'd made a plan to spend an entire night cutting open the pages of all the books in her collection once I'd decided to sever ties with the Club once and for all.

In that hotel room, while waiting for the coffee and croissants I'd ordered, I cut the pages of two of the books the Doctor had just acquired on the Cuesta de Moyano. It was risky to cut all the pages, so I decided to cut only a few of the signatures. If she noticed it before I was on my way to Málaga with Luzmila, I could tell her she'd been cheated. That often happened: a book that seemed uncut wasn't completely uncut; its former owner had cut the pages of one or another signature. But if the pages of even a single signature in a volume are cut, that volume no longer belongs to the category of books with uncut edges.

I was busy at my task when the phone rang again. This time I was rash and answered. It was Luzmila. She wouldn't be joining us for lunch; we'd see each other at the airport. The conversation was distinctly unfriendly; not so much as a "how are you?" Since she'd become a scout, I'd seen her only once, in a pleasant little meeting called by the Doctor at the beginning of the year to explain where she had set each employee's performance goals and to demand that the stragglers get energized if they wanted to remain on the team. The Doctor had five scouts working for her, several fewer than in the company's largest branches. During that meeting, Luzmila and I barely exchanged more than a chilly hello. She'd disguised herself as an aggressive executive, wearing a gray suit and high-heeled shoes with her luxuriant hair pulled back in a braid. She asked a couple of questions after the Doctor's speech was over and was one of the first to leave the room. Someone told her that a few of us were going out for some beers, and she answered with a cutting, "I don't think any of you really feels like having me join you." She didn't so much as glance at me during the entire meeting, though I'd taken care to sit right in front of her. Still, I couldn't work up any ill feeling about having her go with me to Málaga, and was even hopeful that her attitude toward me—palpably disdainful, as if she wanted to forget who it was that had helped her attain her current position—might have changed, and we could have some fun together.

When we saw each other at the airport, our greeting was cold. She'd arrived before me and hadn't waited for me before checking her bags; she didn't want to sit next to me on the flight. We talked a little as we were waiting to board. I remember that she unwrapped a piece of gum and offered it to me, saying, "So there are still a few romantics left in this astonishing world we live in."

"Why do you say that?" I asked indifferently, refusing the gum, which she ended up popping into her own mouth.

"Don't you think it's romantic for someone to see a photograph of someone else and hire a whole organization to find him, catch him, and hand him over?"

"Neither you nor I knows the terms of the agreement, and the final cost of the operation is another a secret we'll never learn."

"That remains to be seen," she said. She folded her arms, gazed at a man who was pushing a cart loaded with sports bags along a corridor, and added, "If I ever find out what those figures are, I'll let you know so you can feel proud of yourself."

Before I joined Luzmila at the airport, the Doctor had confided over lunch that Luzmila herself had been the one to convince her of the value of using her for this case, which was not at all typical. The annals of the Club recorded very few similar incidents in which clients singled someone out and asked the Club to place that person at their disposition. What "their disposition" meant precisely is a question the Doctor preferred not to go into; she only assured me that everything had been decided in New York, and that if we managed to bring in the Nubian, she couldn't say whether the client intended to keep him forever or only enjoy him for a period agreed upon with the Club, at the close of which he would come back into the Club's fold to work as a model, available to other clients. I couldn't help but be intrigued by the fate of the man who was now our most coveted piece, nor could I help but imagine the secret client who had set this whole operation in motion: undoubtedly someone who was completely deranged and filthy rich, perhaps a wealthy New York art dealer or the president of a tobacco company, the kind of man who's learned that nothing is impossible for him and that if he doesn't set great challenges for himself, he will soon grow bored. But how had Luzmila found out about the operation, and how had she dared butt in and ask the Doctor to include her in it? Relations between Luzmila and the Doctor had improved a great deal since the day Luzmila switched to the scouts' team, and the inevitable gossip among certain members of the team sometimes conjectured smoldering scenes between the two women to explain Luzmila's rapid ascent. It was perfectly normal for the Doctor to have thought of me for a risky operation that could have a very positive impact on her future in the organization; my statistics outshone everyone else's, and if that wasn't enough, the area where the desired piece had been located was part of my assigned zone, which I was—or was supposed to be—well acquainted with. But Luzmila? Naturally the argument that it was a good idea to have a woman along to attract the piece's attention was so pathetic that I had made no comment on it whatsoever; it was obviously no more than a pretext designed to block any questions I might have as to why the hell I was being forced to work with a companion who, furthermore, didn't appear to be jumping with joy herself at the thought of working with me.

Since my assistant had made it very clear she didn't desire to exchange any information about the case with me, I decided to go against her wishes. When she sat down in her assigned seat, I turned to the elderly woman already sitting next to her and said in my most affable manner: "Señora, this young lady and I are traveling together, but they've given me a window seat over there. Would you mind changing with me?"

Delighted, the woman stood up and yielded her spot. My Albanian companion pretended to concentrate on the pages of a book filled with glossy four-color reproductions of African masks; I caught a glimpse of some of them out of the corner of my eye, very colorful, minutely detailed, impressive. Later I learned that the Doctor had given Luzmila the book, which was full of photos of Nubians. I myself got out the latest book by my favorite writer, Stephen King, in which I'd underlined a sentence that set forth his narrative method in all its overwhelming simplicity: "In my concept, stories and novels have three parts: the narrative—which has to take the story from point A to point B until it finally reaches point Z; description—which has to create a sensory reality for the reader; and dialogue—which brings the characters to life through their own words."

I'd made a point of sitting next to Luzmila only to bother her and remind her that however much she might pretend to be completely unaware of my presence, I was there. I was the commander of the mission. She could do whatever she felt like doing, but her success would redound to my benefit. Nevertheless, Luzmila spoke to me. She stashed the book on the Nuba in the seat pocket in front of her, threw a glance over my shoulder at the page I was reading in the Stephen King book, and said, "What do you think will happen?"

"Nothing out of the ordinary. We'll find the Nubian Prince, hand him over to the Doctor, he'll be sent off to New York and placed in the client's hands, and the client will do whatever he wants with him—maybe hire him as a gardener to keep from upsetting the children. And there you go."

"Something tells me that's not where all this is headed."

"Yeah?'

"Haven't you ever thought that the Club doesn't take full advantage of its power?"

"What do you mean?" Only then did I close the Stephen King book and turn to meet Luzmila's eyes.

"I mean that the Club is the ideal means by which to achieve more important goals than just satisfying the demands of a pack of slavering sex maniacs."

"The ideal means? More important goals? What are you talking about?"

"How far does your ambition go? I mean, how high are you aiming? The Doctor told me she's going to recommend you for her position if they end up sending her to New York. Would you be happy with an administrative job like that? Do you think you'd be good at it?"

"I don't know. I never gave it much thought. I've toyed with the idea of quitting the whole game—the looking for diamonds in the trash and all that, saving the lives of beautiful creatures, you know. I'd never thought about an administrative position, but when the Doctor mentioned the possibility I got my hopes up. After enough time traveling from dump to dump, from one beach full of shipwrecked refugees to the next, from one shanty-town dive to another, you start getting a little sad and want to make up for all the emotional garbage you've accumulated with a period of well-paid peace and quiet. But I'm not sure if administrative work is for me. It obviously is for you."

"Why do you say that?"

"Because you'd like to apply for the position. Am I wrong?"

Luzmila smiled.

"If you want to become someone you haven't yet become, don't be satisfied with who you are," she said. A scout for the Club Olympus quoting Saint Augustine. To my stupefied look, due mainly to the coincidence between her citation and a moment of turbulence in the sea of white clouds we were flying over, Luzmila added, "If I did reach a managerial position, I would steer the Club toward a more important goal."

"World domination or something like that?"

"Something like that."

The serious demeanor I'd been trying to preserve gave way, and I exploded into a laugh that caused the people sitting across the aisle to look over. Two stewardesses arrived, pushing a drinks cart. Luzmila didn't want anything. I asked for a glass of Manzanilla.

"And just exactly how are you going to achieve world domination?"

"Have you ever seen our client portfolio?"

"No I have not, and that's the truth. Aren't we forbidden to take any interest in the clients? Isn't all that information confidential, and isn't it a crime for the Club to provide it to anyone who isn't management?"

"If you drew the line at anything that's against the rules, you'd never be able to scout a single piece."

"In other words, you've seen the portfolio. Lots of famous people? Priests? High-ranking members of Opus Dei? Public prosecutors? Famous soccer players? Singers renowned for their machismo who nevertheless contract the explosive services of our mulatta dominatrixes?"

"All that information is confidential."

Another uncontainable burst of laughter. This time Luzmila smiled. We were getting somewhere.

"We could use it in a way it's not currently being used. That's the sad thing, that it isn't being used as it could be. Can you imagine? What's more, I think that's what the founder of the Club had in mind—to found a club that would transform unfortunate people all over the world into powerful people, sexual machines who would ultimately take control of the masters of the universe, making them pay for scandalous sex and then putting the screws on them when they learn their secret weaknesses, weaknesses that would destroy their prestige if the public ever found out."

"OK. So blackmail would be the order of the day. Even more money than they're already paying."

"*Much* more money. Don't you realize that all the Club's financial backers are united by a vice they must keep secret? That vice is the magnificent tie that binds them. They're part of a sect, but they don't realize it. All that remains is to consolidate the potential the Club already has. There's dynamite in the files, but no one's ever thought about lighting the fuse. All anyone does is keep us working, keep the Club running by whatever means necessary, and keep the clients supplied with whatever material they demand to satisfy their cravings, feed their vices."

Luzmila seemed to be delivering a speech she had previously gone to some trouble to memorize. I tried to look interested, but while she was talking I said to myself deep inside: pretty weak brew. To give her the impression that I was fascinated by what she was saying, I interrupted periodically with a question.

"But how would you achieve that control?"

She explained in great detail. Blackmail operations, use of a media apparatus that would pressure our victims until they yielded, collection of a kind of revolutionary tax in order to finance our goals, use of our sexual machinery to drive the weakest clients to the edge of the abyss, enslave them, subjugate them to our will.

I asked, somewhat idiotically, "Have you told anyone else about this?"

I was thinking, naturally, of the Doctor. I tried to imagine the expression on her face if she were confronted with this Albanian girl's ludicrous plan but couldn't even begin to.

Luzmila said, "I've told some of the boys about it."

"You hang out with the models?"

"Of course I do. Not just the ones I scouted—some of the others, too. For example, not long ago I met an Argentine you saved. Interesting boy; finest male ass I've ever seen. He seemed depressed."

I didn't want to ask her what was going on with Emilio; I wanted to go on keeping my distance from the fate of the pieces I brought in. It was enough for me to collect their photos in the trophy album that documented my achievements as a scout.

"I've been a machine, and now I'm a scout. No one else I know of has had both experiences. The Doctor herself says so: that no one else has been both. It's only natural that I'd take the next evolutionary step, to management, even you must see that, though you've only been a scout and you don't know what it is to be a machine."

"The Doctor hasn't been a machine either."

"And that's precisely why she's not doing very well. That's why she's wasting an opportunity for more important goals. And that's why her days are numbered."

Her days were numbered? She was going to be promoted to director of the New York office, and Luzmila thought that meant her days were numbered. This time I didn't laugh. The clouds had thinned, and we were heading straight toward a patch of greenish sea, leaving the city of Málaga on the right, the ugly buildings fronting the beach protected by a mountainous mass sprinkled with houses. Slowly, the plane banked over the fishing boats and yachts. Landing was announced. Luzmila retrieved the book about the Nubians from the seat pocket, and I put my book back in my bag.

"Did you know that the Doctor collects books with uncut edges?" I inquired, hoping she'd ask what a book with uncut edges was. Instead she replied, "I know everything about the Doctor. I even know what bad taste she has in lovers."

It had been several days since I'd looked at a newspaper or watched TV. In fact, I rarely read newspapers because whenever I happened to pick one up, it forced me to do as Pontius Pilate and wash my hands. That hand washing was already a critical sign of cowardice. So I was entirely unprepared for what awaited us in Málaga. The city was enduring a garbage strike that had already been on for ten days; the stench had reached even the airport's corridors. This first bit of evidence that we were heading into a very particular kind of hell came to us as we were waiting for our luggage. The air was thick with a sticky smell of rot, and by eavesdropping on other travelers waiting for their luggage, we learned that the situation in the city itself was absolute chaos. In the poorer neighborhoods, the trash had been heaped into actual barricades, and people had begun lighting fires in trash containers to force the city government, which was refusing to negotiate with the unions, to respond in some way. The more resolute columnists were demanding that the army intervene immediately to relieve the afflicted population from the reek permeating every corner of the city. What will the tourists think of us? a Málaga native sighed, ashamed of the welcome her city had in store for the foreigners who had traveled there seeking its much-advertised ideal climate, broad beaches, and waiters with a passable command of English. Luzmila covered her nose with a lavender-perfumed handkerchief, and I did what I could to breathe through my mouth, but I couldn't stave off a wave of nausea that clouded my eyes. I tried to think about something else to escape from the filth that was imprinted on the very air. First I wondered whether, under her clothes, Luzmila was wearing the portable fitness equipment the Club furnished to each of its models so their muscles wouldn't relax for a single moment of the day and they wouldn't have to spend too much time in the gym in preparation for the moment when their bodies would be unveiled. It consisted of one belt that went around the waist and administered electrical charges of varying levels to the abdominal muscles, another belt encircling the place where thigh joins buttock, and two armbands which the men in particular had to wear for several hours each day to keep their biceps powerful. These devices could entail unforeseen and annoying consequences, for instance if you were careless and fell asleep without remembering to switch it off, the waist belt would cause a numbness throughout the entire abdomen, which could be very uncomfortable to the model. Thinking about that led me to imagine Luzmila's underwear, a black thong, straps barely thicker than dental floss winding tight around her hips, then meeting to plunge deep between her buttocks. It didn't do me much good. As if she'd guessed where my thoughts had strayed in their escape from the stench of reality, Luzmila said, "Listen, what it smells like in here is shit. That can't be because of the garbage collectors' strike."

"Yeah, to improve the situation even further all the sewage pipes must be backed up, too," said someone behind me, someone obviously eager to start a conversation with a beautiful Albanian girl.

Then we saw them. There must have been more than thirty Africans. They'd smeared their whole bodies with feces so the police who were herding them along couldn't grab them and put

them on the charter flight that would bring an end to their dream
of staying in the promised land. A few small groups of them had
been bound together with electrical tape. It was a terrible sight,
yet I never thought to take out the Leica and capture it. Most
of the Africans had joined in a hoarse unanimous lament that
sounded like both a shattering hymn and the prayer of a victim
who cannot be saved. When they walked past us on their way
toward the runway we'd just come from, we had to cover our
noses and struggle to keep from vomiting. Not all the passengers
who were waiting for their luggage managed to do so, and the
shiny floor was now covered with revolting, orange splotches.
From time to time, one of the Africans in custody would stop,
throw himself to the ground, and kick the air. The plainclothes
policemen weren't at all shy about taking care of him; they
weren't going to leave their job undone just because a few foreigners happened to be looking on. With great care—though there
was no way to keep clear of the shit that covered the prisoner—
but with grim determination, they'd set him back on his feet, and
if he put up much resistance, one of them would take out a special
pistol and shoot off electrical tape, transforming the prisoner into
a kind of mummy. One of the Africans, the biggest one, managed
to break away from the guards despite being entirely enveloped in
electrical tape; he reached a wall and started beating his head
against it. But his self-inflicted injury wasn't going to do much for
him—probably little more than make the mere frustration of his
inevitable repatriation feel a little less painful.

The caravan of Africans left our group of travelers with a lin-
gering horror that doesn't need to be put into words. Through
the large blue-tinted windows at the end of the baggage claim
area we saw them walk along the runway. One by one, the police
pushed them up a stairway into the depths of the plane, until

they disappeared from sight. Only Luzmila was capable of saying anything when the stairs were retracted after the final policeman had gone up.

"You saw the guy beating his head against the wall? He could be the Nubian we're looking for."

I was silent.

"And even if he wasn't the Nubian, he was a magnificent piece for the Club. He looked like Michael Jordan. What a pity."

Among the most prized of the Club's models were those who looked like famous people; they practically made up a department all their own. The Doctor profited from such resemblances to extract supplementary fees from the clients who hired them: we had clones of models like Tyson Beckford or Naomi Campbell, of tennis players like Anna Kournikova, of actors and actresses, from a magnificent double of the handsome John Gavin—of *Spartacus* days, not the one later typecast as a wealthy businessman—to a young Paul Newman and Brad Pitt; from a fantastic, delicate Audrey Hepburn (I wasn't the one who scouted her), who was often hired to be shown off on gala social occasions, to an explosive Demi Moore, who ended up leaving the Club because of breast cancer, which elicited a stupid joke from Luzmila ("Really? I always thought they were silicone"). I counted a few clones among my captures, but only one was a success; obviously the actors and actresses I like don't spark much passion in others. The successful capture was a boy I found living in a depressive state in Barcelona, only two blocks from the Doctor's office—a colossal stroke of good luck. The boy was a dead ringer for Cassius Clay: the Doctor took one look at him, approved, and very happily hired him. To make my accomplishment sound more impressive, I told her I'd followed the piece's trail for weeks, that I'd seen him once in La Mina—the most exclusive neighborhood of all where poverty and violence were concerned—but hadn't managed to bag him until much later, when my highly professional persistence finally paid off.

I'd been to Málaga a couple of times, but had never combed the city in search of a piece for the Club. I knew that its population of immigrants was large and variegated, but I'd always postponed a closer examination, busy with more urgent matters. Of course it figured on my list of priorities as a juicy spot where I could achieve profitable results with minimal diligent effort. Luzmila, as she confided in the taxi that took us to the hotel, did know the city pretty well, but not because she'd ever scouted for pieces there. During a certain period, unable to bear the Seville heat, she had decided to make do on the streets of Málaga instead, where, because of the proximity of the sea, the summer was less grueling. All she said was "It's a violent city." She refused to offer any evidence in support of this information. The taxi driver was watching us in the overly wide rearview mirror, and possibly considered intervening in our conversation in order to support Luzmila's claim. In the end, he didn't wish or didn't dare to do so. I couldn't help connecting Luzmila's comment with the city's current situation; seen in that light, the very palpable tension in the air was less surprising than the fact that after more than a week without garbage collection the entire city hadn't yet burned to the ground.

We saw heaps of garbage on every street corner, people wearing masks scurrying along the sidewalks, dead rats in the middle of the avenues. I asked the taxi driver if the sanitation workers and city government showed any sign of reaching a resolution, and the taxi driver answered by plagiarizing one of the bellicose clichés that the radio had been spewing since we got in the cab. According to him, "Only the army can resolve this," the garbage collectors were all sons of bitches who wanted to be paid a fortune and get an extra day of vacation, and the city officials were a bunch of spoiled rich kids living in fabulous houses who hired private services to haul away their garbage every night. Meanwhile, the poorer and more populous neighborhoods were in a state of emergency, rats were proliferating to a dangerous degree, and the generalized despair was a powder keg that was bound to explode sooner or later. This description of the situation seemed to make Luzmila happy. She must have thought that this state of affairs was somehow favorable to her, I'm not sure why—perhaps because she was remembering the night in Seville when I told her about my experience on the garbage dump in La Paz.

"Will we be working together? How are we going to do that?" I wondered aloud, as we were waiting at the hotel reception desk. To my dismay, my voice shook a little as I asked the questions. Luzmila had a genius for taking advantage of other people's weaknesses to increase her own power. She shrugged, knowing that no response at all was the worst response she could give. I persisted: "Maybe it's best if we each work on our own, each find our own way as well as we can, but it might not be a bad idea for us to get together once a day, perhaps over breakfast, to see where we are, I mean, so as not to get in each other's way; I'm not talking about sharing our progress with each other but, well, you know."

"Dinner would be better," she answered. "I get up too early; I almost never have breakfast."

In the room, as I unpacked my bags and starting hanging up shirts in the closet, I decided to get to work immediately. Luzmila's presence was goading me on. As she herself had suggested, this was in some way a competition, like the stupid footrace we once got into in Seville. But far more was at stake now. There was no way I could believe the Doctor when she asked me to trust her and assured me that even if Luzmila were the one to capture the piece the promotion to the top post in Barcelona would go to me. Given what I'd learned about Luzmila's ambitions, I had every reason to fear that her excessive interest in working the Nubian case cloaked a plan to top off her meteoric rise by transforming herself in record time from model to branch director. I called down to the desk and asked them to send up a pack of cigarettes. This was an excuse to meet a local, who turned out to be a stuttering redheaded kid. I remembered Gallardo and the Doctor's theory about the essential sickness of all redheaded males. I showed the bellhop the picture with the Nubian and asked if he recognized the park in the background. *"Qué va,"* he answered.

"Do you know of a park in Málaga where blacks go?"

"There are lots of them; they're all over the place. You can't even go out at night anymore. They've taken over all the parks," he answered, widening his eyes, a little intimidated and trying to frighten me in turn.

"You're exaggerating," I said.

"Really, señor, they're all over the place; you run into them wandering around here everywhere; it's an epidemic, worse than the garbage," he answered, adding resentfully, "One time they tried to steal my wallet."

I wasn't inclined to hear out this bit of personal history. Experience, as we know, is deceptive: one judges the world through the prism of what has happened to oneself and considers this a just and legitimate approach, when in fact it is quite obviously the perfect tactic for never learning anything about anything.

Finally, as the bellhop was leaving, after I'd paid him for the pack of cigarettes without adding a tip, he said, with an edge to his voice, "Especially in the prolongation of the Alameda, where they spend the nights, there are thousands of them there; from the Corte Inglés to the Puente de las Américas, it's all crawling with blacks."

Right now I could really use an omniscient narrator. At this point it would be entirely appropriate for my narrative to fly off for a few pages to the steep slopes where the Nuba are resisting the bloody ravages of the Sudanese army, and, better yet, go on to enlighten the curious reader about the epic adventures of a boy who managed to slip through the military barricade surrounding the Nubian villages and undertake a spectacular journey which has yet to be celebrated by a single line of poetry, aboard precarious vehicles that took him to a barge jammed with traveling companions in whose company he attained our privileged coastline. The omniscient narrator for whom I so long could also take us on a side trip to the home of the client who prompted the Club Olympus's latest operation, offering a leisurely guided tour of the costly accoutrements of his palatial home, recounting in some detail his ordinary workday, describing, with a touch of humor, his bored wife—a collector of shoes—and providing a list of his most significant lovers. But I only ever knew one omniscient narrator, and I beat him to death rather brutally. Incidentally, though the rest of that story is of no interest, I will say that Paola pressed charges for the death of her rottweiler, and at the trial the judge refused to take seriously my argument that the dog had cornered me on its mistress's orders. According to him, the animal knew me and was hardly likely to have been obeying telepathic orders or a command issued far too long in advance of its fulfillment. I had to pay Paola considerable damages, and since my salary as a coach hadn't allowed me to save up much, my father was forced to plunder his own savings account to get me out of that mess. When he deposited the check that would protect me from the additional fine levied in case of nonpayment, he emitted another of his dicta: "There's only one thing worse than a dog killer, and that's a dog killer who can't even pay the fine for his crime."

While I was taking a bath, having dumped both little bottles of bath gel into the hot water to create lots of foam, I decided I wasn't going to let Luzmila show me up in front of Club management. I would challenge her ability to capture the Nubian. I would teach her that my experience could outdo both her charm and her inordinate self-assurance. Therefore, despite my earlier plan to let the first night go by without expending any of my energies on the hunt, I put some clothes on, went out into the city, reconfirming that every inch of it indeed smelled like the rotting and gangrenous soul of a demon, and made my way to the prolongation of the tree-lined Alameda, where, according to the bellhop, lay a series of parks in which many black immigrants spent their nights. It was impossible to enjoy the stroll and very difficult indeed to stage any kind of Olympic footrace; the few pedestrians who dared sally across the sea of garbage the city had become were traveling at speeds that denied all hope of challenging them. At the Alameda, I spent a while browsing past the flower stands, whose masked attendants seemed almost ready to give their flowers and potted plants away in exchange for a little conversation. No one was stopping to select a bouquet of roses. I asked when they closed up for the night, thinking I might buy some flowers on my way back from my first expedition. I also inquired about the Puente de las Américas, and they pointed toward it, straight ahead, about five hundred meters distant.

Stretching before me was a wide avenue along which cars were gliding at dizzying speeds. The avenue's backbone was a divider planted with grass and embellished, here and there, with enormous shrubs; a few bags of garbage had even reached that divider, though I couldn't imagine an adequate explanation for how they'd gotten there, no matter how I strained my deductive capacities. Several small public gardens ran on both sides along the avenue. These were patches of darkness, lit only by the few streetlights not yet smashed by stone-throwing vandals. Naturally those parks were the ideal spot for the tumultuous garbage that had long since overflowed every trash container. I saw several locals augmenting one of the piles of trash with gigantic bags; clearly, given the prevailing stench, they didn't mind keeping the garbage around for a while, only throwing it out every two or three days when the odor inside the house became as unbearable as the reek that permeated the streets.

After walking past the deluded bulk of the Central Post Office, a mother ship from a spurious world—the high-flown fascism of the 1950s—and reaching the inscrutable Rorschach test of the Corte Inglés department store, a gigantic igloo dating from the grotesque 1970s, I stepped out onto one of the wide promenades in the Alameda's prolongation, which was bordered with colossal planters on which a few Africans were sitting, their legs dangling above the ground, their talk minimal, their eyes deep and expectant. I decided to speak to a man who was sitting by himself. I showed him the picture of the Nubian and asked if he knew him.

"Why want?" he asked. It was a question that could have elicited a high-voltage philosophical response, and I was about to try to come up with one, but then chose to consider the metaphysical issue nothing more than the result of creative error.

"That's my problem," I answered. "Can you help me?"

"And you me?"

"Of course."

He must have been a little over twenty. The whites of his eyes were traced with a fine mesh of blood vessels. He was well dressed, like almost all the Africans I had passed. Shoes are particularly important to them. He didn't seem bothered by the smell that was torturing the area, and a small but very distinct scar perturbed his forehead. What he told me in his rapidly masticated Spanish—once I'd assured him I might be able to help him if he gave me any valuable information—was of no use to me whatsoever.

"That one I don't know," he said. "I don't know where you can meet one who knows that guy, but ahead are lot of guys like him and with luck he might be in park up ahead, at bridge, with luck they tell you something about this guy there or about one who knows this guy. But don't you go now, it's bad to go now, but go with me and nothing happens, if you go with me, someone I know could know this one with luck and be there in park up ahead."

He rested the palms of his hands on the edge of the colossal planter and prepared to hop down. He was a little taller than me; only then did I notice that his lips had an odd whitish tinge. He went on gesturing toward the park, then put his hands in his pockets and said, "We go?"

I had no intention of letting him go with me. I said, "No, I think I'll look another day, maybe tomorrow."

Then he started up again with "Why want?" I didn't know how to react. I stood there immobilized, unable to choose between walking toward the park at the bridge or retracing my steps. In any case, it seemed clear that if I wanted to get rid of this guy, I'd have to be very harsh. I began slowly heading toward the park, and the black guy matched me stride for stride saying, "With me there no danger, at park they know me, and we can ask one I know who maybe know one you want, so I help and you help, you find who you want and I find help."

I stopped.

"Now look," I said, "you're mistaken. I don't want you to help me. I'm not going to the park with you. How do you expect me to help you? I can't help you."

"You say before you help if I help."

"But the thing is, you're not going to help me. You could only help me if you told me you did know this guy," and I pointed to the Nubian in the picture.

On the following planter—we'd stopped at midpoint between one planter and the next—sat two black men who had directed their attention toward us. One of them got off the edge of the planter. I was afraid they were going to come over and back up the guy with the scar and that things would start to get dicey, so I turned back, whereupon the black guy who was with me grabbed me. The time had come to make things very clear. I said, "Listen, that's enough. Leave me alone."

Perhaps I spoke too loudly. One of the black guys from the other planter, not the one who'd gotten down but the one still sitting on the edge with his legs dangling, decided to intervene. He hopped down, came over, and asked what was going on. He spoke better Spanish than the first guy, who stuck his left hand in the pocket of my jacket and took out the photo of the Nubian.

"You know?" he asked in Spanish. Which seemed to me at that moment a very polite gesture; it never once occurred to me that the two of them might not speak the same language. I took it for granted that although they were able to converse between themselves in a language impenetrable to me, the guy was speaking my language out of deference. The second guy took the photo the other one was showing him. I noticed that his nails were deep yellow, which made the entire scene even stranger. He turned toward the third black and called him over, whether in unintelligible English or his native language I don't know. In a few seconds the third man had reached us. I wasn't sure whether the best way of resolving the situation might not be to let them have the photo and get the hell out of there, shitting in my pants.

"He's a fighter," said the third guy in a refined voice that didn't match his corpulent presence.

None of the three would have passed the first round of examinations for aspirants to the Club Olympus. The third guy had applied far too generous a dose of aftershave, and the sweetish smell that emanated from him in combination with the prevailing stench—for the colossal planters in which frail bushes were growing had also been used to hold bags of garbage—was revolting.

"You know him?" I asked.

"Of course we know," said the second guy.

"See how I help," interjected the first.

"How can I find him?" I asked all three, or maybe none of them, maybe just myself.

"I find if you give me help," the first one promised.

"He fights in extreme fighting."

I didn't know whether extreme fighting was a kind of sport or a dive where wrestling matches were held.

"Saturday he fought and won. He's very good fighter. You looking for him why?" said the first guy, who'd suddenly gone from not knowing the Nubian to knowing more about him than anyone else.

"Look, it just so happens that I'm looking for him. Can you tell me how to find him?"

I felt as if I'd stepped into quicksand. The more I struggled to get out, the faster I was sinking.

"I can, I know," said the third one.

I imagined the three of them in the procession I'd seen at the airport, smeared with their own shit to keep the police from grabbing them.

"I can. Give me phone number, and I call you when is fight."

"No, no." I was growing impatient. "I don't want to see him fight; it's nothing like that. I want to meet him before he fights."

"Go to magnolia park," said the second, referring to the park that the other one had called "up ahead."

When I was in the park the next day, I discovered that it was in fact presided over by a gigantic ficus, but that there were indeed a few magnolias among the dozens of palm trees and other assorted vegetation that my botanical ignorance kept me from identifying.

"I go to magnolia park and find, give me telephone, and I call and meet you with him," said the third one.

In the end I gave in. I gave him my number. He did not write it down. He assured me he had a very good memory for important numbers. Just as I was about to say good-bye, my cell phone started vibrating in the pocket of my pants. I didn't answer the call. As I was walking away, I reproached myself for having been so afraid; those three could have robbed me, beaten me, raped me, but none of that had happened. I headed back to the hotel with a sense of having taken an important step: at least I knew now that the Nubian was in Málaga, and though the fact that he earned his living from clandestine fights was not going to make things any easier for me, that same fact would make him a lot less difficult to locate. I checked my cell phone; the call I'd missed had come from my parents' number. I dialed it, and my father answered. All he said was "Here's your brother." My brother came on the line to tell me my mother was dead; she'd been run over by a bus. The entire neighborhood considered it a tragic accident; my brother and I knew it to be a suicide in disguise.

I don't know if anyone you know has ever committed suicide, but it won't surprise you if I confess that when someone does it leaves your body feeling strange, as if you were living in a mansion where nothing's in the right place, where the mirrors don't reflect but slowly melt, the shadows don't move down the corridor ahead of you but crawl up to the ceiling and hang down from there, completely alien to you, disobeying your movements; the flowers in their planters look like monsters with terrifying faces, your footsteps on the parquet floors sound like a fork scratching a windowpane, the voices in the neighboring houses are like the roar of wild beasts, the hands of the clocks don't move, and when you turn on a faucet all that comes out is a noise that expands against the walls of your brain and stays there even after you've shut the faucet off. All of a sudden nothing is in its proper place anymore. There's no better city in which to learn of your mother's suicide than one abandoned to its fate, its air thick with rot, its street corners colonized by rats, its poor neighborhoods barricaded with flaming garbage cans, everywhere awash in shit. I told my brother what he already knew, that I wouldn't be coming to the funeral. I asked him how our father was, and I think he must have shrugged in response. Don't let your grief overwhelm you, I told myself. But the most surprising part of it was that the pain did not come. I was ready for it, waiting to fight it off, but it decided not to show up at all. Maybe it was waiting for me to let down my guard before taking a swipe at me, but the fact is that although my mind flew to Seville and tried to imagine the scene of my mother's death, I didn't manage to wound or weaken myself. I stopped to buy roses at one of the flower stands in the park. When I ran into Luzmila, she asked about the flowers and I gave her the news—the news about my mother's death, the less I told her about the Nubian the better—but when I said "My mother's dead," she only replied, "Mine, too."

That gave me an opening to ask her something I'd been wondering about for a while: "Why do you resent me?"

All I got for an answer was the quick flash of her gorgeous smile.

"Have you found out anything?"

We were in the hotel café; she'd ordered a gin and tonic, but there was another glass on the table. I sat down as if that other glass were waiting for me and began pondering the tattoo on her shoulder, a little ship atop a green wave, which her T-shirt obligingly left in full view.

"Yes. That there's not one spot in this entire city where you can escape from the stench. You?"

At that moment Luzmila's discovery stepped out of the bathroom: a tall man with black eyes and a jaw carved out of granite, his hair slicked back with gel, and his tight T-shirt underscoring the impressive musculature of his torso. She introduced him, but I've forgotten his name.

"New recruit?" I whispered to Luzmila as I got up, yielding the seat and the whiskey to the other guy.

"A private matter," she answered.

I was glad. So much the better if my Albanian friend spent her time picking up men; it would give me an advantage. But I quickly curbed these enthusiastic predictions; it would be highly uncharacteristic of Luzmila to make the mistake of wasting a few hours with this hunk if he wasn't going to give her any interesting information. Could he be one of the promoters of the clandestine fights? I couldn't know if Luzmila already had information about our Nubian's status as a fighter, and I wasn't about to let that cat out of the bag and give her a shot at it, so I went up to my room without further ado.

The proper thing would have been to spend a sleepless night, muffle my sorrow with a couple of tranquilizers, assemble a large album of mental images, and slowly reflect on my mother's life. But I soon collapsed into sleep after the inevitable minutes spent fighting off the itching that punctually appeared as soon as I stretched out naked in bed.

In the morning I was awoken very early by the telephone: not my cell but the one in the room. Before answering—there's no cure for it, no way to stop, no solution—I told myself: Moisés Froissard Calderón, La Florida 15, 3B, twenty-two years old, scout, seeker of Nubians . . . It was one of the Africans, I couldn't tell which. While I was talking to him, it never occurred to me to wonder how he knew what hotel I was staying in and why, rather than calling me on the cell phone, he was calling my room. Later I realized they must have followed me back the night before. When one of them told me he had a very good memory for important numbers, he wasn't really doing anything to try to remember my number; he already knew they'd follow me back to the hotel.

The conversation was brief.

"I have now what you wanting."

"The fighter?"

"I have. Tomorrow night we can go see his fight."

"No, no, I told you already. I don't want to see him fight. I have to meet him beforehand; otherwise there's no deal."

"What deal?"

I didn't know what to say. I couldn't remember if we'd reached any agreement or if I'd offered them some kind of compensation if they could help me find the Nubian.

"Well, you have to get him to me beforehand."

"Come to magnolia park this morning. There's a swing with children; close by there on bench you sit and wait for me this morning."

"I'm not sure I'll be able to go this morning. Last night"—and I was quiet for a moment before saying—"my mother died."

Before hanging up, the black guy said, "Mine, too."

I didn't quite remember what I'd dreamed, but I was certain that in my dream I became a machine. I'm not sure what kind of machine; I don't know what my function was or what I was used for. I still felt strange; an invisible needle pricked at my chest and the blood jumped violently in my temples. A pack of white clouds was drifting slowly in from the sea; the patches of sky between them looked like a child's watercolor. I don't know exactly when I decided to go to mass. I thought it was one way of going to my mother's funeral, and the Málaga cathedral was on the same street as my hotel, so without stopping to have breakfast I walked over to take refuge in the church's cool dimness. The service had already begun when I arrived; about a dozen solitary old people were listening to the priest as if they truly hoped to find a magical secret in his words, an elixir that would give them the strength and courage to confront the coming day. I tried to stay in my seat for as long as the mass lasted, but couldn't. Instead, I took a curious stroll through the cathedral, which at that hour was still free of tourists in their photographic frenzy. I stopped in front of a *retablo,* where with skilled hands a painter whose name had not been preserved told of the adventures and misadventures of a martyred saint. One of the *retablo*'s paintings was a magnificent illustration straight out of a gay magazine: the saint—naked, young, and very beautiful, his flesh like marble, his muscles pure sculpture, without a single hair to mar his perfect skin—was being tortured by a group of soldiers dressed in their finest clothes. The scene was exciting, and I was surprised to notice that my crotch was starting to bulge. The male saint reminded me of someone, but I couldn't think who, undoubtedly one of the pieces with whom I'd enlarged the Club Olympus's catalog of offerings. Ashamed, I turned toward the priest to see if that would diminish my desire. How strange a thing desire is, slashing out at you suddenly from the middle of the hollow morning, casting its net about you and reducing—or perhaps enlarging—you, annihilating everything false and personal within you, transforming you into pure instinct and need. That's why it's best for desire to have a proper name: the proper name that puts a floor beneath desire to close off its abyss, and a roof above it to shut out its raging storm.

I stayed there, sitting on a painted wooden bench near an old woman who had fallen to her knees to talk to her God. I was thinking about life and the martyrdom of that saint, imagining who the anonymous painter's model had been, wondering whether they'd been lovers and whether the bishop who commissioned the altarpiece was aware of the relationship between the painter and his model, and whether that same bishop, on seeing the painting, hadn't demanded that the painter give him the model's address, then sent the model a message summoning him to the bishop's residence in the early hours of the morning. And all that while, in a parallel narrative, for the brain can permit itself these luxuries and project several movies at once, mixing up their negatives, I was imagining the church in which, at that very hour, the funeral mass for my mother was being held.

I left the cathedral feeling a little disturbed and started for the magnolia park on the prolongation of the Alameda. The morning air was cold, and I felt like walking but wanted to get there quickly, so as soon as I reached the enormous avenue presided over by the massive post office I chose a passerby up ahead to compete against for an Olympic gold medal. The walk seemed very short, and I didn't pay much attention to the many Africans who crossed my path as I drew closer to the park that was my goal. However, by the powerful light of day, I did come to a more exact appreciation of the quality of the city's architecture: unquestionably atrocious. Particularly appalling was a picturesque colossus in the style of Gaudí that copied only his defects, balconies that folded back on themselves, rooftops in imitation of fairy-tale gnome dwellings. Also, I'd seen the news about the death of fifteen immigrants that was on the front page of all the newspapers, and it was jumbled in with the rest of my thoughts: they'd drowned at Barbate beach in Cádiz. The Guardia Civil had taken seventy-three others into custody, an excellent number, very promising. Impossible to keep from thinking of the lives that, because of the Doctor's special mission, I wasn't going to be able to save. The high season for shipwrecks was beginning, and you had to be constantly on the lookout or the best pieces would slip through your fingers. I also thought about my mother's burial and asked myself again and again who it was that the saint being tortured in the painting in the altarpiece reminded me of. This assortment of thoughts kept me from internally broadcasting the succession of Olympic footraces by which I reached the park, but even so I didn't lose my concentration; the farther your thoughts stray during these kinds of activities, the better your legs react, with no complaints about your speed, carrying you as if you were levitating over the sidewalk.

On the colossal planter that stood at the entrance to the park, which contained a single bush prostrated before dozens of kilos of garbage bags, the heavyset black guy of the previous evening was sitting waiting for me, now deprived of his deep gaze by a spectacular pair of mirrored sunglasses that gave back to the world whatever the world presented to him. His shoes glittered as well, and the sun rebounded off them, daubing their toes with two gleaming drops of light. I won't dwell on the nuances of the stench in that part of the city.

"Manager here, waiting to talk," he said. And we went into the park along a gravel path, leaving behind the bald patch of dark sand where some swings had been installed, though it must have been years since they'd enjoyed a child's merriment. Here and there, engaging or disturbing figures peopled this park, which was large enough to allow for all sorts of nooks and niches, little plazas with dried-up fountains, stretches of lawn untouched by the sun, which stayed high above, threading its light through the crowns of the trees: a pair of diminutive old men who had no choice but to stroll together, though without saying a word to each other (a retirement center was nearby), a woman keeping guard over an army of bags of clothing, who passed the time reading an impressive tome and ripping out each page as she finished it, a group of hippies who spent the morning lying on the shadowy grass deciding what place in the world to run away to next once they'd recovered from their laziness, and blacks, many blacks, the masters of the park, who tolerated the presence of the odd white but adopted a bellicose stance if a visitor belonged to any other group of immigrants—North Africans, Peruvians, Chinese.

We sat down on one of the benches around a dead fountain, whose basin formed yet another depository of garbage which, as it rotted, manufactured the highly effective reek that had conquered the city and placed firemen and soldiers in a state of alert after negotiations between the garbage workers and the city government again broke down. (Within a few months, a distinguished sociologist would publish an interesting study of the increase in crimes of passion and domestic violence during the garbage strike.) On the other five benches that completed the perimeter of the little plaza, other Africans were waiting, all young, all well dressed. How did they earn their living? Where did they get their money? What did they do all day? The manager was a young man, I put him at a little over thirty, heavyset, with a shaved head, small eyes, and a deep voice. He received callers two or three times a day and always in the same way: he sat on the edge of the basin and would summon one of the men waiting on the benches, the man would explain his problem or proffer his request, and the manager would recommend a solution or tell him what he had to do. The bench left unoccupied by the man consulting with the manager was quickly taken by another man, who until then had waited in the shadow of one of the boundary stones that lined the gravel walkways. What were they all asking about or requesting, and who was he? The black who was acting as my guide said he would tell me later, but for now I should be quiet. The only thing I asked him, before the manager called us over, was what his name was.

"I don't know: manager."

"No," I said. "I mean you. What's your name?"

"Carlos," he answered.

"Where are you from?"

"Guinea."

"How long have you been here?"

"Long time."

And he asked me to be quiet again because the manager had given us a look that demanded silence as he attended to a boy who, judging by the condition of his running shoes, was asking the manager to get him a new pair. Despite the ban on speaking, I insisted on giving Carlos a vital test. I asked him where he lived.

"Around here," he said, anger souring his expression.

THE NUBIAN PRINCE 137

"And how do you earn a living?"

"We won't be called if you talk."

At that moment we were called. I didn't hear the manager's voice, but he must have signaled to Carlos somehow that we approach. We sat down on the edge of the fountain, Carlos on one side of the manager and me on the other. Though I had held out my hand to him, he only bowed his head slightly in greeting and patted the spot to his right where I was to sit.

"We look for fighter."

"Which fighter?"

Again I was pleased that they were speaking Spanish, regardless of whether they were doing it for my benefit, in order to include me in their dialogue, or because they had no other language in common. Carlos told me to show the photo to the manager. For a moment I thought I'd left it back at the hotel, but finally I found it; I'd cut it down so it would fit in my wallet. The setting, which was probably the very place we were in, was gone; all that was left was the resounding image of the Nubian.

"Boo," said the manager. I didn't know if it was an interjection, a monosyllabic word in his African language, or the moniker by which he knew the Nubian. I asked and learned that Boo was the Nubian's name.

"Tomorrow he fight," said the manager.

"Ah," I interjected, "but I need to meet him before tomorrow."

"Why you want?"

"I'm interested in him, that's all. I have a proposition for him that's going to interest him a great deal."

"Fights?" the manager asked.

"I can't say anything about it," I said. I wanted to improvise something, but nothing came out; I could have claimed to be representing a famous gym that was signing on the greatest extreme fighters and wanted to offer a lot of money to the Nubian and his representative, but nothing came out. Of course I was very clear on the fact that if I wanted to win his trust, I couldn't breathe a word to the Nubian about the existence of the Club Olympus and what it had in store for him. My mission consisted in taking the Nubian to the Doctor. I had no doubt she would take care of the rest, coddling him along until he was fully convinced that he had to travel to New York to satisfy the esoteric longings of a millionaire who had laid out a vast amount of money for his services. But I had nothing to do with any of that. I remember I once succeeded in persuading a pair of Romanian shantytown dwellers to sell me their son, on the pretext that he would be playing soccer in Barcelona. When I took the boy to the Doctor, he was still expecting to be sent to a soccer training camp. How the Doctor fixed things so that the Romanian boy ended up being one of the Club's sexual prodigies—one of its most efficient machines—was a mystery I had no interest whatsoever in exploring.

"Talk to me," said the manager, a tempting but inadmissible invitation. What was I going to tell him? Yes, he was the bridge that would carry me to the Nubian faster than I'd ever dreamed I'd reach him. But my imagination was drained, and I couldn't come up with anything to say that would convince him I represented the Nubian's salvation and had come looking for him in order to save his life.

"He's great fighter," said Carlos.

"I don't doubt it," I said.

"You want to set up match with big bets," the manager informed rather than asked me. I suppose I must have been fed up and gave evidence of this with an ill-considered snort, which troubled the manager's calm and made him give me a petulant look. I decided to speak.

"There's a lot of money at stake, a lot of money for Boo, I have a fantastic deal to offer him, but I can only offer it to him, not to anyone else, any intermediary. If you can help me find him and talk to him, I'll make it worth your while, and if you can't, then we're both wasting our time here."

The manager weighed my words. For a moment I thought he hadn't understood anything I'd said, and I was about to translate it into English, without knowing if he would understand that. He scratched his cheek, offered me a broad smile, held out his hand for me to shake—which I did without altering the expression on my face in the slightest—and said, finally, "Here tomorrow at eight, we go see Boo fight crazy Yankee soldier, then you talk to Boo, you and Boo alone."

As I walked away from the magnolia park where I'd counted far more palm trees than anything else, I felt the burning heat of a gaze boring into the back of my neck. It felt as if the outline of my body were being watched by a sniper posted on a nearby rooftop through the scope of his weapon. Thus do we live, continually within the infernal circle we don't know how to escape, watched by the invisible assassin who will pull the trigger sooner or later. I turned around to see if I could detect the source of the blaze that had erupted against the back of my neck, and a hand was raised to me in greeting above a patch of shadow it took me a while to recognize. It was Nadim, sitting alone on the edge of one of the colossal, useless planters that cluttered up the pathway. She jumped down and came to me. I watched her walk over as if in slow motion, I watched a slight smile begin to form on her face, which was looking much better, and I paid particular attention to the sunlight exploding around the top of her head, which made it look almost metallic, and gave her a small halo.

"It's been a while," she said.

And that was true. So much had happened between that dusty sunrise in the train station of a town whose name I can't recall and this reeking noon in which we met again that the measure of real time was distorted by the sum of adversities we both had passed through. Nadim was not Nadim; she was named Irene. She was wearing loose gray pants and white tennis shoes without laces. On top was a white T-shirt bearing the words "Ledig House, New York City" in red letters. Since at first I'd stood dumbstruck, not responding to her greeting, Irene asked whether I remembered her or not. She put this to me in excellent English. Then she wanted to know if I'd had time to develop the pictures I took of her with my Leica. I laughed and felt a stupid look appear on my face; just because someone has paid a fortune to get on a dilapidated barge and leave Africa, and then spent several days defying death before being shipwrecked, you imagine that that person will be a savage who won't know what it is to develop a photograph.

"Want to have a drink?" I stammered.

And she gestured toward a bar where several groups of blacks filled all the outside tables.

"Better inside, it won't smell so bad," said Irene. And we walked over. Neither of us said a word during the fifty meters we covered to get there, though a couple of times I raised my eyes from the ground, where they were dragging along behind our shadows, to the pure exactitude of her profile. She had her hands in her pockets, and one pocket made a metallic sound at every step, keys hitting against coins.

Over two glasses of pineapple juice we talked. I began by telling her I hadn't yet developed the photos but would be very happy to give her one as soon as I did, as long as she didn't disappear on me again.

"I'm sure I don't look good in them," she said, adding, with a flirtatious glance that slightly wrinkled the corners of her eyes, "Are you still mad at me for stealing the camera?"

I ignored the question and wanted to know how she'd reached

Málaga and whether she'd found a job and a place to live and if she'd managed to locate someone she knew there.

Like each and every one of the Africans who packed that avenue, she had an extraordinary story behind her; she carried with her a densely populated tragedy, full of dead family members and broken dreams and legends about neighbors who'd managed to reach a country where things were less difficult. Now she was aglow with unfounded happiness, as if the mere fact of having survived the crossing and escaped from the coast guard enabled her to forget that there was no guarantee she could stay where she was and earn a living—"earn a living," that eloquent expression by which language wisely tells us what a brutal thing work is.

Irene was from a small city in Mauritania, from one of the few well-off families in the region—her father was in the military. Against her parents' wishes she'd moved to the capital to enroll in the university. Things started getting ugly for everyone, and when she found out that a group of her brother's friends were negotiating with a big wheel who handled travel to Morocco for those looking to embark from there for Spain, she decided to go home to her parents, convince them that she realized she'd made a mistake and was coming home to stay, then take advantage of the moment to steal a good part of their savings, return to the capital city, pay for her ticket to Morocco, and embark on the adventure whose denouement I already knew. She told me all this as if it were of very slight importance, implying that here in this very bar were at least a dozen girls who had far more impressive stories to tell.

"And you? What are you doing here? You didn't come looking for me, did you?"

I shook my head, holding in a belch.

The bar suddenly fell silent as the tomb. As if they'd had some premonition, those sitting outside rose from their seats, abandoning their drinks, and came inside, each one noiselessly finding a space at the bar or one of the tables. On the gigantic screen that hung on the back wall, a news bulletin had come on about another shipwreck on the coast of Cádiz. The images were all too familiar: Guardia Civil lifeboats trying to recover a drifting drowned body, a policeman throwing a cable from a helicopter down to a young boy who waved his arms, unable to cross the distance that lay between him and the lifeline that could lift him from the water. Nine bodies had been recovered, though there were no official figures on the tragedy yet. Those who had been rescued were now in the hands of the Red Cross, among them two pregnant women. Those two might be allowed to stay. The others would be repatriated. A shattering cry seared the air when the camera panned across the row of corpses lined up on the beach. In its wake came a growing rumble of voices. Irene didn't want to look at the TV screen and didn't understand the words that accompanied the images.

"Let's go," she said.

After a quick walk spent snaking our way around mountains of trash—I saw a rat cross an alley from one heap of garbage to another and found it the most normal thing in the world, proof that the stench was affecting not only my sense of smell but my spirit as well—we entered the pedestrian zone in the city center, which like the rest of the city had been emptied by the repulsive situation; the perfume shops alone were doing a roaring business, selling barrels of cologne to protect the air inside your home.

"How do they all make a living?" I asked Irene.

"It depends. The Nigerians control the heroin business, the Sudanese run the secret fights, and some of the others make do by converting to Islam and asking the rich brothers in Marbella for help. And some need the help of an NGO; there are organizations that try to find apartments we can share. An organization called Málaga Shelters has a whole building where they put people who are waiting to be repatriated."

"Are you staying in one of those apartments?"

"Yes, I have a friend here in Málaga, and she's letting me stay in her room. There are twelve of us in the apartment, but it's a big place with two floors. The neighbors aren't happy about it, but we're not likely to stop by and ask the girls next door for a cup of sugar; we don't want them getting all worked up about us, and we don't complain when they get home drunk at three in the morning and put on very loud music. They're American students who came here to get laid and learn Spanish; they can do as they please."

"And what are your plans? I mean, I don't exactly see you as an extreme fighter, not really, and as for heroin . . ."

"I'll look for a job, like everyone else. My friend is a cleaning lady for several houses, and she told me she could find me some work. To get your residency permit, you have to hold out for three years, and if you're going to stay here for three years, you have to work. But it's hard to find work if you don't have a residency permit. I've got to learn Spanish."

"A nightmare vicious circle."

"That's what it is. Of course there's always another way, right?"

"There always is, especially when you're beautiful."

"And even when you're not."

"But that means getting mixed up with some ugly mafia types."

"Of course your Club isn't any kind of mafia."

"Of course not, I can promise you that. As I told you, if it were a mafia, we wouldn't be looking for exceptional girls."

"Thanks for the compliment."

Irene seemed angry. It probably disgusted her to remember my offer, and I wondered whether she had ever pondered the terms of my proposal during her journey to Málaga. It seemed unlikely that the recollection had tempted her, not even as an emergency exit through which to abandon a reality that was intent on destroying her.

"And this prince you're looking for, he's for the Club?"

"That's right."

"If he's a good fighter, you're not going to have an easy time winning him over."

"They earn a lot?"

"It's not that. I'm sure they don't earn as much as the ones who organize the fights, but those guys aren't going to just let your prince wander off and become a whore. What's more, I'm pretty sure the fighters have a fairly easy life; they're watched closely, of course, to make sure they don't take it into their heads to ruin the business by wandering off, but they eat a lot. I'm sure they're well nourished."

"But the prince doesn't have to become a whore; this particular case is more complex—quite unique actually."

I explained the situation to Irene, and she tried to imagine the face of the sicko who'd initiated this whole operation, the nameless individual who saw a photo in a magazine and asked the Club Olympus to find the person in the picture and serve him up on a silver platter.

"Have you ever fallen madly in love with someone you'd only seen in a photograph?"

I shook my head. "I have," she confessed. "It was a rugby player from New Zealand. There was a picture of him hanging in the barber shop in my hometown."

I was on the point of asking her why the hell someone had

hung a picture of a New Zealand rugby player on the wall of a barber shop in a town in Mauritania, but then decided it was one of those things I was better off not knowing. Compared to the one I could imagine on the basis of the facts I already knew, whatever story she could tell me would seem vulgar or trivial.

"Who knows? Maybe he just wants to sit down with him and have a chat," I said, getting back to the Nubian and the client who was asking for him. "I've heard of stranger things. People who prayed to a picture of a whore as if she were the Virgin. People who borrowed money from the bank so they could pay for an hour with a boy. Millionaires who treated themselves to a party with ten or twelve models from the Club Olympus, then had the models fuck each other in the swimming pool while the millionaires relaxed around the edge, watching them and sipping good gin without feeling the slightest temptation to touch a single millimeter of that gorgeous flesh."

I invited her to have lunch with me. I suggested my hotel on the pretext that my camera was there and I felt like taking a few more pictures of her, better ones than those I'd shot in the dusty train station. She agreed to join me on a pretext far more convincing than any of mine: it was certain to be more pleasant in the hotel than in the unbearable street. Of course I didn't tell her that in addition to taking some pictures of her—though I couldn't consider her a piece scouted by me for the Club Olympus, and therefore she couldn't go in my pantheon album—I was also hoping Luzmila would see us together. I wanted to make Luzmila nervous, make her see that my talent had won me a prize contact with the black community in the person of this exquisite and adorable lady, and that my quest for the Nubian—though I didn't know what progress Luzmila had made—might be meeting with very rapid success. I called the Doctor from one of the hotel's phone booths while Irene waited for the tropical salads we'd both ordered. I told her that things were going well; although I hadn't yet seen the Nubian, I had located him. All the blood rose from my body into my head, my heart palpitated wildly, and my lungs shrank within me when the Doctor replied, "Really? I take it you're referring to the same Nubian who is, apparently, up in Luzmila's room right now."

I dropped the receiver, signaled Irene to go ahead and eat without me, got into the elevator, trying to restore my normal breathing pattern as I rose from floor to floor, then stood in front of the door of Luzmila's room and knocked. It was opened by a tall man of truly fearsome aspect, the endless expanse of his chest illustrated by a baroque tattoo in which I intuited, rather than saw, womanly curves and sea waves. He did have one defect, however: he was white. Luzmila's voice emerged from behind him, inviting me in.

"So this is the Nubian you've come up with?" I asked.

"Well, we'd need a little shoe polish for that, wouldn't we?"

"Then why the fuck did you tell the Doctor that . . . ," and I shut up as the guy who'd opened the door looked at me in some confusion, unsure whether to let me have it for addressing his lover in that tone of voice or to disappear for a while and leave us on our own. Luzmila ordered him to take a shower, and the giant meekly obeyed.

"Don't get all nervous. I only told her that I had him here in my room, not that I'd signed him on and was sending him to her by express mail."

"But you made me look like an idiot."

"Well, that's what you're good at, after all."

"I'm sick of your stupid games, I really am. I don't know what you're trying to do. What's going on? You came to Málaga to get laid by every marine who got off the ship that docked yesterday?"

"How did you know he's a marine? I'm impressed," said Luzmila, who was starting to paint her nails. She was wearing a see-through camisole and had her hair pulled back and wrapped in a green scarf that matched the little wave tattooed on her shoulder. I didn't know what else to say and turned to leave, but Luzmila held me there, sweetening her tone.

"I'm sure you've made a lot of progress, but I'm also sure you're going to need me when you want to bring things to a conclusion, so I'm only letting you pave my way for me. The best thing would be if you told me what you've been up to and I took over for you. I'm sure you're in over your head, and I've seen on the news that a pile of blacks and north Africans are arriving on the coast. Some drown, others don't, and that's your specialty, that's what you're good at, isn't it? You've got your contacts among the cops and all that, so the best thing would be for you to leave this in my hands and head off to Cádiz to hunt more pieces."

"That's certainly what you'd like and maybe you've even told the Doctor so, but I'm going to call her right now and tell her there's still no sign of the Nubian and there won't ever be any sign of him if she sends me off to Cádiz to look for shipwreck survivors."

"Now, now. Where's your humanitarianism? Think of all the good you could do. Don't you know why you do this job?"

The question hit me hard on the jaw and left me deaf.

The marine came out of the bathroom. He gave Luzmila a questioning glance, and she beckoned him over.

"I must let you go now," she said to me. "If you want, we can talk tonight and come to an agreement. It's so hard to leave the room. It smells so bad everywhere." And with that she turned to the marine, whose only garment was the towel he wore knotted around his waist.

Irene and I were finishing up our dessert when Luzmila came down to join us, no marine attached. She evinced no surprise at seeing me with a beautiful African woman, but greeted her as if they'd met the day before. She asked Irene all about herself, and even though Luzmila's English left much to be desired, they immediately understood each other as accomplices in the same tragedy, as if they each knew enough to complete a puzzle between the two of them—a puzzle I would be incapable of fitting a single piece to. Only when it was time to order coffee did I remember my mother, buried that morning. It had been hours since her image had troubled me, since I'd asked myself how my family was doing, or punished myself by imagining the process of decay that had begun in her body only a little while earlier. I had to go to the bathroom for a moment, and I'm almost positive Luzmila took advantage of my absence to place herself on even more intimate terms with Irene or tell her something that would undermine my authority. Be that as it may, the fact is that Luzmila, having had her fill of the marine, must have resolved that the time had come to get moving and not forget entirely about the mission from which her uncontrollable urge to fuck anyone and everyone she wasn't trying to scout for the Club had made her take an unexpected break. She spent the entire afternoon with us. We stayed in the hotel, in no mood to go out into the street, and when I said it was time to go up to my room with Irene to shoot the promised photos, Luzmila added herself to our group without the slightest protest from Irene. Of course, why on earth would she have protested? By that time Irene may already have been mulling over the idea of joining the Club Olympus as a model, swayed by the cannily timed propositions Luzmila had been making throughout the afternoon. I felt as if she were stealing my job out from under me but couldn't complain about that either because I realized, when I tried to verbalize my objection, that it would sound like the faint bleating of someone who didn't know how to make the most of his position but consistently lost all his important pieces and jeopardized his victory, and therefore had to find a scapegoat because even he didn't understand how the hell he kept on making one mistake after another.

"I like your friend," Irene said when Luzmila had left my room for a moment to take a phone call.

"Uh-huh."

"You saved her life."

"She told you that?"

"More or less."

"Well, it's true. She's the first person whose life I saved in this business. Only a couple of years ago she was a beggar in the streets of Seville, going from café to café to plead for food. She even had to turn tricks on the Alameda de Hércules sometimes, and that's the cheapest place in the city for that kind of business."

"You say that as if begging were a shameful thing, as opposed to fucking one of the clients of your Club."

I begged her pardon. I also wasn't happy with the pictures I was taking; they seemed awkward or, even worse, meaningless. Irene looked like a well-brought-up young lady offering a reporter from a glossy magazine the exquisite comfort of her private room. When I take a portrait, I like to isolate the figure I'm shooting from any kind of setting; I prefer uniform backgrounds, a dark drop cloth or a white wall, and there wasn't a single corner in that overdecorated hotel room where I could position Irene to isolate her. Not that I so dislike the Arnold Newman type of portrait where the background is meant to reveal the essence of the person portrayed, who occupies only a small space in the middle of his own portrait, yielding the rest of the picture to the objects that will say much more about him than his own image. But I feel closer to the school of Irving Penn, who always put the people he shot in front of a gray drop cloth, nothing more than that; he never offered any kind of background to hint to the viewer about the virtues or defects of the soul of the person portrayed. Of course I'm closer to that type of portrait largely because the people I was shooting were of such extraordinary beauty that nothing could have competed with them for centrality in the final image, and also because when I took their pictures I knew so little about them that even to suggest a setting in relation to the subject would have seemed terribly contrived.

Luzmila was, in fact, the first of the pieces in my pantheon album. When I really wanted to drive myself nuts, I would spin a private hypothesis about that album of mine, telling myself that I had the mind of a collector and was therefore incurably melancholic, that my need to photograph the pieces I caught and to choose the best negative, enlarge it, and stick it on a page, protected by a sheet of plastic, was evidence of a psychic ailment whose cause I would have to investigate at some point by trolling through the murky depths of psychoanalysis. However jeeringly I put it, I knew I wouldn't be able to keep from sending my thoughts somewhere in search of an explanation that would satisfy me, but then, whenever my thoughts set out in that direction, hard as I tried to come up with something, I would end up tired and with nothing whatsoever to show for the effort: simply the collection of images that was there like a mausoleum where I stored all those who owed their lives to me. Luzmila told me: it certainly is true that you've never fallen in love with any of the pieces you've caught for the Club, but it's just as true that you're hopelessly in love with all the pieces you've caught, in love with your life's work. You must be the only scout in the Club Olympus who truly believes that our mission is to save lives.

"You don't believe that?' I asked her innocently. And she exploded with laughter.

My job was to save lives, it was that simple, and there was Luzmila already saved and Irene about to be saved to prove that fact to myself and give me wings to go out in search of another piece to rescue from the undeserved mud. Could it be true, as Luzmila said, that my problem was that I was incapable of developing feelings that could elevate me, and the most I could aspire to as a measure of the impact someone was having on me was to desire him or her? But as I've mentioned, my desire at that point was taking a long vacation in some remote, uncharted archipelago—unless you count the episode in the cathedral, which was quite funny if you ignore the macabre circumstances of its happening on the day of my mother's funeral, I hadn't managed to arouse my desire for ages. It was increasingly difficult for me to conceal my lack of appetite when the Doctor made her demands. Nevertheless, I was beginning to realize that I felt an odd sort of fascination mingled with tenderness for Irene, a fascination of indeterminate origin, and I was toying with the idea of inviting her to stay with me beyond Málaga, even after the Nubian was found and scouted. The thought that she might enter the Club as a model made me feel ill. After all, another of the time-honored methods immigrants use to obtain their residency papers involves convincing a native to fall in love with them, or arranging a marriage of convenience, and I was beginning to consider such an offer in my head, though merely as a working hypothesis, as yet unsubstantiated by enough data to be taken seriously or removed from the category of hypothesis and promoted to that of seductive possibility or urgent solution. After several hours in that hotel room with those two ladies, all three of us slowly getting drunk together, I stretched out in bed thinking about how strange the whole thing was. Though I tried to push the image of my mother's first night in the cemetery out of my mind, I felt as if I could hear the rats squealing in the street and the sound of strange footsteps on the cemetery gravel, while in the house that had always been my home my father drank his first glass of milk as a widower and wondered whether to switch on the TV and dilute his bitterness with some idiotic entertainment, stupid competition, or wooden performance—my brother always said the essential purpose of those late-night shows is to convince their viewers that the best thing they can do for society is fall into a deep depression; he also maintained that such shows were entirely funded by the pharmaceutical labs that manufacture tranquilizers and antidepressants—or else he could leave the TV off and watch his own reflection on the dark screen. When I was a boy, obeying my mother's sharp order, I learned to reel off at top speed my first name and both surnames, my age, and my address—in case I got lost and had to ask a stranger for help—and in exactly the same way I now repeated my full name, my age, and my address and added: my job is to save lives.

Irene had fallen asleep in Luzmila's room; we'd all gone up there to pillage the minibar after a surly waiter informed us the café was about to close. That was when my Albanian colleague proposed, "Shall we share her?"

I didn't know, or didn't want to know, what she was talking about.

"You're obviously the one who found her, but I'm the one who's persuaded her to join the Club."

"You've persuaded her?"

"Practically."

I was dubious and disappointed. I'd finally managed to spend a few hours with someone who was beautiful and poor without thinking about the possibility of making money off her good looks, and now Luzmila had taken the wind from my sails, having been hard at work behind my back the whole time, a very efficient machine indeed, a fail-safe machine.

"This trip will be our crowning success," said Luzmila, relentlessly bent on sapping my morale. "We can agree," she added, "to put me down as the one who scouted Irene, and list you for the Nubian. I need to improve my statistics. I haven't scouted many females—it's one of the weak spots on my record."

"Do you know why you don't do well with women?"

The question was intended to return the blow that had deafened me up in her room.

"Well, I'm sure you do, since you're such an ace at female psychology."

"Want me to tell you?"

She nodded, saying that if I couldn't answer the question she had asked me earlier, she'd appreciate it if I would at least answer my own question to her.

"Because you know what you're getting them into. I don't; I've never had to lie there under some client, but you have, and you know that however many hundreds of euros they were paying, not a single one of those men deserved to have the pleasure of your body. You don't work well with women because you don't want to get them involved in this; you know you're not really rescuing them from the mud."

"Well, what a fascinating angle you have on the situation. You could write a dissertation."

"Which one of the clients you had was the worst? Which was the best?"

She actually deigned to answer the questions. She reviewed, none too exhaustively, her working sessions as a Club model. Most of the clients who chose her were executives passing through the city who'd been told by previous clients about the existence of a beautiful Albanian girl whose cachet was vertiginously on the rise. Among them she recalled with special affection a retired soccer player who'd decided to spend all the money he'd saved during his time as a privileged star of the stadiums as fast as possible, reasoning that if he didn't spend the entire amount, a judge would force him to divvy it up between his two abandoned wives. No client had ever disgusted her by asking for something unrealistic or repellent, all of them had behaved more or less like gentlemen, avid gentlemen, and she would often obligingly mount them to accelerate their orgasms.

"That's against Club rules, isn't it? Don't they tell you not to take care of a client too quickly because then he's going to think he's paid a lot for very little and won't ask for you again?"

"Even so, they all came back, and I always stayed with them for the whole allotted time. They asked me about my life or told me moronic stories about themselves. They all liked to have me invent some incredible adventure in a boat full of half-dead refugees, or tell them how I spent almost a week lost on a mountain without eating. All very idyllic."

"Really? That's not exactly the way I heard it—concerning your skills," I said, trying to get a little mileage from what the Doctor had recently confided. "I have it on good authority that not a single client ever asked you back for a second session. Were you really once lost on a mountain for a week?"

"Maybe. I've forgotten. Who told you no client ever . . . ? The Doctor's talked to you about my time as a whore?"

"We say 'model,' not 'whore,' Luzmila. None of them fell madly in love with you?"

"Only because I didn't want them to," she said, angered by my doubts about her skills and by the Doctor's betrayal.

To change the subject I delivered an accusation: "I don't believe you've been spending all your time getting it on with marines without even trying to find the Nubian. I know you're hiding something."

"If you want to," she said obligingly, "we can each run through our discoveries to see where we stand and who's closer to reaching the Nubian."

"Fine. No problem. Ladies first."

Luzmila helped herself to another miniature whiskey; it was the last one. The alcohol I'd ingested was beginning to claw at the back of my throat and the pit of my stomach. But I wasn't about to let the night end here.

"I know as much as you do," she said.

"Very clever. What do I know?"

"Aha, a question of real philosophical significance."

"Philosophical significance indeed," I replied. Neither of us was going to tip his hand; we were both convinced that any gift of information would not soften the other's heart and would not be reciprocated.

"All right, if you want to play cat and mouse, we're not going to get very far, especially since there's nothing left to drink."

"I don't want to; I'm fully prepared to share everything I know. We're working as a team, aren't we?"

"What would I have to gain by hiding information from you?" she replied, slipping off her shoes and lying down on the bed next to Irene. She stared at the sleeping woman a long while, then said, "Pity about those enlarged pores, but there must be a solution to that, I imagine. I've also noticed that she has a cavity."

"You looked at her teeth?"

"Of course—that's important. Very important."

"You're quite the consummate professional. Are you finally going to tell me what you've found out about our Nubian?"

"The guy you saw me having a drink with yesterday was a contact: extremely elegant, highly refined, deeply conservative, and bored with life to an intolerable degree. Someone told me to call him, that he could help us; he knows a lot about the Africans in Málaga. As soon as he saw the photo of the Nubian, he said, 'People notice a specimen like that one.' Then he told me about the underground fights you heard about this morning in that park where you went to waste your time and get ripped off by a bunch of losers. He's involved in the fights; I don't know whether he's one of the promoters or just bets on them. In any case, he was useful. He brought me the real promoter—a guy who's nothing but a vast collection of scars on a long, lean body—I don't know if he's in the *Guinness Book of World Records* but if he's not it's only because he doesn't want to be. I didn't even see his whole body, only what his clothes didn't cover, but that was enough to imagine the rest. With him was the giant you saw in my room this afternoon; that marine is none other than the contender who's going up against our Nubian in the fight you think you're going to be attending because you've made an agreement with two scam artists who'll swindle you the moment your back is turned."

I couldn't get over it. Reeling with surprise, alcohol thickening my tongue, I managed to ask, "And you fucked the marine because you're trying to drain his strength so he won't hurt our Nubian?"

Luzmila proved to me once more that she was capable of laughing wholeheartedly when the occasion arose. Irene shifted on the bed and said something we couldn't decipher.

"No, stupid. I fucked him because he was very, very good, and because he'll be dead tomorrow."

"Dead?" I was shocked and couldn't hide it.

"It seems that our Nubian is invincible. He's been killing off soldiers, neighborhood karate champions, racist security guards, and professional boxers looking for easy money who thought extreme fighting was a joke. However much muscle that marine has on him, he still won't be able to take it for very long."

"And it was the guy with the scars who told you all that."

"Of course. I told him that my interest in the Nubian is purely sexual and that I'm prepared to pay a magnificent sum of money to carry him off with me to my mansion. The scar guy keeps him locked away along with the other gladiators, God only knows where. The Nubian is a gold mine because even though he always wins, there's always a big group of fans who dream of seeing him defeated and think that if they support his opponents by betting on them, they'll make them believe they can beat him. Of course tomorrow's fight will be packed to the rafters with marines who'll bet their every dollar on their brother-in-arms. Things could get ugly when our marine gets torn into tiny pieces."

"I do not believe a single word you are saying."

"Well that's just great. Here I am, keeping you informed, offering you my help, and you won't take advantage, out of mere pride. OK. Great. Go on with your own movie, then, show up for your appointment tomorrow with those two scammers, and you can tell me all about it later."

"How do you know about my appointment in the morning?"

"Because for all your much-vaunted experience, you've never learned to keep to yourself what you should keep to yourself."

I looked down at Irene and realized that Luzmila had persuaded her to repeat every word of what I'd told her.

I got out of bed early on the morning of the match with a stabbing pain in my head and the feeling that my entire body was a single open wound, and ran to the cybercafé on the same street as the hotel to do a little investigation on the subject of underground extreme fighting. During my brief, alcohol-infused sleep, my dreams had fabricated agonizing images of dimly lit combats, broken bones, and bloody faces, the worst part being that every scene was contaminated by the stench that came billowing up the hotel's facade and in through my open window. I overheard, during my hasty breakfast, that the city government had hired an army of street cleaners and tractors to clear out certain particularly hard-hit areas—the wealthiest in the city, naturally. Constant fights continued to break out in the poorer neighborhoods, and the preceding night's altercations had claimed several victims, one of them a boy of twelve, felled when a rubber bullet fired by the police to disperse protestors ricocheted against his temple. On my way to the cybercafé I saw two bulldozers removing the mountain of garbage that had grown up in front of the hotel; a dump truck stood ready and waiting to haul it away.

I Googled the words *extreme fights, underground, Málaga* and came up with nothing. Then I eliminated *extreme* and found an article published in the local paper, *La Opinión*. It was very poorly written, in a pompous style—obviously its author was trying to conceal his lack of information behind his purple prose. The description of the fighters was particularly laughable. A few atrociously tacky passages read more like an account of a fashion show than a fight to the death. As far as I could glean, the underground fights were held in rather inaccessible locations— obviously—were attended by individuals from all walks of life (??), and very, very, very large amounts of money were wagered on them (!!). The fight the newspaper's reporter attended was "hellish"; the contenders were a "Herculean Negro" and a Turk "with the air of a butcher and an aesthetically incorrect mustache." The winner was the Herculean Negro, perhaps the very Nubian we were looking for. The Turk had to be carried out on a stretcher and hospitalized. What sort of explanation was the hospital given for the state the aesthetically incorrect butcher was in? The author of the article intuited that the implied hospital was no more than a turn of phrase; in all likelihood the badly injured Turk was abandoned to his fate in some ditch between the inaccessible spot where the combat had taken place and the city of Málaga: "a line of glittering light on the horizon." The author claimed to have succeeded in interviewing one of the promoters of the underground fights but he failed to cite a single line from the conversation, as if the simple fact of having achieved this interview was sufficient proof of his professionalism. Not much was clarified by this article; it did confirm that the underground fights took place at some spot quite removed from the city limits and that they were attended by a crowd that apparently managed to keep the event secret enough to avoid being disturbed by the police. Certainly if the police did nothing to stop these matches, it was probably—or assuredly—because of their own interest in having them take place; perhaps the promoters charmed them with a suitcase full of euros, enough to finance their invisibility. That the press—that alternate police force—hadn't profited from the story's many attractions in page after page of scabrous prose, stirring the populace to clamor for an end to this scourge, might mean that, though fully aware of what was going on, the journalists had preferred to keep their eyes closed because the situation was still a new one and didn't yet have the power to provoke much public outrage—perhaps because not enough people had been killed, or because the fights involved gangsters and mafias with whom it was best not to clash.

Whatever the case, I decided to pay a visit to the local newspaper's offices, find the reporter whose name was on the piece, and see if I could garner something a little juicier than what appeared in his article. I was in luck. A harried individual, recently emerged from the shower and exhibiting symptoms—such as the skin stretched tight over the bones of his face—of not having spent a very good night, had just arrived at the newsroom. His teeth were yellow with nicotine, and his voice was hoarse. He acted surprised that anyone would be looking for him at so early an hour and spoke to me in front of the coffee machine in the hallway, continually shrinking back as if he were fearful I'd come to attack him for something he'd written. When he learned the reason for my visit, he didn't seem relieved; he may have suspected I was a police investigator looking for privileged information in order to initiate judicial proceedings, or a colleague who, having read his scoop, was hoping to improve on his work with sharper prose and a more probing curiosity. I told him I was a big fan of these kinds of fights, that I liked to bet money on them, and that after discovering his article on the Internet, I thought he might be able to tell me about upcoming matches; I'd heard one would be taking place soon. What he told me, between stammers that conveniently allowed him to leave a lot out, was of barely any use; he remembered neither the name of the black contender nor any detail of his physiognomy. I tried to jog his memory by showing him the photo of the Nubian, and he didn't recognize him, though he confessed he'd been sitting too far back to see any more of the fight than a dark blob hitting a light blob until it was covered with red. It wasn't hard to see that he was lying, and not just because his hands were shaking and he couldn't meet my eyes. But I was intent on finding out where the fights took place. I understood that he didn't want to disclose the name of the source who'd taken him to the match, but I hoped he wouldn't have any scruples about giving me details on the locale.

Then he started to question me, at which point he did meet my eyes. This often happens with the journalists who cover celebrities; they use it as a form of self-defense. It's a familiar sight on the news shows devoted to disemboweling famous people: a gang of journalists fire all kinds of abuse at the person in question, and as soon as the targeted star accuses them of lying, they grow indignant, calling themselves professionals with long records of proven integrity, and reload their weapons with venomous saliva to assail their victim anew and keep him from making any reply, because every question they're putting to him comes loaded with its own perverse answer. That was precisely the way my harried reporter went on the attack and started interviewing me. He intuited that I was keeping a high percentage of what I knew to myself, and that he could brandish what he knew in my face as an exclusive scoop, thereby heightening his own prestige as a reporter willing to run a few risks to get a highly charged story. I was enjoying the situation and returned the reporter's interest by telling him I'd heard rumors that an extreme match was taking place that very night, and the "main event"—I was starting to talk the way he did—would be a fight between the undefeated Negro and a crazy marine off the ship that had docked a few days earlier. He raised his hand to his receding hairline, scratched a centimeter of his forehead with the tip of a nail, and said, "That's serious." Then he told me that the police didn't lift a finger to stop the fights, on condition that they remained free of scandals, deaths, and public altercations between the opposing sides. The bouts were held on a private estate—"the people who go to these fights are very swank"—which contradicted the paragraph of his article that claimed the audience came from all walks of life. The sanctum where the secret fights were held was a kind of vast shed, specially equipped for the purpose, and very, very, very large amounts of money were wagered.

"What do they mean by scandals?" I wanted to know.

"You know. The fights are stopped when one guy has clearly proven his superiority over the other, which is stretching the rules of extreme fighting a little bit—normally a match doesn't end until one of the two contenders has lost consciousness. The moment someone gets killed, the police will intervene. And if there's trouble in the stands, same story. Of course there have been deaths anyway, but the bodies are left in a gutter and made to look as if they were beaten to death in a bar fight or anything else that won't connect them to the business of the matches. That's why if a marine is going to fight today, and if he loses and gets badly injured, things might start getting difficult. How on earth are they going to cover that up?"

"Do you know who the estate belongs to?" I asked, which was a mistake any way you look at it, far more like a policeman's question than that of a gambler eager to lay some bets. The reporter shook his head and tried to get me to tell him who had whispered the news of tonight's fight to me.

I didn't say anything. A girl came over to the coffee machine without so much as a hello, slipped some coins in, and waited for her tea to be delivered. The girl stared at the machine, the journalist bored a hole in one of the floor tiles with his eyes, and I pretended to whistle a casual tune. When the girl finally disappeared, clutching her plastic cup, the journalist said he couldn't help me and that he was entirely uninterested in the underground fights which had already caused him more than enough headaches; no one on the editorial staff had been the least bit appreciative of him for having been brave enough to report what he'd already reported.

"Come on," I encouraged him. "It can't be as bad as you say. Why don't you take me with you tonight? Or at least give me a phone number where I can find out more?"

"Wait here," he said. He took a long time coming back: four coffees' worth to be precise, extracted from the machine by a woman who looked as though she'd misspent her youth in that newsroom, a boy who appeared to have chosen the wrong profession, a man who could easily have passed for a door-to-door encyclopedia salesman, and the girl I'd seen earlier, who, unsatisfied with the tea she'd carried away after interrupting us, was coming back for a cappuccino.

"It must be hard to work here," I said to her.

Her behavior implied that she did not speak the language in which I had addressed her.

Finally the harried reporter came back with a folded slip of paper on which he'd scrawled the number I was to call if I wanted to attend that night's fight. As we said good-bye, he told me, "It's a hundred euros to get in."

Not ten steps from the front door of the newspaper offices I was already dialing the number he'd jotted down for me, which was completely illegible—the sevens looked like ones, and the twos looked like fives. Finally, on the third try, I hit the right number. I was surprised that a woman's voice answered. I said who I was and why I was calling. She asked me who had given me that number, and I told her. She left me on hold a few moments and then put me through to a guy—as I spoke to him, I imagined the scars covering his body—who gave me an address where I had to present myself before five p.m. in order to buy my ticket. Why was I doing all this? Was it only to show Luzmila that I, too, could get tickets for that night's fight without any assistance from her? How could I possibly have believed the two blacks and expected them to get me into a fight for which the price of a ticket was a hundred euros? Or had my plan been to slip in as part of the Nubian's entourage? Or maybe the two Africans had been hoping to use me in order to watch the fight? In any case, I went back to the hotel. Luzmila and Irene were still sleeping. I called my brother to see how everything was going and how the old man was. My father answered, and I heard a new vigor in his voice; he seemed like another man. He even indulged in a luxurious bit of affability and asked me what I was up to. After which he went so far as to give me a piece of advice: "Don't get into too much trouble, son."

There is a rule that does not appear in any manual for the achievement of perfect coupledom. It ordains that the degree of complicity and, if you like, of love between a couple can be measured by the length of time one member of the pair is able to bear life after the other has passed away. The shorter the time, the greater the love. For example, the great poet Juan Ramón Jiménez didn't last very long at all after his beloved Zenobia's death, but Jacqueline Kennedy lived on for ages after John Fitzgerald was assassinated. Of course the rule is somewhat tricky; we'll never know how long Zenobia would have lasted if Juan Ramón had died first, nor will we know if John Fitzgerald would have been able to go on living for much longer if Jackie had been the one assassinated. Be that as it may, if we're willing to grant any kind of validity to this rule, then my parents loved each other far too much. They broke all the records. Not long after our conversation, my father took all the pills from his medicine cabinet, forced them down into his stomach with a couple of glasses of Scotch, and to forestall any doubt whatsoever as to his intentions, proceeded to turn on the gas after having closed all the windows and sealed them with duct tape.

My sudden transformation into the son of two suicides gave me a certain air of a man with a past, a tumultuous history of grief and terrible uncertainties upon which I could discourse with lamentable cynicism or cynical lamentations. My pedigree would have been further improved if my brother had committed suicide as well, but all he did was inform me of the most recent tragedy once my father was in the tomb. Apparently my father left a note that read, "Better in poor company than alone." Such was the eloquent lesson he bequeathed to his sons, the culmination of a lifetime's devotion to the noble art of making do for oneself. His admonition seemed to be a warning that our family bloodline doesn't deal well with solitude, and though I don't recall ever having *not* been alone, I've also learned since the old man's death that he was right about two things. First, that it is undoubtedly better to be in poor company than entirely alone; second, that if one makes do for oneself, there will probably be no other solution than to put an end to one's achievement with one's own hand, because there's no more reliable way of ceasing to make do for oneself than by destroying oneself.

The true pathos of my father's final days came dramatically to light a month and a half after he was buried, when my brother looked at the phone bill. In the extremely brief period between my mother's death and his own suicide, my father appears to have spent all his time calling clairvoyants and phone sex services. The total amount due for these calls was more than three hundred euros. The phone bill listed the duration of each call and the hour at which it was made, so it was easy to deduce that my father had spent one whole long night talking on the phone to charlatan astrologers who promised him a golden future they could read in the stars, or to husky voices that told him all the things a hot, horny lady can do for a charmless insomniac. Some nights, trying to feel what my father felt, I find myself getting out of bed and picking up the phone to call one of the numbers where desperate people consult the future or try to procure an orgasm, but I always hang up before dialing the last digit.

Following the instructions I'd been given, I obtained a ticket for the night's match. I was also given directions to the estate where the evening's events would be held: four fights in all. I went back to the hotel and called Luzmila. Irene had gone off to pack her bags. She'd agreed to be evaluated by the Doctor and become a model for the Club. When I heard this, the blood accelerated in my veins. Luzmila kept trying to persuade me to let her take credit for the catch in order to improve her statistics. I showed her the ticket for that night, and she looked at me as if to say, "Boy, you really are completely hopeless," and bemoaned the fact that I hadn't trusted her. She rummaged through her leather purse and pulled out two tickets.

"We'll have to invite someone to go with us," she said.

By the time we got there, the first fight was already well under way. The taxi driver had no trouble finding the estate, though he had to leave us at the front gate because cars weren't allowed on the grounds. It was highly restorative to leave the reeking city behind as we climbed a highway up a dark mountain crowned by a moon just millimeters short of being full. The silence was like an invisible substance you could breathe. When we got out of the taxi, the invigorating air slapped us full in the face. The fights were held in a kind of warehouse, a shadowy structure with high ceilings and a musty odor. I can't begin to estimate how many people were inside, but I can state with some confidence that not many more could have squeezed in after us. Our tickets were checked several times before we reached our seats. At the third check—this one at the door of the warehouse—the two guards gave each other a questioning glance and one disappeared behind a gate to look for a supervisor. Luzmila asked whether there was some problem, and the guard answered that we'd have to wait a moment. The problem was Irene. Blacks were not allowed inside unless they were fighters or part of a fighter's retinue. Fortunately for us, the supervisor was the very guy who'd been so useful to Luzmila on our first night in Málaga. Greeting her euphorically— "You've come!"—he scolded the guards for having kept us from going in. He took us to our seats—resolving, in the process, the slight problem of my having a ticket for a seat several rows away from the two women—and whispered something in Luzmila's ear. Meanwhile on the dirt floor inside the ring, a middle-aged Arab was being punished mercilessly by a marine with biceps so large the entire Old Testament could have been inscribed on them in small print. I must confess that I was impressed, both by the place and by the ardor with which the public was celebrating the beating the North African was taking. One eyebrow had been sliced open, and his nose was no longer a nose but a blood spout. He was trying to stay on his feet, but the American wouldn't let him stand, delivering one blow after another in a fearsomely efficient display of full-contact fighting. About thirty seconds after we arrived, the referee decided, over the crowd's vociferous protests, to save the Arab from dying right there before our eyes. Once the first fight was over, the light illuminating the ring grew brighter and other lights came on as well, revealing a group of thirty or forty riotous marines. Those who'd placed money on the winner were going over to make good on their wagers, while the rest stayed behind in their seats, smoking cigarettes or drinking from little bottles.

Irene, sitting next to me, said, "I don't know if I'm going to be able to take this."

"I'm sure you can," I said, but noticed that my own heart was beating very fast and my mouth had suddenly gone dry. The one who took it all in without appearing the least bit affected was Luzmila, who was commenting at length on the sex appeal—to my eyes nonexistent—of the winning marine, as the pummeled body of his opponent was carried off by four men. The marine was short, with his head shaved like a Cheyenne warrior; except for a slight bruise on his left cheek, his person bore no mark of violence. He wore only a pair of shorts in the well-known colors of his nation's flag. A long line of fans was congratulating him, and one spectator behind us said, "Oh, come on, there's never any serious danger in the lightweight competitions."

His companion, a platinum blonde who was smoking a small cigar through a gilded holder, seemed reassured, after having taken fright at the state the Arab had been reduced to.

Irene said, "I'm leaving."

But I stopped her. I told her we could always escape to the bar, and that was what we did. I didn't want to leave without seeing the Nubian, but I didn't have much appetite for watching two more fights before he went into action. The little I'd seen so far was more than enough.

With the exception of the laceless tennis shoes, which she still had on, Irene had been dressed for the evening by Luzmila. In the taxi on the way to the fights she'd seemed very animated, almost happy, as if she were excited about finally seeing in person the Nubian we'd gone to so much effort to locate. Luzmila was showing her off as if Irene were a trophy she had won from me for the Club's treasure chest. Once we were in the bar, which was far too dimly lit and tended by a grumpy kid who hated us for having bothered him just when the second fight was about to begin, I brought up that subject while we sat with our elbows on the bar, since the four or five tables in the room were uninvitingly heaped with glasses, bottles, and ashtrays.

"I'm thinking it over," said Irene. "I need time, I don't know if I'm ready for it, but Luzmila says that in that place you both work for they prepare you very well, that she herself was surprised by how easy it was to handle her first jobs. At first she was just like me and thought she'd never be able to and yet . . . I remember you told me she used to turn tricks before she joined the Club. I asked her about that, and she said you were lying, that she'd never had sex with anyone for money before then, and certainly not in that place you mentioned which is full of starving street people."

I dismissed all comment on this with a fed-up gesture. And confessed: "I've been thinking this over very carefully. I think this trip to Málaga has been decisive in some way, even if only because it's here that I learned my mother was dead—she was buried yesterday—but anyway, that's the least of it now. The truth is, I've been thinking, and it's certainly true that the Club seems to have a lot at stake with this Nubian business, and if things turn out well I could stop working as a scout and move up to become a manager, which I'd like to do because I'm getting a little fed up with shipwrecks and slums and beautiful children living in garbage dumps, and thinking all that over, the new opportunities that will open up to me if I finally become a man with an office job and all, I realized that—I don't know quite how to say this to you—that, well, scouting someone and taking them to the Club is not the same thing as being there in the Club waiting for pieces that other people have scouted to arrive—and then you have to decide whether to let them join the modeling team or not, which I imagine is not as sickening a job; the thing is, what I want to tell you is that, well, I'm sure Luzmila has painted a very attractive picture for you, and it's true that there are lots of good things about it, I mean, it's true you won't easily find another job or an employer in Spain that will allow you to earn more money with less effort than the Club Olympus, but there are also some drawbacks, you know. It isn't so true that it's very easy to leave once you've started; you'll see that the contract that binds you to the Club has some teeth to it, it's natural, they're going to agree to pay your expenses, and on top of that you'll make a lot of money, enough to live very well, but if you earn a lot for them, if you earn as much as they expect of you, they're not going to let you get away so easily; they'll string you along, asking you what city you'd most like to live in, and you might think I'm just running off at the mouth here and making no sense at all, and you're right, this makes no sense; it's only that, thinking about you as a model for the Club, well, it makes my stomach churn. I guess that's because I know more about you than I ever knew about any of the other pieces I've scouted, or because I like you more, or because you and I are kind of in sync, I don't quite know how to tell you . . ."

I stopped and took a little sip of my orange soda. Irene said, "Are you asking me to marry you?"

And she gave me that gorgeous, dazzling smile of hers which widened her eyes and slightly wrinkled her forehead. I returned the smile. I racked my brain in search of something to say, some bit of conversational loose change that would keep me from being unmasked by the silence, some cliché that would give me time to recover the thread of what I was saying, though I wasn't at all sure what it was that I really wanted to say.

Irene took the floor.

"I don't know what to do. As I said. I'm thinking it over, but I still haven't made up my mind, though Luzmila wants me to go with her when she leaves in order to simplify the paperwork or something. But I also think that if I stay here in Málaga, there won't be many opportunities for me, especially given my condition."

"What condition?"

"Your colleague has told you nothing," Irene stated rather than inquired.

I shook my head and prepared for the worst.

"They told me it would be much easier to stay in Spain if I was pregnant when I got there, so I got myself pregnant. I waited until I was sure before setting out. I let several boats go without me before finally leaving on one. Things are much worse here than I expected, and the truth is I really don't like the idea of ending up with Málaga Shelters, waiting for them to decide to repatriate me. Because there's no other solution—you're the one who told me that when you took me out of that police station, didn't you? What's changed since then? Didn't you want to save my life, the same way you saved the lives of all those other people like me who didn't have so much as a place to drop dead in?"

"True," I said hesitantly, "but I suppose I've realized since then that I don't want to save you; at least I don't want to save you the same way I saved the others."

"Luzmila warned me you'd try this, so please, I'm asking you, don't push it."

"That I'd try what?" I asked, again fearing the worst.

"Well, just what you're trying. To seduce me, get me interested in you. She told me you always do this with pieces other people have scouted. You get all softhearted, tender, charming. And all you want is to go to bed with the piece while you still can without having to spend a lot of money. Don't try it on me, please. Luzmila has already warned me. She said: he'll try to go to bed with you, and then claim that the two of you can stay together; he'll promise to straighten out your situation by some other means, and all that just so he can go to bed with you now because he knows that if he wants to go to bed with you later, he'll have to sacrifice a large portion of his savings to afford the luxury."

It was as if a steel beam had landed in the pit of my stomach. Everything I'd eaten that day was churning in my intestines. I felt the muscles in my face splintering, and a drop of sweat branded a white-hot streak down my back.

We could hear the crowd roaring, the frenzied shouts, an amalgam of harsh voices rising to a crescendo so loud it was painful. And suddenly a silence froze every throat. The bartender ran to see what had happened, and I followed. A few voices had come back to life already by the time I finally saw what it was: one of the contenders, a boy, little more than a child, the type who thinks that going to the gym and taking tae kwon do makes him able to face down anyone or anything, was lying on the dirt floor of the ring, his eyes very wide open. His opponent, an African, had scrambled out of the ring, protected by ten or twelve blacks and a few uniformed guards, to hide in the dressing room and avoid even worse problems. The bartender said, "He's killed him, he's killed him; I told him so, I told him not to fight; he's killed him." And ran toward the ring as if his life depended on it. I turned back to Irene and asked her to wait for me right where she was. The body was taken away and the silence threatened to take possession of the very air of the warehouse, but as soon as the employees carrying the dead pugilist disappeared, a murmur started up again, bets were called out, and the two new gladiators who were already parading toward the ring were welcomed with applause. I went over to Luzmila's seat not because I was worried that the outcome of the previous fight had disturbed her in any way, but in order to try and infect myself with her confidence and peace of mind. Indeed, I found her there chatting happily with an admirer in his fifties who wore a carnation in the lapel of his brightly striped jacket and had thoughtfully distributed several bottles of sickly sweet perfume about his whole fine person. Luzmila was holding a glass of wine in her left hand and in her right a long cigarette, which she was gradually shortening one smoke ring at a time. Irritated by my sudden presence, she begged her elderly swain's pardon—which fleetingly distracted him from what was going on in the ring, where the two latest contenders were being introduced, both black this time and one of them a mammoth, every centimeter of his body carefully greased—and yelled at me, "What's itching you now?"

Her use of the verb *itch* jolted me as if with an electric shock. Could she possibly know about my nocturnal affliction?

"Things are getting ugly. I don't like the look of those marines at all. I don't suppose you have a plan for evacuating our Nubian if those wild animals decide to avenge their brother?"

Luzmila gave a snort. She asked about Irene and was stunned that I'd left her alone. I was about to berate her for what she'd had the nerve to tell Irene about me, but before I had time to say a single word Luzmila had already left for the bar. The fight began. The black who looked like a sumo wrestler ran at the other one as if he were a bull rushing blindly from its pen. The other faced the charge head-on, showing signs of having been a boxer, then delivered a nice clean uppercut that stopped the mammoth in his tracks. The sumo's brain must have filled with fireworks for a few seconds, but instead of taking advantage of that to try and get in a new blow, his opponent chose to move away. It was clear that the smaller man knew his strategy: he was going to whittle the big one down, slowly and patiently, keeping his distance, knowing full well that if the sumo managed to get at him he'd be crushed, there'd be no way out, he'd be easy prey. So he danced and danced, with supreme style, getting in a few timely blows that gradually weakened the giant, who was slowly transformed into a bag of marinated meat, entirely at his opponent's mercy. There are no rounds in extreme fighting, the contest is continual, and neither fighter can hope for a bell to save him. I was fascinated by the way the sumo wrestler was melting into thin air. Furthermore, the fight was going to be very profitable for the house; judging by the crowd's regretful reaction, not one person there had wagered a thing on the formidable fatso's defeat. When the tower of grease started to sway, the other man knew the time had come to put his opponent out of his misery; the boxer left off floating like a butterfly and stinging like a bee and moved in to send his enemy sprawling at last. And that was when he almost made a mistake, because the sumo wrestler seemed for an instant to have saved up enough strength for a final assault. But the smaller one's reflexes saved him; he put things back in their proper place with a pair of direct punches. Then he picked up some momentum by running across the ring, hurled himself into the air, and smashed his skull against the fatso's face. The big guy crashed to the floor as if someone had fired a shot from the bleachers. Once his opponent was down, the boxer straddled his chest and delivered seven punches to his opponent's face, one after the other, until the referee ordered him to stop and pronounced the fight over. Disappointment was clearly etched on the fifty-something admirer's face as he served himself another glass of fine wine from a bottle he was holding between his lacquered shoes. Dragging that massive body out of the ring was going to take more than four employees. Irene and Luzmila came back, and Luzmila asked, "Did I miss anything?"

I could only whisper, "It's been quite a show."

But the best was yet to come. First to jump in the ring was Luzmila's marine—he, too, wearing shorts in the colors of his nation's flag—looking as if he could easily topple a whole regiment of boxers. There was a tattoo on his back I hadn't noticed before: a mastiff with golden fangs. He looked twice as tall in the ring as he had in Luzmila's room; it was as if every part of his body had been pumped up. But there was also a certain sense of fragility about him that I can't quite describe, as if it were all no more than a facade, as if a valve were hidden in some part of his body and if that valve were uncapped, all the air would go out of him. Then, finally, our Nubian emerged. I couldn't contain my jubilation when I saw that his assistant was indeed the manager

I'd spoken to in the park with the magnolia trees. I was about to say to Luzmila: look, see there, it's him, the man I met, the one who promised to bring me here. I now had reason to be dismayed at having given up on meeting with the manager at eight that morning; if I'd come to the fight with him—in exchange for I don't know how much money—I would have had the chance to strike up relations with the Nubian much earlier. I couldn't imagine how in the world Luzmila was going to contrive a meeting with the Nubian after the fight was over—assuming of course that the marine was unable to stand up to our man. I asked her, and she answered, without taking her large eyes off the Nubian, "I made an agreement with the guy with the scars; he's bringing me the Nubian tonight for a thousand euros. Now that I've seen him, I think that's a real bargain."

"*Mamma mia,*" murmured Irene, her hungry eyes riveted to the Nubian's spectacular body.

He measured about a meter ninety. His mouth was sensual with full lips of the kind that are easily caricatured, the kind that female TV stars dream of achieving through surgical procedures that never result in this kind of perfection. His deltoids seemed to have been created by one of those master sculptors of the Renaissance who carved the gods they dreamed of in stone. But the most sensual thing about him were his legs: long, flawless, not too muscular, at least not in appearance, with enticing, gleaming skin. His head was shaved, his fists and ankles wrapped, and all he wore was a pair of tight yellow briefs that closely followed the outline of his rock-solid buttocks. Inevitably, he brought Gallardo's definition back to mind: beauty is whatever gets you hard.

The fight was devoid of emotion. It lasted precisely forty-eight seconds. The marine threw out a few kung-fu kicks and a few desperate flails with his arms. The Nubian dispatched his opponent without wasting too much energy, or at least that was how he made it look. He pounced on him, immobilized him, slung him over his shoulder, and sent him crashing to the ground. He didn't give him a chance to recover but cut off his breath by pressing one forearm against his neck while sinking the other fist into the center of his chest again and again. We could see the marine's terrified eyes begging him to let go. There was no pity. When the Nubian got up, the pack of marines started throwing bottles into the ring. Their comrade-in-arms was now a scarecrow whose face, at least, the Nubian had had the delicacy not to disfigure. But the melee stopped there, having been brought under control with no more than a couple of punches and a few bleeding eyebrows. Almost without anyone realizing it, the Nubian vanished, following his manager. The interior of the warehouse was now bathed in an unpleasant white light, and the thundering crowd began to break up as everyone pushed toward the exits, excitedly going over the incidents of the evening. Luzmila ran to collect the money she'd won for having wagered that our Nubian would knock out the marine in less than a minute. My arms crossed and my gaze hypnotized by the blinking of one of the lights on the ceiling, I stood to one side with Irene, her dark skin slightly paler than usual, whether from the effect of having seen the Nubian god in action or because of the unpleasant lighting which depleted all color, I don't know.

"What did you think?" she wanted to know, I suppose because it made her uncomfortable to stand there in silence.

"I was impressed," I said in all sincerity. "I would never have believed a fight like that could be so exciting."

"Me neither."

And to keep the silence from casting its shadow again and making us more uncomfortable, I asked her what she was thinking of doing about the baby.

"It's not a baby yet."

"I suppose Luzmila's told you the Club will pay for the operation."

"Of course."

"Who's the father?"

"A guy. Someone, no one. Who cares?"

At that moment my phone rang. Luzmila's name appeared on the little screen. She was calling me from the door to tell me I had to get over there with Irene right now; she'd managed to get seats for us in the van that was taking the Nubian back to Málaga. What Luzmila could not do, no one on the face of the earth could accomplish. Nevertheless, I took my time getting to the door; I was not at all convinced that I wanted to travel in that van. I told Irene to follow me, and on the way to the door, along an aisle between rows of now empty seats, I ran into the journalist from *La Opinión*, who had attended the match after all. At first he tried hard not to recognize me, but he had no choice when I asked him if he was planning to write something about what we'd just seen. He clearly didn't want anyone to suspect him of any such thing. He confessed to having attended purely as a fan of the sport; he'd been forbidden to write another word about the secret fights, and he wasn't about to risk anything with those people—you had to take them seriously. I asked if he could give me a ride back to Málaga, and he said he wouldn't mind, so I told Irene she should join Luzmila and go back to the city with her, and we'd see each other later, or maybe not; I'd find my own way home.

This was, no doubt, a way of throwing in the towel, losing all interest in hunting the Nubian, and delegating everything to Luzmila, given that she was the one who'd taken the essential steps toward placing this prodigious piece in the Club's vaults. I considered this—prematurely, as it happened—a major defeat, and it lowered my spirits down to my ankles, but it could also be viewed as one of those pyrrhic victories that it's best to try and make the most of, rather than sadly licking the wounds to your self-esteem. Perhaps I wasn't as good a scout as I thought; maybe I wasn't really the best scout in the Club, though the Doctor took pains to assure me that I was every time I was assailed by doubt. I had no idea how Luzmila was going to persuade the Nubian to go back to Barcelona with her, and it made me smile to think that she was spending a thousand euros to have the pleasure of him for one night—perhaps preparing a delicious welcome for him with Irene as the warm-up act—and yet still might be unable to persuade him to go along with her plans. I imagined a scene in which she told the Nubian about the beautiful dream he would step into if he trusted her, and the Nubian turned his back on her, saying he'd rather stick with extreme fighting; it brought him enough income to dream of the possibility of establishing himself in Spain, bringing his family here from the remote coastline where they were vegetating, opening some kind of business—a discotheque for immigrants or a twenty-four-hour convenience store in one of the neighborhoods jammed with illegals—which would allow him to earn, day by day, the right to become a legal resident. Now that I knew I was incapable of reaching the Nubian myself, my only remaining hope lay in the possibility that Luzmila might fail. Seen from that perspective, the prospect of being rewarded with an office job in Barcelona lost much of its charm, however strongly I condemned myself for continuing to sink my hands into the muck of shipwrecks in search of a piece that deserved to be saved before the Guardia Civil flung it back to the misery from whence it came.

I immediately set the record straight with the harried journalist, Nicolás Bermúdez Aliaga his name, NBA to friends and readers of the newspaper, telling him I was sorry to have passed myself off as someone who gambled on the extreme fights just to get some information out of him. In fact, I assured him, we're colleagues. I saw your article, thought I might be able to do something with the story, and showed up in Málaga after hearing the rumor that some fights would soon be taking place. Nicolás didn't get upset but took it very well; he must have figured he would have done the same in my place. He even gave the steering wheel a cheerful thump and said, "I knew you didn't look one bit like a gambler." He asked me who I worked for, and since it's always been my policy that once you start to lie you shouldn't shy away from any exaggeration or absurdity however extreme, I said, "I'm the Spanish correspondent for the *Guardian*." It was clearly a little risky, but he swallowed it, threw me a sidelong glance, gave a quick whistle of admiration, and asked if I had enough material to write a decent story. Without giving me time to answer, he added, "I hope you're going to credit me and my newspaper in what you write; that would be a big score for me." "Of course," I murmured, and now freed from all qualms, I began digressing at length on the impression the magnificent Nubian had made on me, assuring him that the most valuable approach to take in a piece of high-quality literary journalism would be to cast the Nubian as the article's protagonist, making his particular case, by logic and induction, emblematic of all others like his. My driver's face crumbled; he searched for my gaze across the spectral space of the rearview mirror, thought for a moment about pressing the button on the tape player to make the silence a little less weighty, and finally said, "That was my idea. Well, that's still my idea."

"What?"

NBA asked for a cigarette. I ransacked all my pockets as if by some miracle one might suddenly have appeared there so I could satisfy his urge. I'd smoked my last cigarette at the fights.

"Well, we can stop somewhere around here, at some kiosk on the beach—anything's better than Málaga. With that stench that makes your eyes burn."

We were driving toward a lake of light that was only a precursor to the immense darkness of the invisible sea. The road's succession of sharp curves gave you a feeling of flinging yourself into the void in the path of other suicides. The wind whipped the bushes that lined it on both sides. I opened the window for some fresh air and didn't even notice when NBA pulled off the highway onto a narrow road that ended at a bridge across which Torremolinos lay sparkling. Gigantic letters hanging from a parapet spelled out the town's name. The sound of late-night traffic reached us, spiraling through it was an ambulance's siren.

"It's a heart attack," NBA informed me. He could tell what ailment an ambulance's passenger was suffering from by the sound of the siren. He claimed he could, anyway, and I chose to believe him. We were approaching the beach; a row of colored lights marked the places that stayed open until dawn. Not all of them had attracted much of a crowd, and we went into one where, apart from the bartender, there was no one except three

Nordic types drowsing alongside three local girls they'd picked up and didn't seem to know quite what to do with.

"That was my idea, exactly that," NBA confessed after the cold flame of two beers had been lit on our table. "I met Boo a while ago, the guy you call the Nubian for whatever strange reason. When I met him, he wasn't fighting yet; like most Africans here, he was selling pirated CDs, with a blanket on the ground and a couple of bulging backpacks. He would sell them in the park or at the port, just like most of the others. I became his best customer and finally managed to exchange something more than a few phrases with him. At first these were very limited dialogues, you can imagine; it's hot today, weather talk like that. But then I realized it was best to visit him when there weren't many people crowded in front of his blanket. I gave him a cigarette or two and won his confidence. He's Sudanese, as you know, and there's some civil or religious war going on there, a pretty brutal one, apparently, though news of the Sudanese army's continual massacres never reaches us here; we don't hear about the terrible prison camps or dramatic punishments inflicted on many people simply because they belong to an ethnicity that didn't convert to Islam. Boo managed to get to the Ivory Coast and found employment there in one of the endless cacao fields, where he worked from dawn to dark for small change. He was able to survive like that until the bad luck that always shadows him reappeared in the form of a military uprising. Things got ugly, and he joined a group of desperate people who'd decided to try and make it to Europe. Next, I would guess, though he never told me, comes a period of hunger and wandering, contacts with various mafias, and finally the possibility of travel to the white world. You can imagine; all these guys have their own epic story to tell, and every one of those sagas puts the story of Ulysses to shame. There are hundreds of Penelopes scattered across Africa, and not one has a poet to tell her tale. Until the Penelopes themselves got tired of waiting and got out of there themselves, occasionally accompanied by their Ulysses. Boo, for example, came across with his girlfriend, but lost her along the way. Their ship went down as they reached the coast, and fifteen of the seventy people crammed aboard drowned. He couldn't even stay on the beach to wait for the waves to return her body; he had to run when the Guardia Civil appeared at the top of a dune. He saw his girlfriend's body on TV in a bar in Almería. Then he was arrested, he and another eight people who were with him. They were taken to police court, and although he speaks fairly presentable English, he pretended only to speak and understand Sudanese—if Sudanese is a language, I don't even know. Since there were no interpreters available, or the interpreters were on strike because they hadn't been paid, the judge had no choice but to let them go. That happens a lot; it's a real stroke of luck for a lot of the illegals who get arrested. The interpreters and the poorly run administration that doesn't pay the interpreters. It was what got him out of that bind."

"But how did he get involved in the fights?"

"First things first. As I was saying, we were getting to know each other better, to the point where he'd let me treat him to a coffee and a sandwich. The poor guy must have thought I was a Good Samaritan, and who can say whether that's not what a journalist really is, in the end."

Even you don't believe that, I thought, but go on. He went on.

"'What do you know about those fights?' Boo asked me one afternoon. I knew nothing, absolutely nothing. I didn't even know that extreme fighting was happening around here. I asked him to explain, and he said he'd been contacted by someone who'd heard he'd once been captain of his country's wrestling team, no less. He did that for a while after he left his village, mainly because, though they didn't pay him anything, at least he got a bunk to sleep in and three meals a day. He'd had forty-two fights and won all of them before the time limit. 'In my village, fighting is a tradition,' he said. 'We're taught to fight from the time we're children.'"

"Jesus Christ, maybe he's a real Nubian after all," I marveled.

"That was how he became a fighter here, and when he got started I thought there was an article, a good investigative piece, in it—but a dangerous one because it's the kind of journalism that of necessity entails shutting down the gold mine."

I didn't understand what he meant but let him go on and nodded so he wouldn't get bogged down in some theoretical explanation that would have been hard to take at that hour of the morning.

"Do you have some way of getting in touch with him?"

"Oh no—I've become a fan of the fights, and I follow him as a spectator, but as far as I know they keep the fighters very secluded so they won't get away. For example, tomorrow would be a good day to visit him, but it's impossible to predict where he'll be; he's just as likely to go over to the area around the train station looking for a whore to spend a few hours with as to spend the whole day watching TV in one of those bars along the prolongation of the Alameda that the blacks have colonized. You see them there, and you wonder: How do they do it? Where do they get the money to have cell phones and cars, and spend the whole day drifting from here to there without appearing to do anything at all? But that's an entirely different question, of course. The point is that on the days following a fight they let them go free to release some of the pressure. They usually give them a day or two of vacation. If they've taken a bad hit, sometimes more. I'm sure they'd all like to get out of the racket. They've seen more than a few men die, or if not die then be battered until they were worse than dead, and afterwards dumped in a ditch somewhere to be awoken by the cries of seagulls, not knowing who or where they are. Later you see them wandering the streets in a very bad way, not even their friends and family take care of them. So the people who run the business keep the fighters under very tight control. The fighters are the hens who lay the golden eggs, and until the hens stop laying, they're kept under close watch. I hope you're going to quote me in your article."

"Well," I argued, "you haven't really told me anything that just about anyone couldn't have just dreamed up without being too far off the mark."

The comment hit home, touching the nerve of his honor as a professional who never, in no case, under no circumstance, would invent a fact to help him out with a story. He then started talking about immigration as the great drama of our time, throwing out reliable figures, three hundred thousand immigrants in Spain, a 21 percent increase in illegal entries, police actions targeting the illegals who were trying to get in, which were forceful but ineffective against the various mafias that were bringing them in. He insisted on trying to interest me in all this, without regard to my weariness and the fed-up feeling I always get from cold, dry numbers, however much he emphasized, with words taken from the standard lay catechisms of our time, that behind every one of those numbers were innumerable dramas full of pain and sorrow. Just then I remembered what my job was—to save lives, to prostitute the beauty of a few of the elect who were discovered in society's worst subbasements. I felt an urgent need to put my talents back to work. I picked up the towel I had thrown in half an hour earlier—which like a dove shot down in midflight had fallen over my entire career as a scout—and raised it once more.

"Can you take me back to my hotel?" I asked NBA, who blushed at the question. The big ninny thought I was making an indecent proposal. As we said goodnight, he gave me his card, and I promised to call him if I had any further questions.

I supposed that by then Irene and Luzmela would be celebrating Boo's flawless anatomy, and after some hesitation went up to Luzmila's room to have a look and find out how things were going. I couldn't mask my surprise when I learned that upon hearing Luzmila's proposition from scar guy, Boo had begged off, saying he was very tired and maybe tomorrow. So the two of them were ransacking the minibar once again, with the tips of their fingers all wrinkled—according to Irene—from having been so close to touching the Nubian god and not having done it. African magical realism, I thought, but decided to ask Luzmila what the next step was.

"He'll come by tomorrow morning, after a good night's sleep."

She was mistaken. He did not come by the next morning or that afternoon, and the Doctor was growing impatient and feeling cheated by the failure of her two best scouts. When she suggested sending out reinforcements, I asked for a couple of helicopters and was refused.

"He looks like a very sensitive guy," said Irene, feeling more and more at home in that hotel room.

"Don't expect any of the clients you'll be servicing to have a body like Boo's," I said. Luzmila manifested her displeasure with a snort. Then she came over to me and with a slight tremor in her voice spoke the following question into my ear: "Would you like to look for your mother with me?"

I tried not to give her a dumbfounded look but did anyway. Some things you don't play around with or make jokes about, but Luzmila would do anything to drive me crazy: she had mastered that art with incomparable efficiency and ease. She'd grabbed my arm and was looking directly into my eyes, which were trying to be flaming but were probably no more than lukewarm. By then Irene had lost all interest in us; she lay her wrist across her forehead, to cast a bit of shadow over her closed eyes, and switched off.

Luzmila said, "The Ouija board. We can find your mother, ask her how she is. It works really well for me. It's true. I always find the dead person I'm looking for, and evil spirits never come."

She let go of my arm and went to get the Ouija board from her suitcase. I watched her as if she were a machine you could not control with a spoken command, a machine created by another machine that now obeys only itself. She sat down on the floor in front of the board and waited for me to join her. Perhaps because I, too, have some quality of a machine created by another machine about me, I decided I was self-sufficient enough to participate in this farce and go along with this game as part of our eternal competition, our unending Olympic race—just to show that I had the strength to withstand all types of strategies intended to send me over the edge, from the pettiest to the most delirious. When she saw me move toward her, she asked me to dim the lights a bit, so I went over to the little dial and turned it slightly until the lightbulbs emitted no more than a faint, creamy glow. Grateful for this gesture, Irene removed her wrist from her forehead. I sat down in front of Luzmila and had a look at the board, a circle rimmed with the letters of the alphabet. Luzmila placed a small cup in the center of the circle and asked me to put one finger on it, and take the finger away when it started to move. But would it really move? I asked Luzmila how long she'd been making these incursions into the world of ghosts, and she said not long. I wondered if she'd met anyone famous, any notable historic figure.

"I once summoned Fidel Castro."

Wouldn't you have laughed?

"I know why you're laughing, but it's true. He told me he'd been dead since 1960. He was killed the year after he came to power. The Americans found a double to replace him and have kept him in power against all the odds ever since, because it's in their interest to have someone they can demonize, someone who messes everything up so badly that it's more than obvious the Yankees are the only possible salvation for Cuba."

"Maybe it wasn't Fidel," I replied. "Maybe it was just some joker who didn't have much luck during his lifetime and is now taking his revenge from the other side by pulling the legs of people like you who dabble in this kind of thing."

"Think whatever you want. But you'd better take this seriously, or we're not going to find your mother."

I'd never participated in a Ouija session, though there was a period when, like every other teenager, I was interested in the world of the spirits. (I'd wake up every morning saying to myself: Moisés Froissard Calderón, La Florida 15, 3B, investigator of electronic voice phenomena.) Along with a couple of other young idiots with too much time on their hands, I'd sneak out late at night to abandoned houses, switch on a tape recorder with a blank tape inside, leave it there, then go back later to pick it up and listen to the cassette in the silence of my room, hearing, in a long wail that sounded like a radio station that's just out of range, a voice from the beyond. From time to time we'd pick up a noise we would try to decode into intelligible words. The scariest ones were like children's voices saying ordinary things ("It's cold," "Come get me," "Mommy"). Other times we only picked up a yowling cat or the skitter of a passing rodent or the conversation the wind elicited from the walls. But I had never dared attempt anything with a Ouija board. And now Luzmila was trying to locate my mother's voice somewhere in the unfathomable cosmic broth that seethes on the other side of death. When she asked my mother to make her presence known, I almost burst out laughing and would undoubtedly have done so if the little cup hadn't started moving like mad, pointing to letters at the edge of the board. I snatched my hand away as if a bee had stung me or I'd had a sudden cramp (correction: as if a bee with an electrified stinger had stung me). As I followed the zigzagging cup, the phrase it was composing out of the letters it pointed to gradually took shape in my mind: *Estoy aquí, hijo.* I'm here, son.

I was choking on my saliva. I looked for Luzmila's eyes, but they were fixed on the cup which now stood at the letter *O;* maybe she was wondering whether to intervene by returning the cup to the center of the board or to allow the spirit that had been summoned to go on unburdening herself. My stomach started to hurt, and I felt someone's gaze boring into my right temple. For a moment it felt as though my eyes were going to burst out of their sockets. I had goose bumps.

"Ask her something," Luzmila whispered.

I looked deep into her eyes, trying to detect a spark of cruelty, a gleam of sarcasm, trying to convince myself that she was only trying to weaken me with this little show she was putting on. I didn't find it. She even seemed frightened, as if what she'd said earlier about her experiences with the Ouija board had been made up and this was the first time an actual spirit had showed up for one of her morbid games. But I was incapable of uttering a single word. Fearful that the dead person we'd summoned would grow bored with our silence, Luzmila put her finger on the cup and started pointing to letters until she'd written "Who are you?" Then she returned the cup to the center of the board, and it started pointing to letters again.

Its answer was "Moisés, I am your father. I know all about you now. No comment."

Searing panic surged through me. My father wasn't dead—I mean, I didn't know at the time that he was dead—and of course he didn't know what my job was, he knew nothing about me; we were just two strangers joined by a random connection that had frayed with the passage of time. The thought that my father knew what kind of job I had, the things I'd done, the people I'd been with, was far more disturbing to me than the possibility that he was dead. It also crossed my mind that he might have met the same fate as Fidel Castro, that he had actually died many years earlier and been replaced by a stand-in without anyone noticing.

This time I did get to my feet. "That's it for me," I said. "I don't need to know any more about this, it's pure shit, my father's not dead, and he doesn't know a thing about me."

I felt as if a set of talons were digging into my shoulder while a light snow fell onto my chest. I bolted from the room in horror, then decided to give the Ouija board's talking corpse the benefit of the doubt and prepared myself for the worst. I punched in the number of the apartment on La Florida and let it ring three times before hanging up. Afterwards I doped myself with pills so I could get some sleep and toppled onto my bed, cursing Luzmila and wondering whether I should go back to her room in case the corpse had gone on talking in my absence. After a night of intense itching in an anguished half sleep with nothing in my head but the terror of waking up to the knowledge that my father was not only dead but also knew everything about me, I got up brimming with impatience (Moisés Froissard Calderón, La Florida 15, number 3B, treasure seeker) and went back to the magnolia park, hoping someone there would be able to tell me where the Nubian had decided to wander to on his day off. I'd worked on extinguishing the previous night's itch with particular violence, and as a result was having a little trouble walking. The excavators and dump trucks had succeeded in attenuating the rank smell of the city's air, though it continued, tenaciously, to reek. I met Carlos, the man from Guinea, whose first question was whether I'd had an accident—he had noticed I was moving with considerable difficulty—and who then proceeded to reproach me for not having shown up the day before. Once he found out I'd attended the match, he wanted me to tell him every detail of Boo's fight with the marine. (The very next day in Barcelona I saw in *La Opinión*—which I picked up at one of those newsstands on the Ramblas where you can get every paper from anywhere in the country—a brief note signed NBA, according to which a marine had been savagely attacked by a band of blacks during a brawl. He was now lying in an intensive care unit with several broken bones.) Carlos offered to accompany me on my search. First he took me to a large shopping center near the train station which was indeed swarming with Africans. Carlos stopped to question someone he knew who looked at me suspiciously, forcing me to lower my gaze. My cell phone rang, and that was when the news of my father's death was confirmed; he'd been buried that very morning. I didn't even try to act surprised for my brother, though I wasn't up to telling him about my session with the Ouija board. I promised to go see him and help out with all that needed to be done, the sale of the house, the inheritance, all of it. My brother had to run; he was writing a speech for the minister—an introduction to some conference on immigration and culture. I asked him what he was going to say, and he answered, "Same as ever, you know: Andalusia has always been a welcoming land, without those who came from elsewhere we wouldn't be here ourselves, and without those who left this place to go elsewhere other communities wouldn't exist either, that type of thing." I applauded him with a smile before hanging up.

"I've got it," Carlos told me. "I know where he is."

"My father's dead," I told him, putting the phone away in my pocket.

"Mine too," he replied.

And there was Boo, wearing a baseball cap, formidable and alone, the splendor of his torso and the perfection of his arms rendered legible by a tight, shiny black T-shirt. He was sitting at the back of a seedy bar, pictures of drum majorettes on the walls and the floor covered with hazelnut shells. He had a liter bottle of water and a sports magazine in front of him and was consuming an endless sequence of sunflower seeds. Carlos pointed him out but said that his mission ended there; he wasn't about to go near him. There weren't many people in the place: just two alcoholics in their sixties who looked as if they'd seen things none of the rest of us could even imagine, and two other clients who seemed to be taking a short break before climbing back onto the roof to reopen fire on passers-by. After Carlos had made himself scarce, Boo was the only African there. I had given Carlos a hundred euros, and he was offended; he regarded the thing as a cruel joke. He asked me to give him my cell phone, too, so I added another hundred euros to what I'd already deposited in the palm of his hand. He walked off cursing me, but that served my purposes well because it attracted the Nubian's attention.

I headed toward Boo, wondering what the hell I was going to say. I was struck by how young he was. The night before I had put him at about twenty-five, but now I thought he couldn't be more than twenty. His face looked very boyish, and I noticed a little dimple in his chin I hadn't seen before, in the photo or during the fight. I said hello, and he didn't even glance at me. I noticed with concern that there were several white patches about the size of tears on one of his arms. Vitiligo, I thought, a real problem if he's not treated soon. I asked if I could sit down, and the Nubian made no movement of assent or refusal but simply went on eating his sunflower seeds and tossing the shells into an ashtray. His method was to break the shell with his front teeth without placing it inside his mouth and without ever taking his fingers away from the shell; the exceptional speed with which he did this allowed him to consume vast quantities of the seeds, which he selected out of the palm of his hand. A half-empty bag of seeds was on the table; it must have weighed half a kilo when full. I'm one of those people who cracks open the shell of a sunflower seed with my molars, which means I have to release the seed inside my mouth. Two different ways of confronting the world.

The Nubian had noticed I was having trouble walking; however much I tried to hide it, it always showed, and the twenty steps I took to reach my spot in front of him had given me away. The burning in my groin was merciless, I had to make a strong effort not to grimace in pain. I counted to ten, held my breath, tried to calm down, and miraculously the itching went away for a moment, waiting to come back and wreak its havoc on me again later.

"An accident?" he asked. An ancient ice glittered in his gaze. His teeth were a fistful of pure snow, and on his monumental lips I noticed slight cracks which he erased almost immediately—he must have noticed I'd spent too much time staring at his mouth—by taking a swallow of water, then passing his quick pink tongue—closer to white than to red—across the surface of his lips.

There, facing me, was Boo, and I had no pretty story with

which to cast a spell on him. I felt both worn out and worked up, and decided to spell out the truth rather than resort to some tall tale to get his attention. The truth was so implausible that if he was at all sensible he'd understand that no clown in the world would show up and reel off a story like that unless it were absolutely true.

I told him the unadorned truth about why I'd come looking for him, skipping only a few intermediate episodes and personalities. His eyes opened indescribably wide until they filled his entire face, or at least that's how I've stored the moment in my memory. The image must be distorted because I feared that his eyeballs were going to explode, proving that he wasn't a man at all but a human fractal designed by a psychopath. If I had to draw a picture of that moment, it would show a single expanding eye that erased all other features from his face, an eye that later appeared to me in nightmares flying over my head or enveloping me in its own sticky substance, immobilizing me, drowning me. I had to stop talking and turn to the bar to ask the bartender for a bottle of water. Only after the water arrived did the Nubian recover his normal facial features; his eyes deflated, and everything returned to its proper place, including the terrible itching in my crotch. I took out the photo where the Club's enigmatic client first saw the Nubian and thought: he must be mine, or, I want to be his—we'll never know which. Have any of you ever fallen in love with someone just from a photograph? I don't mean "desired someone," even the chastest among us has gone that far, I mean really "fallen in love," or better still "fallen madly in love" to the point of obsession, to the point where you put everything you have in the service of a quixotic and delirious quest for that person. Whenever I thought of the engine behind this whole search, I'd feel more and more curious about that client veiled in shadow and secrecy. And I sorely missed having an omniscient narrator who, as I gradually revealed to the Nubian the reason I was sitting there in front of him, would describe the Club's client going about his daily business, softly humming a tune in the bathroom or buying a magazine in some airport, this deep fixation constantly churning in his soul: he must be mine, or, perhaps, I must be his.

As I'd foreseen, the story struck the Nubian as being so entirely beyond the bounds of any rational discourse that he had no option but to take it seriously and believe it. When he picked up the photo I handed him and saw himself, he gave an affectionate, childlike smile that softened his chiseled features with tenderness. I was glad he decided to ask me some questions, even though I could only answer a few, since most concerned the client. It neither tired nor bored me to answer, again and again, that I knew nothing at all about the client, that I wasn't trying to hide his or her identity, and that I didn't feel any particular loyalty to him or her, quite the contrary. And while my utter ignorance concerning this person and this person's desires or plans for the Nubian—by the way, I asked him if he was a Nubian, and he shrugged, didn't know what that meant; "I'm from a village on the slopes" was all he said—had prompted me to make certain guesses and deductions, it did not enable me to provide any confirmed information.

"Is it a man or a woman?" "I don't know." "Where does the client live?" "I don't know." "What kind of work does this person do?" "I don't know." I did tell him what kind of work the Club that would be employing him did: saving lives, that simple.

"Those two are keeping an eye on me," he said then, with a slight, imperceptible movement of the chin toward the two snipers sitting at the bar. I realized the time had come to launch into the second movement of my symphony. Now that I'd told him the story, I had to place particular emphasis, using the violins and the percussion, on the opportunity that was being presented to him. The backbone of my argument was that if he agreed to accompany me, he would escape from his foreordained fate as a fighter, the inevitable lost match or incurable injury, the gutter where he'd lie abandoned beneath a sky crowded with frozen stars.

"I like to fight. I like knocking white men down," he said, wounding my backbone with a well-placed dart. "There's a song in my village," he added, "which goes, 'I don't sing because I'm happy/ but because I don't have food / I sing so you'll give me a little change and I can eat / Maybe after I have eaten I'll sing because I'm happy / and then I won't need your change to make me sing.'"

Without knowing what to say, I smiled. In my mind I switched *sing* to *fight* and looked down at my knuckles because I couldn't hold his scorching gaze. But then he offered me a truce, adding, "Soon enough they won't find any more opponents for me around here, and they'll have to take me somewhere else where I'm unknown and people will still bet on the others."

I invited him to imagine the client's identity. Perhaps the client owned an advertising agency and would make him a famous model whose name no one knew but whose image would recur obsessively in the dreams of hundreds of thousands of people. Perhaps the client was an elderly female art collector who felt that no art was superior to the human body itself; perhaps she simply wanted to show him off to her visitors, placed on a pedestal for a few hours each day with a fig leaf covering his groin, admired by the old lady's friends, whose avid eyes would rove across his skin while they sipped their tea. He liked that and smiled again. Maybe the client was a beautiful woman, tired of corrupt men, who yearned for the wild elixir of a new, true, and fiercely immaculate creature. Whatever the case, he could always just give it a try, then move on afterward. Of course his place in the Club Olympus would always be guaranteed; he could become one of its most valuable assets in no time, a gold mine, a thousand euros for an hourlong session. He wanted to know, the little angel, what we did to save the lives of the people we hired. So I told him. Sex. We sell sex at very high prices. We have an inexhaustible roster of clients willing to pay through the nose for sex. He said, "Women only." I said, "That can be negotiated, you can make some kind of an agreement, I think they'd accept that from you. Of course you'd earn much less money, but it's possible, yes, the model can set his own conditions if it suits the Club to hang on to him, but the main thing is for you to come with me to meet the client who has made all this happen, and if you don't like what you're offered there, then you'll still be welcome to join the Club." And he, dropping his fistful of sunflower seeds onto the wooden tabletop, answered, "I'm going to tell you a story. A story my grandfather told me. A story all the grandfathers tell all the children in my village. Something from our ancestors."

I prepared to listen, feeling the intransigent gaze of the two men who were watching us on the back of my neck and registering a blissful cease-fire between my legs.

"One night a long time ago when the world was still a flat, smooth surface that ended at the abyss where the dead dwell, some white hunters came into my village and kidnapped its handsomest man. They took him away, and the warriors who were supposed to defend the town could do nothing to stop them. My grandfather was just a boy then, and the handsomest man in the village was his father. But if you ask any child in my village about this story, he'll tell you the same thing: that the man they took away was their grandfather's father. Once they'd taken him, we no longer knew what was happening to him, what they

wanted him for, whether they had killed him for something he'd
done or sold him as a slave. But my grandfather dreamed about
his father every night. He saw him as if on a TV screen, though
he never knew what a TV was; he could follow his story clearly.
They put him on a boat with other warriors, and crossed the sea.
During the crossing, all the other warriors died one after another,
all except for my grandfather's father. Later they put him on display in a cage that also held a monkey. The cage was in a zoo.
Every day thousands of people came to see the cage where my
grandfather's father stood. But many of those people were
wounded by the sight of him there and protested the way he was
being treated. Their protests had an effect; the director of the
zoo, to whom the white hunters (who, just like you, were following orders) had sold the warrior, decided to let him out of the
cage every morning before opening, so he could go wherever he
liked, as long as he didn't leave the zoo. At night they let him
back in so he could sleep on his bed of straw. But people
protested again: they wanted the warrior back in his cage; he was
the main attraction, they would visit the zoo only to see the warrior hiding high in some tree; they would pursue him across the
whole zoo, no longer stopping in front of the animals' cages. The
warrior was forced to defend himself and stood up to his
harassers; he made them run away, all except for the bravest one
who was undaunted and wanted to fight, and my grandfather's
father killed him with the second blow. Then the dead man's
friends went to the zoo to hunt the warrior down. My grandfather dreamed about what was happening to his father every
night, and he was sure that every night his father dreamed about
what was happening to him, for it was daytime in my village
when it was night where the warrior was. My grandfather
dreamed that his father was being hunted with guns, and that the
director of the zoo felt obliged to protect the warrior and get him

out of there. He managed to find a job for him in a bottle factory in a faraway town, lost in the desert. But the news that he had killed a young man who challenged him quickly followed the warrior, and the other workers started ganging up on him in circles of six or seven. The warrior had no choice but to defend himself. He broke two of one man's bones and split open another's nose, but he couldn't take on all of them at once and he got beaten up and stabbed several times. Until he couldn't stand it any longer. One morning, before the seven or eight who were the ringleaders of the group that wanted to settle accounts managed to corner him, he tracked them down one by one, without giving them time to react, and smashed each one into a lifeless pulp. Then he climbed onto the factory's roof, opened his eyes wide, and jumped. My grandfather woke up at that moment. He never slept again after that, never again."

A peal of thunder rolled outside, and someone loudly proclaimed, "There's a big storm coming this afternoon." As if this were a command of some sort, the ancient, unrelenting melody of rain pounding against asphalt was immediately audible. "Just what we needed, garbage plus rain," the bartender opined. I went on searching for some response to Boo's Nubian folktale, without success. Hard as I tried to hit on the precise moral that lay concealed within his fable, I couldn't come up with it. The itching reawoke down below.

"Every time I hit a white man, I remember my grandfather's father, how he ended up, how the whites put him on display to entertain their children. You can't understand that," he told me. Passersby were crowding into the bar to take shelter from the cloudburst.

I dared to speak.

"What I'm offering you is a chance to free yourself from that story, or from the end of that story anyway. I'm offering you a gateway to a better place, a place where you'll be respected, lusted after, desired, and lavishly paid for your services. You can decide on any time frame you want: you can say, in three years, I'll make enough money to stop doing this. That's if you agree to join the Club rather than staying with the client who's longing for you."

I felt ridiculous as I said this, but I suppose it was my obligation. What I really felt like saying was: Let's go, Boo, let's get out of here; to hell with all of this, the fights, the rain, the fucking garbage, the fucking Club Olympus; let's get out of here. I'll help you. Go wherever you want to go, do whatever you want to do. I'll pay. As if it were that easy, as if I really could turn myself into a magic lamp which, rubbed by the chosen hand—that is, the hand of my choosing—could make any desire a reality.

"Can your wonderful client turn back time and make everything different?" he asked, serving me up a very useful answer.

"Neither the client nor anyone else I know can turn back time, but all three of us together can make things different: the client because he or she chose you, me because I found you and told you about the client, and you because you can decide to do what's best for you."

Then he started talking some more about his village; I was afraid he was going to remember some other indigenous legend on which to base his decision, some other illustrious ancestor to pay homage to. He told me that every night he asked the gods to let him wake up the next morning a boy again, in his village, where things were as easy as watching the flocks or daubing himself with ashes on feast days, where everything was foreordained and all he had to do was fulfill what was expected of him in the knowledge that he wouldn't be punished if he didn't stray from his duty. But instead he would wake up on his musty cot, would see the sun coming through a barred window and hear the first sounds of the day, the first smells, sweat and snoring, and would wonder all over again: what am I doing here? His village no longer existed—there weren't any more boys taking care of flocks or feast days with masks and ashes; for a long time now there'd been nothing in those thatch-roofed adobe houses except the ghosts of the people murdered in the last raid—all of it was destroyed. He didn't have a place to go back to. How could I combat the woe of Boo's melancholy?

"No one has a place to go back to, really," I told him, remembering my father, my mother, but not mentioning their deaths because I didn't feel like hearing him tell me that his parents were dead, too. All the parents are dead, I know that; we're all impassive orphans, that's fine.

The rain outside was gathering force, and the number of people seeking refuge in the bar was also multiplying. Boo's handlers still hadn't taken their eyes off me; I could feel their gazes embedded in my back. "What a storm!" I heard someone say. "It's exactly what we needed," someone else answered. I remembered the scene in the movie *Magnolia* when frogs rain down from the sky, and I flashed back to the day my mother threw a wrap around my shoulders when I was overcome by a fit of weeping because, like one of the pathetic characters in that movie, I had lots of love to give. In the streets running down the mountain slopes to the city, the rainwater was gradually starting to flood, carrying along the several days' worth of garbage that the trucks hadn't yet gotten to. The city's emergency services were on the alert, and the red lightning of a fire truck's siren shot through the room where we were sitting and exploded against Boo's face. As if he'd been hit with a fistful of paint that affected not only the surface of his skin but also the distillation of his thoughts, stirring up his insides, shaking him, he said, "Let's go."

I thought he meant we should go someplace else, which was clearly a bad idea with all that water falling from the sky just

then. But a new gleam in his ancient eyes told me he was agree-
ing to go with me. I wasn't worried about his handlers. They'd
follow us for a while, but we'd lose them the minute we got into
a taxi; they didn't look as if they'd be willing to spend a single
euro on hailing another taxi and coming after us. I decided, even
before getting up out of my seat, that we'd go straight to the airport, that I'd call Luzmila and tell her she could get lost: the
party was over, and the Nubian was in the bag. But there was no
way to leave the bar; the rain was no longer a collection of drops
or a forest of lines, but a thick uniform fabric that immediately
blocked any plan to step out the door. The street's paving stones
were no longer visible, and the mountain of garbage that had
been heaped on the corner just a few minutes earlier was now
adrift and dispersing. I watched a black bag with a banana peel
sticking out of it float past and collide with a stoplight; it broke
open, spilling all its garbage. Though I asked him to wait for the
storm to stop or at least ease up, Boo walked out of the bar with
his head held high as if rain could do nothing to him, as if it were
a problem that only affected other people. Within seconds,
before he'd gone even ten meters, he was soaked. His handlers
didn't move from their seats, certain he wouldn't get very far. But
they must have grown anxious when they saw me disappear out
the door after him. My three main concerns were not losing sight
of Boo, protecting my Leica, and not losing my balance. Water
was sloshing around my ankles. I saw the green light of an available taxi and called for Boo to follow me. He did. We got into the
taxi, but it couldn't move; it was boxed in among other cars that
were stalled. "You should just get out," the taxi driver shouted
back to us. "We're not going to be able to move. I'm sure some
pipe must have burst," he added in a voice tense with fear, as if
he were begging us not to leave him alone. We saw the sewers
spewing out shit, the wet garbage taking over the street; the sight

was worth a photo, but I didn't want to risk the camera in the attempt. The taxi driver switched on the radio but wasn't persuaded by any of the programs he sampled until I asked him, please, to leave it tuned to a lugubrious announcer who informed the public that the Bureau of Civil Protection was advising all citizens not to leave their homes.

"Even the ones who know their houses are about to collapse on top of them?" the taxi driver shot back, but diminished the impact of his cynical riposte by celebrating it with a bristly little laugh.

Police cars and ambulances were all trapped in the city's traffic-snarled streets. The garbage that was finding a home for itself everywhere as the water level rose began suggesting elegiac lines to the many poets in the city's cafés. Drivers hurled invective at each other, but there was no place to pass another car without the risk that a sudden torrent of water would bring about a total loss of control, disabling the steering wheel and transforming the car into another of the many objects swept along by the force of the flood. Not half an hour had elapsed since the cloudburst began, but it felt as if we'd spent the whole afternoon trying to take shelter from it. I saw fear in the Nubian's gaze; his teeth were clenched, and he shut his eyes from time to time and moved his lips in an almost imperceptible murmur that was clearly a prayer. In this he was responding to the advice of the voice from the radio, whose information, news, and announcements all seemed intended to advise the public—especially those who'd been injured or lived in flimsy houses or houses that stood near the slopes where the water was hurtling down in torrents—to pray, simply to pray, because no one was going to be able to help them until order was restored. But order could not return until the rain had stopped, and the sky didn't seem ready to offer any reprieve. It was ironic, I said to myself, that now that I had the Nubian, now that he had decided he was willing to come with me, we were halted by an afternoon rain-shower. We couldn't stay in the cab any longer, even though the rush of water was continually intensifying. Every moment we spent in there was only making our situation more difficult. I recalled having seen, in my strolls downtown from the magnolia park, one of the big red signs that mark the stations of the national train system, and I asked the taxi driver if there was a train to the airport.

"Every ten minutes," he said. "What's more, it runs under-ground to the outskirts of Málaga, and if the tunnel isn't under water, the train will be operating. If you make a run for it, you'll get there just fine; it's right there; turn down that street and go all the way to the end."

I got out of the taxi without even checking to see if Boo was fol-lowing. I made my way forward, taking whatever shelter I could in the doorways along the street I was trotting down, and with every bound I made, I plunged up to my calves in the vast expanse of water that now covered everything. The Nubian caught up with and passed me. I watched him pull ahead as if he were levi-tating over the water, as if he could rest his foot on the liquid sur-face without it sinking in. By the time I reached the stairs of the train station, full of pedestrians seeking protection from the rain, Boo had already bought our tickets. As we waited beside the tracks, not knowing how to begin to dry ourselves off, we started laughing. Then I remembered Luzmila and called her. She didn't believe me. She wanted us to wait for her at the airport.

"I can't make any promises," I said. "It's too dangerous. We're being followed."

"But how are you going to get him on board a plane when he doesn't have any papers?"

That's why Luzmila is better than I am; she foresees such prob-lems before they arise. She would never queue up at an airline ticket counter with an illegal immigrant in tow, hoping to succeed in buying him a ticket with neither passport nor identity card. My agitation was keeping me from thinking clearly, but I didn't want to give Luzmila time to get to the airport and solve the problem herself; for a moment I thought the only solution would be to rent a car and drive to Barcelona. But I had a flash of illumination when I saw two black men sitting in the airport, their flashy luggage resting on a cart. I went over and explained our problem, pointing to Boo. He had no papers and needed to get on the next flight to Barcelona. Would one of them mind buying a ticket in his place? They looked at me as if I'd just offered to purchase their mother. Then they looked at Boo and were perhaps affected by the sight of him. They were Dutch. One of them joked, "You wouldn't happen to be terrorists now, would you?"

"Well, you're not flying to Barcelona with us, so you've got nothing to be afraid of."

He didn't find this funny. The other guy generously took pity on us. (Generously to himself, that is: he wanted three hundred euros for buying the ticket and loaning his name and documents. It was risky, but I saw no other way out and paid.) We had no trouble boarding the plane: no one asked Boo for any documents at the Guardia Civil passport control station, and at the departure gate he only needed to show the stewardess his ticket.

It was Boo's first time in an airplane. He closed his eyes as the plane began taxiing down the flooded runway. The sky, now a dazzling silvery gray like the back of a giant fish, had come down to rest against the mountaintops. The plane had a little trouble gaining altitude and with a whine flew out over the sea, which seemed to be within reach of our hands and adhered to the windows on the plane's left side as we circled back to the coast. Down below I could see that the main road running along the seafront was overrun with garbage, and littered with hundreds of trapped cars. Thousands of disemboweled garbage bags covered the promenade along the beach, and shit was splattered everywhere. It was the ideal scenario for a great escape, a supreme metaphor that epitomized all my opinions about the world, or about my own world anyway, which was not a tub full of guts, as a Faulkner character says, but a city buried in its own garbage.

THREE ‖‖‖

I met the Doctor in her Barcelona penthouse. She served me a fruity wine along with a platter of cheeses, some of them not entirely inedible, and a bowl of dark, taut grapes, each topped off with a little daub of light. On the pink wall was a new acquisition from Tom of Finland's *Slave Market* series: a large mustached man wearing a mechanic's uniform, its top buttons undone to allow the viewer to appreciate the breadth of his chest, astride an executive with a finicky little mustache who would be completely naked if given the chance to slip off his tie.

"There never was any client to satisfy," I said after taking a first sip of the wine.

"Yes there was, and yes the client is happy."

"Right, but it wasn't a mysterious client, nor was it a mission that originated in the New York office, nor is the reward what you promised me."

"Everything in its time, *chiquillo,* don't be in such a hurry. The client was me. I saw the Nubian and said to myself: we've got to have him. But since I haven't noticed you showing much enthusiasm for any of my plans lately, I thought it best to ensure the project's success by making up a story about the New York branch. I know that gave you some real incentive because you'd like to occupy my throne, wouldn't you?"

"I don't know. The truth is, I'm not sure anymore."

"Oh, come on, my sensitive young lad, one must never fret over anything; nothing that really matters ever happens, and once it does happen it no longer matters."

"It's not going to be easy for you to make use of him," I warned. "He only wants to perform services for women, and you don't have enough female clients to make him pay off. Not even if you charge five thousand euros per session."

"Come now, come now, you're a full-fledged pessimist. There are other possibilities. As for his servicing only women, well, that remains to be seen; it all depends on our being able to convince him of just how pleasurable things can be when you go the other way, doesn't it? You didn't by any remote chance try to give him a little demonstration, did you, with yourself as guinea pig?"

I didn't even smile. She went on.

"In any case, if we see we're not making as much off him here as he could undoubtedly earn, if we don't manage to squeeze out enough of his potential, then we'll send him to Paris or New York; there are plenty of women in our client portfolios there; they'll appreciate our Nubian warrior's true worth. Whatever happens, I have big plans for him, very big plans."

"I hope I'm not being too forward if I ask what those plans are."

"Of course not."

The Doctor coughed, suddenly choking on a grape seed. She drained the contents of her wineglass in one long swallow and asked me to refill it.

"A couple. A magnificent couple. The Nubian prince and his royal consort. Those two magnificent finds you scouted in Málaga. They'll be ideal for all the clients who want threesomes—and that's how we'll gradually make the Nubian give in about only doing sessions with women. We won't need to pressure him much. I'm thinking about training him with Margot, the wonderful transvestite Luzmila roped in last year. That could be a first step. We'll see. I've got lots of plans. And there are quite a few male clients who are willing to pay just to watch; don't tell me that my Nubian royal pair isn't going to be deliciously appealing to that crowd. Six hundred euros per event for the session itself, and three hundred more for the image rights, you know, all the fantasy sex the clients will have after it's over. Provocateurs of desire—a magnificent profession. I've been thinking a lot about that idea; you seem to write it off as completely unrealistic, but it isn't, it isn't at all. Think of it: all you'd need is some mechanism that would regulate people's lust and prevent them from simply being able to masturbate over anyone they feel like as if they were masters of their own desires. No, señor, if they use someone else's image to benefit their own sexual satisfaction, they're going to have to pay for it; I'm very clear on that point. But anyway."

I made no comment. I was remembering another of the Doctor's soliloquies in which she described her plan to write the biography of one of the Club's models as narrated by his cock. She'd come up with a title: *Una, grande y libre. Lone, Large, and Free.* She continued:

"I've picked out ten or twelve names on our client list who'd line up for a treat like that this very minute. I'm really delighted with your work; the two of you are a great team. And Irene! What a surprise, she's marvelous, she's already got an appointment for the operation, and of course she'll need a little fixing up as well. The one who doesn't need any fixing up at all is the male—what a specimen—don't tell me I don't have a good eye; the moment I saw him in that magazine I said to myself: wow, this one cannot get away. I haven't tried him out yet; he's terribly inhibited. I put him in an apartment with some other blacks so they can start filling him in on things; he's going to see so many movies we'll be lucky if he can keep from fucking his roommates and the doorman of the building. But don't start getting jealous on me; you know who I like best. You've done great work, and now it's my turn; you know that. You hunt them down, and I transform them into machines. We have to talk about money, of course, and I'm sure you're going to ask me for a vacation, and you need one—Luzmila told me all about your parents; you don't know how bad I feel about that—you really deserve a vacation, you do. And I'm going to give you one, even though it's high season for shipwrecked refugees along the coast and Brazil looks like its about to go belly-up and that really is like taking candy from a baby, Brazil, but we still have to negotiate with Paris about whether we'll be the ones to go looking for Cariocas or whether the Americans will handle them; they seem especially interested in sending some of their own scouts. And you know that this year's African famine is hitting Mali. Which is really good luck for us because there are some incredibly beautiful children in Mali, the Dogon, a very odd tribe who believe they're descended from extraterrestrials—I was in Mali once working as a nurse—what beautiful people, the women more so than the men, who are a little effeminate, a little fragile, but that's good for us too if the famine hasn't done them too much damage by the time we get there. I'm going to let you have the vacation you need because I'm going to need you this season more than ever, but before that, what do you think of the new print I just bought?"

I woke up amazed and with a slight headache: Moisés Froissard Calderón, La Florida 15, apartment 3B, impotent and ethereosexual. I'd been quite unable to satisfy the Doctor, who lay naked beside me, talking in her sleep, undoubtedly reliving some tortured scene from her time as a nurse without borders, down in the depths of the world. She always said she hated to sleep because she was assailed by hellish little vignettes she wished she could flush out of her head, cleansing her spirit of the rubbish of poverty, pain, and death. A sweetish, sickening smell wafted across the bedroom from a vase full of jasmine. I remembered my itching problem, and just the thought of it was enough to set off a tingle in my scrotum. I swore to myself not to touch the skin down there, which had been brutally savaged over the last few days, but I didn't keep the promise, though I was careful to use only my fingertips to relieve the itch. A pair of quinces ripening on a ceramic dish looked as if they'd been purchased in quite the upscale grocery store. The street below sounded like Friday night on any street lined with any city's most popular clubs. I hadn't planned on doing it, but when I went to the kitchen for a glass of water my old idea about damaging the Doctor's collection of books with uncut edges came back to me. I picked up a knife and began slitting the pages in the remaining volumes of the Doctor's collection, grinning all the while. I didn't leave a single book intact. In some cases I cut open the pages of only one signature, in others two. Afterward a few shreds of paper were left on the table. I swept them into a little heap and popped them in my mouth to eliminate all evidence of my crime.

Since I was a child, I've been goaded by an insatiable curiosity, particularly whenever I've felt compelled to commit a forbidden or improper action; consequently I began inspecting a stack of folders that lay on the floor next to the shelves. The Doctor's craving for order made the task easier; there was no need to immerse myself in the files one by one: for the front of each of them, in the painstaking handwriting of the smartest girl in the class, bore a title describing its contents. I didn't take the time to satisfy my curiosity concerning the various outstanding bills or statistics on the models. I did stop to look over the client information folders, but that turned out to be no more than an endless list of names, ages—what else could those numbers in parentheses be?—and professions. There was nothing there to give me an idea of what kind of services they asked for or how often they asked for them; all that information must have been stored in some inaccessible file on the hard disk of the Doctor's computer. Even so, I calculated a few statistics myself, just for fun, and learned that the average age of the clients was forty-seven, that there were twenty-two men for every woman, and that the most common profession was that of businessman, followed, distantly, by that of lawyer. There were nine doctors, three professors, two writers, and a priest. I read through the names of the clients one by one and was surprised I didn't recognize any of them; I was hoping to find someone famous, an actor or actress whose face would be familiar from magazine covers, a TV anchorman well known for his adroit shifts from woman to woman, a government minister. I did notice that quite a few of the names on the list were foreign—lots of Germans, not many Italians, a Greek—but didn't stop to calculate the proportion of foreigners to Spaniards because I'd already spent too much time playing detective and didn't want the Doctor to catch me going through her secret files. Even so, I couldn't help casting a quick glance over the files with information about the models, and though my curiosity was not driven by any eagerness to find out where the pieces I'd hunted were now, I did inevitably run across some of their names. It shocked me to see a cross marked next to the name of Emilio from Argentina. Other models' names were also marked with crosses, though not many, only six or seven more—and these files didn't have a lot of information, either: names, prices, statistics. What had he died of? What could Emilio have died of? A traffic accident? A sudden, horrific disease? Suicide? Of course it didn't say; there wasn't even a note to indicate that this particular model had stopped working for the Club, that his services were not available, that he was no longer on the team. It was possible that the Doctor simply marked with a cross—but it wasn't an X, it was a cross, a crucifix—the name of anyone who left the Club, giving him or her up for dead.

Rumors that circulated in the scouts' idle conversations and the office where the Club administrators worked gave me reason to believe that suicide was not entirely unheard-of among the members of the modeling team. It was considered, in some way, a natural death: the machine can give no more of itself but remains capable of making one last, very human decision. And then came the crude joke cracked by the typical scout who thinks he's above circumstances and immune to death notices: you're fucked whatever you do, he'd say in pompous tones, you risk your ass to save their lives, and to thank you for your effort they kill themselves. There was another joke that went: you bring them over to help them amortize their debts and where do they end up? In a morgue. It was odd and disturbing or maybe just disturbing to notice the sound of *amor* in both terms, as if love had any part in what we were doing, between amortization and a morgue. I restocked the rifled files, lit a cigarette, and let my eyes wander across the horizon of dark windows outside the living room's glass doors. I remembered an article I'd read somewhere about the high rate of suicide among actors in porn films, which was even higher for those who worked in gay porn. Furthermore, among these, very strange fact indeed, there were many more suicides among those who played bottoms than among those who played tops. From which it could legitimately be deduced that it is better to give than to receive, or at least the givers aren't so prone to thoughts of suicide. It really was bizarre, but the article listed thirty or forty cases of suicide in the preceding five years, and 70 percent of them—or maybe more; I don't want to exaggerate or falsify the data, but it may well have been more like 80 percent—were actors who played passive roles, those who had to suck and take it in the ass and hear the top man

whispering "bitch" or "whore" in their ear while he nailed them
with his massive member—and there's no need to describe just
how massive the members of the top men in gay porn films are.
Emilio must have been a bottom, of course, his magnificent ass
had to be put to use, and most of the shots of him in the catalog
were taken from behind, to show off his greatest treasure, his
gift, the reason the Doctor set his price as high as she did.

My thoughts ran back to my first captures, the trip to Argentina
and my thrill at having found, at last, a fantastic job that would be
the envy of all those who wished me ill. Judging from the photos I
kept in my pantheon album, I had saved seventy-three lives, Boo
would make it seventy-four, though I hadn't yet taken a picture
of him to make his salvation complete. I wondered how many of
the seventy-three were dead now. And suddenly I was visited by
a new image, an image that had never before flashed across my
mind, and its devastating force made me close my eyes: I was in
a trench, an enemy was coming to kill me, and I crawled under
the lifeless bodies of my fallen comrades; I hid beneath them like
a soldier taking cover under a friend's corpse. That's how I'd
been saving my own life, hiding beneath all those bodies who
now seemed to want to escape from my photo album—more of
a pantheon than ever—and stand before me, dead, so I could see
myself hiding beneath them, using their corpses to defend myself
against an invisible enemy I could not withstand. I knew I could
try to exonerate myself with the thought that everyone probably
does the same thing, and that's how we all defend ourselves, by
fashioning armor out of the debris at hand, but I couldn't come
up with any convincing evidence that anyone else would have
done exactly as I did, and in any case that was no excuse. I had
no strength left to convince myself of the contrary and repeat
what I'd told myself so often to keep going: I'm saving their lives;
I'm offering them something better than what they have; they

were diamonds lost in the muck, and I dug them out, cleaned them off, and put them in a shop window where they could shine; I put a sticker on them with a price that bore some appropriate relation to their true worth.

I went back to bed, pulled the blanket off sleeping beauty, and contemplated her naked body, which, through assiduous use of a tanning bed, was uniformly bronzed. She was wearing her electric ab stimulator belt. When had she put it on? I had no idea. The instruction booklet warns of the danger of using the device beyond a prudent amount of time—half an hour at maximum. But the Doctor needed to punish her belly in pursuit of a firmness it would never possess. I ran a hand over her icy back. Perhaps because spontaneous gestures of affection were unusual between us, my hand only managed to cover a couple of inches of spine before she woke up.

"What are you doing?" she asked, her sleepy voice tinged with anger, though I couldn't tell if it was because I'd awoken her or because I hadn't been up to the task of satisfying her earlier.

"Do you know why I do this job?" I asked.

Her only response was to grab the edge of the duvet and haul it back up over herself, after first taking a second to disconnect the ab stimulator.

I went back to Seville without saying good-bye to Boo or Irene. I knew I'd be seeing Luzmila again soon, and as far as the Doctor went, we'd agreed on a ten-day vacation. It was clear from her insistence on seeing me as soon as that time had elapsed that she was afraid I might not show up at Club headquarters ever again. My native city welcomed me back with a white-hot heat wave, and all the business related to my parents—especially the sale of the apartment—foiled any plan to devote those days entirely to thinking about my future and deciding whether I was going to go on saving lives or find something else. With the money from the sale of the apartment plus the savings I had managed to amass, I calculated that I could give myself a year's sabbatical without too many privations. I kept the collection of books my mother had bound in her favorite dresses—lined up on the shelf, they had a colorful visual impact that really was quite touching—as well as my father's bicycle, which was old and black with rusted spokes and worn-out tires. My brother was going to hang on to my father's collection of biographies of the wives of illustrious men. I was unable to spend more than three days in my parents' house; at night the itching drove me crazy, subjecting me to long, painful bouts of insomnia that left me walking around like a zombie by day. One night, to make some use of the insomniac hours and find some pastime other than twisting and turning in bed, I had the

idea of doing further research on electronic voice phenomena. I
left a portable tape recorder in the room that had been my parents' bedroom and waited. Forty-five minutes later I went back to
turn the tape over and record side B. I picked up the results the
following morning but didn't dare listen to find out whether some
voice from beyond the tomb had been recorded, whether my
father or mother had wanted to leave a soundtrack of their presence. From then on I carried the tape with me everywhere, in case
I managed to convince myself at some point that the time had
come to listen to it.

I couldn't seem to concentrate on what I was going to do after
my vacation, whether to prolong it and so get myself fired from the
Club's scouting team, or return to the field and add another
seventy-four lives to the seventy-four I had already saved, and then
demand that the Club administration reward me with an office
from which I could observe the business with a greedier eye. Not a
day went by—I could exaggerate and say that not an hour went
by—without my thinking of the Nubian prince and his consort.
They worked their way into the few dreams I had, in some of
which they went so far as to ask me for the royalties they were due
because I was making use of their images. Not all my thoughts
were salacious; I didn't always use them to rouse my appetite from
its stupor, or at least I didn't always use both of them; little by little
I was establishing my preferences, but I was very careful not to
clarify them entirely, always leaving a little room for doubt and
denial. I did no more than imagine how things were for them, what
they must feel; I needed an omniscient narrator again, a voice that
could recount everything in its true form, all that was happening
that I couldn't see or even imagine vividly enough to make it credible to myself. They were in intensive training in order to become
perfect machines for dispensing pleasure and procuring handsome
remuneration as rapidly as possible. I went over Boo's brilliant

fight with the marine again and again, and I could not deny that the thing making a hole in the pit of my stomach and sending a burning shaft from there to the base of my groin was called desire. And it was not desire that assaulted me when my attention turned to Irene, perhaps because Irene had disappointed me (and yes, the fact that Irene had disappointed me because she decided to become a model for the Club explains quite a bit about me). Someone who disappoints someone else is never responsible for the other's disappointment; the disappointed one alone is at fault for his own bitterness: he's the one who wanted to subject another person to his expectations—a person who was perfectly free not to fulfill them.

At some point it occurred to me that I could cross the divide separating scout from client. The client is the person in charge of transforming one of the immigrants you scout into a machine, the Doctor once told me. My idea was to hire the Nubian prince and his consort, of course, though the mouthwatering spectacle that Boo and Irene together were going to offer the Club's clientele was not yet in the catalog because each member of the pair was still being fine-tuned to perfection. Perhaps the Club's trainers were trying to establish a close rapport with them, or maybe they were wasting their energy trying to teach Boo to enjoy sex with men (which would have been a real con job, because in his work for the Club he would never be experiencing sex with men; in the Club there was only sex between a machine and a client's thirsting lust; in fact, the club's models were no more than soda pop vending machines, extremely expensive vending machines).

Be that as it may, I was toying with the idea of dipping into my savings to indulge in that particular diversion, and at night, as I tried to control the urge to scratch my itch—without ever succeeding, however hard I tried to lose myself in flights of fantasy to escape the unbearable discomfort that had forced me to trim my nails down to the quick so I couldn't do myself any more harm than I'd already done—I would imagine the scene: Boo, Irene, and me, the two of them naked, performing their star turn, and me, sitting in a chair in front of them, smoking a cigarette and watching them like an impotent millionaire who accords himself these pleasures from time to time, more to punish himself than to attain some impossible erotic stimulation.

One night, my last night in Seville—I was planning to spend the rest of my allotted vacation at the beach, not watching for the arrival of new hordes of immigrants who'd be arrested the moment they made their first footprint in the sand, but relaxing and getting a bit of a tan—my brother invited me to dinner at his apartment with his girlfriend, a distinguished lady with lovely manners. I have no idea why, but I decided to respond truthfully when they asked me what I'd been up to lately. My brother unwittingly delivered a hollow prologue to the news, mentioning my many excursions across lands of dire poverty to which I'd tried to bring a little spontaneous joy. All color drained from his face when I enlightened them about what my job actually was. Unexpectedly, my brother's girlfriend was interested in finding out how my work was classified by Social Security, which category it fell under. When I told her I counted as a freelance worker, and paid my taxes as self-employed, she came out with a lengthy and very expert discourse on the advantages of taking out a private insurance policy and investing in a very attractive pension plan that would give me security for the future, because the pensions for self-employed workers are the lowest the state gives. My brother couldn't believe it—not his girlfriend's questions, but my job. His questions required only brief, informative answers. Nothing he asked required me to explain *why* this was my job, which was fortunate, because I didn't have a convincing speech on that subject at hand. How many of these immigrants have you hired? How much are you paid for scouting one? Things like that. From the expression on his face, it was impossible to tell if he was fascinated or depressed, whether what I did disgusted or delighted him.

To get them to tone down their curiosity, I told them that I had decided to reveal the truth about my job, after five years of devoting myself to it exclusively, for the simple reason that I'd now chosen to quit. But the exculpation I was seeking was entirely unnecessary, for it had never even occurred to them to condemn me. That surprised me, and I told them so, saying that if I'd known no one was going to be shocked by it, I wouldn't have kept my occupation a secret. My brother's girlfriend told me that a lot of exciting things must have happened to me in such an adventurous line of work. But she didn't ask me to tell her about any of them. They displayed such a lack of interest in the details of my experiences that I was almost traumatized; it was very clear that they had an entirely vulgar idea of my epic feats. But my brother's girlfriend—and, by extension, my brother himself, by that miraculous contagion that so often happens between couples—was one of those people who think that nothing could possibly be interesting enough to keep her silent for more than a minute. In that respect she much resembled the Doctor, but at least the Doctor had seen so much that she wasn't shocked by anything she heard. In a subsequent phase of the conversation the subject of immigration was broached, and here my brother's girlfriend raised anchor and sailed forth onto the fabulous ocean of the politically incorrect. She applauded the government's repressive policies. She was the sort of person who transforms a small personal experience into a general rule, a dogma. Like the Cuban woman who wrote an article assailing the dignity of all North Africans because once, in Venice, one of them stole her Louis Vuitton handbag, my brother's girlfriend hated all blacks because one of them had once grabbed a backpack away from her and run off with it. Experience can be deceptive, I told her: if you let yourself be guided by experience, you'll end up supporting the first Hitler who happens along. My brother disagreed; he maintained that experience is the most reliable measure we have by which to evaluate things, and that if we don't learn from what it teaches us, we will lose ourselves in nothingness, nihilism, total desolation. At moments our chat ascended into real intellectual heights.

I was stunned by the deep change that had taken place in my brother. His new job and his distinguished new girlfriend had entirely stripped him of all the insolent cynicism he'd always had at the ready in our shared bedroom, never missing a single opportunity to take a pot shot at anything. I left his apartment in a bulimic state of mind, feeling as if I'd just acted in a play, the kind of play where a group of family members get together over dinner and discover, even before the first course, that they are among mortal enemies. By the time dessert arrives they know they'll have to use their knives for something other than slicing up the cake.

I think this helped me decide to go on doing my job, though I could be deceiving myself; it may be that the decision was never in any doubt, and the most I did during those gloomy days was try to clarify for myself just how far I wanted to go in the Club Olympus. I didn't have too many other alternatives, apart from my idea about the sabbatical year or the possibility of risking my savings and my share of the proceeds from the sale of my parents' apartment on some business deal. I shelved the plan to spend a few days on the beach and opted instead to return to Barcelona and follow at close hand the progress of the Nubian royal pair. I'd been expressly forbidden to do this, but I'd figure out some way to find out what was going on. I couldn't stop thinking about them. During the few hours of sleep I managed to get they would always appear, sooner or later, transformed into resplendent machines dispensing desire.

I went to Barcelona by train; I felt like watching the landscape change gradually rather than crossing the sky in a white tunnel and being dumped in a new city with no time to adjust. But the trip wasn't merely slow, it was leaden; all my seatmates were engrossed in conversations so unbelievably dull they made me yearn for the efficiency of air travel. Fortunately, the woman next to me, who tortured me with the details of her dysfunctional relationships with the women married to her sons, who were all far superior to their wives in intellect and education—she was one of those people who could never write her autobiography because it would take her as many years to write it as it had taken to live it—got off the train in Zaragoza. Once my seat-mate's voice no longer prevented me from attending to my own matters, I plunged into a session of self-examination with the very clear intent of perplexing myself. And I succeeded. Romping through my head, stamping, kicking and causing trouble, was the phrase with which my father had chosen to take his leave of the world: better in poor company than alone. And yet, except for those innocent months as a junior soccer coach, when I was with Paola, I'd never been capable of sustaining a single romantic relationship worthy of the name. And my attempt to review the list of my friends ended quickly because I couldn't think of anyone on whom I could pin that badge of honor. I felt that my brother was

lost to me, too, now that I'd seen him in a world so distant from
the one we'd shared, stripped of his wounding barbs, serious and
domesticated, seeming almost British in his refusal to be daunted
by anything, and evincing the kind of colossal composure that
would enable him to wear a mayonnaise stain on his shirt as if it
were the official seal of his university or a war wound of which he
was enormously proud. All this left me alone on a bleak plateau
where my father's last words, more than a warning, seemed like
an order that demanded to be carried out. The reflected image of
my face on the train's window—superimposed on a row of yellow
letters that informed me I was sitting next to an emergency exit,
a magnificent random metaphor—suggested a series of morbid
questions to me such as: what on earth did you do to get to this
point? But I quickly abandoned these melodramatic thoughts to
indulge in my caprice: all I had to do was close my eyes and imagine myself sitting in a hotel room and smoking a cigarette while
on the king-size bed in front of me the Nubian royal pair showed
off their recently acquired skills. I've never felt particularly concerned about my future, nor have I been troubled much by uncertainty as to my fate. Yet now the black wings of a new despair
spread over me, their broad shadow leaving me in the dark, doubt
raining down all around. I'd lost confidence in myself and was
afraid I might go on doing what I'd been doing out of simple iner-
tia, unable to reverse the slow dwindling of my hopes to find
another way of making a living, unable to try out a different path
that would transform all my years as a scout into a notebook full
of anecdotes to enliven nocturnal conversations, anecdotes I
would tell as if another person had been their protagonist, as if I'd
done no more than witness them.

I was still in that state of uncertainty when I saw the Doctor. I
caught up with her in the Club's bar, which is not at all one of
those places with naked girls grinding up and down a steel pole,

but a very calm spot where the liveliest thing to be heard some nights is a Leonard Cohen record.

"You miserable son of a bitch. I'm not going to fire you because I need you, but it's all over between us," she said. Certainly a rather inflammatory greeting. I had no trouble figuring out that she'd finally noticed her collection of books with uncut edges had been savaged.

"I'm delighted to see you looking so well, too."

"What have I ever done to you to make you want to do something like that to me?"

I was about to respond with some farfetched bit of insolence, but she didn't give me time.

"I can understand how someone might squash a mosquito against the wall, but it's very hard for me to understand why someone would get out of bed and cross the whole apartment to go outside and kill a mosquito in the stairway."

Her exceedingly mysterious metaphor left me standing there with my mouth hanging open.

"But let's forget about that. I'm a professional, and I'm trusting you to be one, too, so please sit down. I have excellent news for you."

I did not believe her. I sat down, raised an index finger, and caught the eye of one of the waitresses in low-cut blouses; she knew what I wanted.

"They're opening a new branch in Athens."

I tried not to get my hopes up. And rightly so. My drink arrived at the table.

"I'm going to recommend Luzmila to the board of directors as a candidate. We've got to get her off the streets. She gets so depressed, and she'll be an excellent administrator."

"And that, I suppose, is the excellent news you wanted to welcome me back with?"

I'd had just about enough of her smile and drank the clear, bitter beverage to cool down the roof of my mouth.

"What that means is that for now I'm not counting on her for
the most interesting missions; the poor thing will have to go to
Paris to be evaluated. I'd thought about sending her to Mali, but
I'm going to do you a big favor and send you."

"Wow. Instead of punishing me by recommending me for an
office job in Athens, you're sending me to a place ravaged by
poverty with hordes of starving people everywhere—I can't thank
you enough. If I ever have a daughter, I'll name her after you, that
is, if the civil registry allows you to name someone Beelzebub."

I had not managed to wound her.

"So get your things ready because you've got to be back here
within less than a week."

"You're forgetting I'm still on vacation."

"Stop pulling my leg."

"How is our Nubian royal pair doing?"

She was amazed by my curiosity. I was breaking one of the
basic rules for Club scouts.

"You know you shouldn't ask that question; it's no longer any
business of yours, and you can't expect an answer."

"I wasn't asking as a Club Olympus scout. I was asking as a
client."

This time I'd hit a vital organ. She drained down the rest of her
drink. I raised a finger in the general direction of the bar, and the
waitress hurried over to take care of her.

"Could you repeat that?"

"I don't think that will be necessary."

"They're not ready yet."

"Fine. I just wanted to put myself on the waiting list, and since
I don't think there are any other names on that list at this point,
I'll probably be number one."

"It's going to cost you a lot of money."

"There's no employee discount?"

"Not even for me."

"No problem. How much are we talking about?"

"I haven't set the price yet. Which one are you interested in? I'm guessing it's him. Girls just aren't doing it for you lately."

"The fact that *you* are not doing it for me lately doesn't mean other women aren't. Never take yourself as an example of anything; it will always lead you into fateful error. It's also an unfair way of looking at things, don't you think? If a guy doesn't get excited about being in bed with you, that doesn't mean he can't ever get excited. Because if you take that as a general rule and deduce that the guy can't get excited about any girl, then you'd also have to deduce that you can't possibly excite any guy. And I'm sure that's not what you think. So please don't draw any conclusions from what is really just your own cheap spite."

"The day after your little fiasco I tried my luck with a different pistol and that one fired, so I deduced that the problem did not lie with me. But why is it that you don't seem at all grateful to this company for having helped you discover such an important fact about yourself?"

I was beginning to lose my cool. I knew we were heading for a place I didn't want to go, but once this conversation had started, who could stop it?

"I don't know what you're talking about."

"Come on, hombre, give me a break. It's not such a terrible thing to be gay."

"Just because I couldn't get excited about you, you've concluded I'm gay? Some detective you are."

"Whether you want to admit it or not, it's as clear as day. That's why I'm asking if you want me to reserve a date for you with the Nubian prince. Because you like men."

"Well that's rather drastic, isn't it? So late in the game and you start talking like a nun. It's pathetic."

"Answer me. It's simple. Do you like men?"

"That depends. The prime minister doesn't do anything for me at all. Neither does any bishop I've ever seen. I could supply you with a list of a thousand men who don't do a single thing for me. And another list of a thousand men who do. And the same goes for girls. For example, you would be on the list of girls who don't do anything for me. But Irene would not be. Of all my problems, this is the only one that really doesn't even deserve to be called a problem. An official inquest on my sexual identity at this point in time? Come on. You surprise me. I had no idea you were so upset by my loss of interest in your curves. To give you a final, unfortunate example: if I had to choose between spending some time with the Nubian man and spending it with you, I'd spend it with the Nubian man. And if I had to choose between spending time with the Nubian girl or spending it with you, I'd choose to spend it with the Nubian girl."

"OK, fine. But what if you had to choose between spending time with the Nubian man or the Nubian girl?"

"I've already chosen—that's what I'm trying to tell you. I'd choose to spend it with both of them. Or rather, they'll be the ones spending the time; all I want is to be there watching."

I realized it was hard to get the better of the Doctor in discussions of this sort but I had managed to get in a few good hits. I could see she was starting to get a black eye, though I, too, had needed more than one standing count.

"So then: a date with the Nubian man?"

"I prefer the couple, even if I have to use up my entire savings. The bad thing about working in this business is that it leaves you disgusted with sex. Everything is such a lie, so dirty. But I'll pass up the chance to deliver a sermon like some priest or commentator on the TV morning news. Even I wouldn't believe my own rancid spiel."

"Give it time. Sex doesn't disgust me in the least. I'd even be prepared to give you another try, now that I no longer have anything to fear for my uncut books."

I was surprised but didn't take the bait.

"That's why I want to see those two together before they turn into machines."

"Why?"

"I've never seen two people fucking because they love each other. Never. I've never had the chance to see that."

"Those two don't love each other."

"They'll love each other when they fuck in front of me, I know they will. Don't ask me how I know, but I know. Anyway, I'll make myself believe they love each other. And a few months from now it won't be the same. They'll be two perfect machines trained to drive your perfect clients crazy with pleasure. That's why I want them imperfect. Because I'm your most imperfect client."

The Doctor pretended to wipe a tear from her cheek with a napkin. "You're going to make me weep."

"Let's get this over with. When can I hire them?"

"The day before you go to Mali."

"Fine. Monday, then. Tell me the price beforehand."

"Don't worry, I won't forget to do that."

I was leaving now. I took the last sip of my drink, picked out the lemon wedge, and sank my teeth into it. I always do that. But before I got up, I asked one more question. I wanted to know what had happened with Emilio. I don't remember whether I put it that way, maybe I said, "What's happened to Emilio?" in any case I wanted to emphasize the cause-effect relationship that certainly existed between whatever it was that Emilio had experienced and the Doctor; what I really wanted to ask, but didn't dare, was "What have you done with Emilio?"

"Are you're asking as a scout or as a client?"

I didn't answer. She let a few seconds go by. Then, very neatly and meticulously, she extracted the lemon wedge from her glass and was about to bite into it but glanced at me and offered it to me. I accepted. Slowly, very slowly, she pulled a cigarette from a gold cigarette case I'd never seen before and lit her Zippo with a single hand, pinching the upper part to reveal the little wheel that activates the flame. After letting out a great cloud of smoke from the first, deep, inhalation, she said, without looking at me, "He got indigestion from eating lobster or something like that, maybe it was crayfish or shrimp, I don't know, some kind of food poisoning that resulted in sudden death."

Perhaps by attaching that adjective to the word *death* she was trying to attenuate the horror of the news, but it didn't work; death by food poisoning could hardly have been sudden. From the little I knew about it, the paroxysms of the body's natural attempt to hang on to life and fight off the poison delay the final moment with terrible pain, racking bouts of vomiting—the body's refusal to accept its defeat—and accelerating anguish. And the Doctor was in no hurry to reveal a fact she didn't know I was already aware of, something that transformed the accidental death she was trying to sell me into a strange kind of suicide. The fact was that Emilio was terribly allergic to seafood. I found that out shortly after meeting him, the first night I invited him to dinner. He refused to eat a salad because of one tiny shrimp, and when I asked for seafood bisque he got very nervous, as if the mere fact that someone at the same table was eating seafood might be dangerous, as if the mere smell or sight of a dish containing seafood could cause his skin to break out in a rash or his stomach to go into convulsions, forcing him to seek immediate medical attention. I asked him about it, and he told me he was allergic; if he so much as tasted a single shrimp, he had to go to the emergency room: his whole body broke out in hives, and his face puffed up monstrously. So that was how he chose to say good-bye to the world: by treating himself to a gigantic lobster feast, as if he wanted to die beyond his means.

Boo's footsteps across my living room floor sounded as if his shoes—black ones, with a gold buckle at the instep—contained two large frogs. Clearly he was wearing them for the first time, and the brand-new soles croaked at every tread. Irene, for her part, was towering atop a pair of stacked heels, and the sound she made on my floor was more like a trotting horse. I'm looking at them right now in the pictures I took during that session: I used up two rolls of film, but have only one; the second was left in the entrails of my Leica, and my Leica disappeared, you'll soon find out how. I had warned the Club not to reveal the identity of their first client to the Nubian royal pair. When they saw me in the doorway, Boo glanced at Irene in perplexity, and Irene looked at me as if wondering whether to make a sarcastic remark or simply laugh. She was wearing an incongruous wool cap over her head, and when she took it off I was surprised to see that her head had been shaved, no doubt to heighten the resemblance between the two Nubians.

The conversation was halting and lurched fitfully along without daring to linger on any specific topic, veering wildly from conversational clichés to improvised comments not intended to make sense of the situation but simply to keep silence from flooding the room with its strangeness. Until the moment of truth finally came, its arrival announced by Boo with a simple "Well,

OK. But: why?" I had absolutely no confident answer to deliver, and rather than lose track of everything as I spun out some long, impossibly meandering reply, I came out only with a "Because" that sounded like the crash of a valuable vase shattering into a million pieces before the panicked eyes of its owners and the look of "Earth, swallow me now" on the culprit's face.

This party was costing me eight hundred euros, a special deal that the Doctor made for me out of pity; she'd given her star students strict orders not to let me take part in their encounter. But now that I had them right there in front of me, my excitement was anesthetized, and I felt more like chatting with them than urging them to hurry up and remove their clothes. They resisted my eager attempts to find out how they were, if they were happy, if they had any regrets. Finally, nervous about how things were going and perhaps wanting to prove to herself that she could do this and was not going to waste the opportunity to debut in the number for which she had been so carefully rehearsed, Irene went over to Boo, kissed him on the mouth, and led him toward the futon. The Nubian followed her lead, and I took my place across from them. In a few seconds they were both lying naked on the blue duvet; Boo's legs and crotch had been depilated, and Irene looked thinner, which made me wonder whether they'd already performed the abortion—which was unlikely because she wouldn't have had time to recover. I started getting excited seeing them there, so insecure, so real, making false moves, glancing at each other from time to time as if to ask whether they should stay like that or change position, two real people with all the awkwardness of youth, inhibited by the presence of a stranger. It'll be bad for business if they do fall in love, but that's a risk we've got to take, the Doctor had told me with regard to the danger that her two newest stars might ruin everything by indulging feelings that were expressly forbidden. All of a sudden

I was sure they would fall in love, if they weren't already in love, if they hadn't already fallen in love during the days of rehearsal they'd been put through. An even better revenge than messing up her collection of books with uncut edges, I thought. If the Nubian royal pair did fall in love, it didn't necessarily have to put the Doctor's business at risk, since, after all, they only needed to hide or repress their feelings in order to keep the Club's administration from separating them. But it was hard to believe that if they really did fall in love, they were going to be able to go on doing that kind of work for very long. Soon enough it would no longer be just the two of them, with a client who was paying only to watch; other clients would pay three times as much to join them in bed, or would want to see one or the other of them alone. You've got to have a mind like a bomb shelter in order not to care that your beloved has a price that will put her in the hands of any stranger. I interrupted their kisses and caresses with a question: "Are you in love?"

Boo looked over at me, but Irene pulled his chin back to busy his mouth with a kiss. Then she got on top of him, straddling him. This was not a good position, from my perspective; all I could see were the Nubian man's long, muscular legs, and his partner's rounded back and firm buttocks. So I shifted to a vantage point from which I could better enjoy the scene. They weren't doing anything to exaggerate the sound of two bodies making love: no melodramatic moans or furious panting. From time to time Irene would let out a long sigh, and that was all the music they made. Her movements were slow. The Nubian man's arms were reaching up to her, his hands resting on her shoulders. From time to time she would turn her head to one side and bite one of his fingers. I felt like going on talking while they were doing it. I got closer. I was one step away from the left side of the futon. I switched on the lamp on the night table, filling the room with orange light. Boo had his eyes closed now, and she was looking at him and trying to control her breathing. Gradually, delicately, they were starting to move faster. I decided to go ahead and sit down on the futon itself. Then, as I was enjoying the sight of Irene's belly button, which looked like a dark eye, and without my so much as reaching out to run my hand over either one's skin, Boo pushed his partner off violently and grabbed me around the neck. I couldn't say anything. I remember being surprised to see that his cock was not of exceptional size and was an embarrassing pale pink in color. Now we were both off the futon. Irene was still lying there watching it all happen; maybe she didn't understand what was going on or was more surprised by my daring than by her partner's reaction. Boo's eyes were two chips of rock-hard black ice, and their gaze made dire panic well up deep in my brain. The back of my neck was jammed against the wall, and my hands were clutching the wrist of the hand Boo was using to cut off my breath. I desperately needed air but couldn't speak a single syllable to beg him to let go. I noticed that my feet were no longer touching the floor. As if he knew to the second the amount of time it takes to lose consciousness, Boo loosened his grip on my neck just when I thought I was about to faint. I fell to the floor, doubled over, my mouth desperately gulping air into the depths of my lungs, my eyes wide-open and staring at the Nubian's feet; there were a few more of those white patches on his instep, and the word *vitiligo* appeared in my brain because the brain is a recording device that registers trifling details even in the most dramatic situations. Irene was trying to calm the Nubian down, but without moving from the bed. Boo squatted next to me, grabbed my hair with both his hands, and dragged me into the living room, unmoved by my howling. There he pulled me to my feet. I was still trying to take in air and now felt as if my whole scalp were on fire. After that I remember only that Boo smiled at me and I saw him make a quick movement, raising his forearm—his weapon of choice—and smashing it into my nose.

Next came a long journey through a province of welcoming shadows and then, in the distance, a strange voice asking my name. I opened my eyes, and the ceiling was a thousand kilometers above me. It rose even higher when a woman's face intervened between the ceiling and the rubble that was left of me, asking my name again and again. "Why do you want to know?" I managed to answer before sinking back into the darkness. When I finally emerged from that shadowy province, where I saw a tree on which children were growing and a swimming pool full of amputated arms that didn't scare me or turn my stomach but instead brought me a happiness I had never known before, I was surrounded by darkness. I needed no benevolent guide to explain what had happened; one look in the mirror confirmed that the beating Boo had given me could easily have cost me my life.

The next day the Doctor visited me, with orange streaks in her hair and a bright red spot on one of her front teeth. She told me that when I didn't respond to her repeated calls to ask how things had gone with the Nubians and why they hadn't returned to their apartment—my very naive boss lady was afraid I'd run away with them—she persuaded my concierge to give her my keys, and when the concierge told her she'd heard a brawl but had decided not to worry about it, to let it run its course, that kind of thing sometimes happens in a young master's house (*en casa del señorito*—that's what the concierge said, or that's what the Doctor told me she said, things that happen in a young master's house)—the Doctor entered my apartment fearing the worst, sure she was going to find my corpse. And in the bathroom she found something very similar to my corpse, with its head in the toilet and a stream of blood flowing from between its buttocks.

(The Nubian had decided to cap off the festivities by raping me; it took ten stitches to sew me up.) I could add nothing to this except "All I remember is that his dick wasn't that big." The Doctor raised her hands to her head, and I noticed that her nail polish was bright blue. I felt pain in bones I didn't even know I had. My nose was like a rotten peach constantly dripping blood that soaked right through the bandages, a faucet there was no way to shut off. I had to breathe through my mouth, and eating became a rather sordid operation because I had to chew quickly in order to take another breath and I had to do that with the remains of the first bite still dancing around inside my mouth.

The Doctor brought me news of the Nubian prince and his consort. "They've run away. Both of them. Damn them, *malditos,* they don't know what they're going up against here. But I've got detectives out looking for them, and it won't take long to catch them. They're going to have their fill of Africa for a very long time."

I didn't need to inquire any further; she'd arranged for the police to capture and repatriate them, the worst punishment that could be given to an African immigrant.

"Especially that Nubian bastard who did this to you and made me lose a fortune. Sudan"—she burst into a laugh—"I'll be happy to think of him in Sudan. The moment he gets there, they'll teach him a couple of things he's never wanted to learn. And the other one, that sly little vixen, to run away with a piece like that Nubian. Where will they go? What do they want? You do your utmost to give them the best of everything, to give them a chance to rise above the shit they're living in, but all they want is to go back to the shit. Well, they're going to find out. And at the end of the day we've been lucky because you're part of the Club, and, OK, yes, the damage they did to you is considerable, but imagine if it had been some other client. Then there really would have been trouble: it would have been a tragedy; they would have forced me to resign, a catastrophe unleashed by those two. They just weren't ready yet—in fact a good part of what happened was your own fault; you were in such a hurry—they weren't ready for anything, they needed more time; it was a mistake to send them to you, but you were so eager to see them together. What did you do? I'm positive you didn't stick to our agreement; I'm sure as soon as you saw them in action you thought: nothing will happen if I get involved in this, too. And you tried to lie down next to the girl, or touch her, or to touch him, even worse; tell me the truth; you forced them to fuck you, and that was what triggered the beating, right? You don't have to tell me the truth. Anyway, there's no justification whatsoever for this, none at all, even if you did get carried away and wanted more than your share of the bargain, there's no justification for this. And in any case, once it's been done, well, OK, let's try to take care of it, but to go and run away on top of it, to make matters even worse? He must have thought he'd killed you. And if he thought that, it's because he wanted to kill you—or maybe he didn't want to and realized he'd gone too far. But for him to leave you there in the bathroom with your head in the toilet, I know the bastard flushed it, your hair was wet, it was the worst thing I've seen, and I've seen some very ugly, terrible things, but a bloodbath like that, no, I really hadn't. I don't know where they are right now, but I promise you their days are numbered; they'll be caught, and then it'll be a quick plane ride back to Africa, they're going to get pretty fed up with Africa. No one plays games with me."

I spent twenty-seven slow, corroded days in the hospital and twenty-seven endless, lacerating nights. My nose, as the doctors explained to me with a level of minute detail they could have kept to themselves, had been transformed into an orgy of miscellaneous cartilage that had taken several hours of painstaking surgery to repair. The whole surgical process had been extensively photographed to impress students of maxillofacial surgery and prove to them that with enough skill nothing is impossible. The tear in my anus kept me from walking, as you can imagine; going downstairs had become as daunting a challenge as climbing Mount Kilimanjaro. If I wanted to sit down, I needed five or six sizable pillows to take the edge off the stabbing pain. But the wound that caused me the worst pain was a bite on the right cheek which had become a pustule the size of a large coin. I didn't remember having received that one either. I imagined Irene, walking over to what she perhaps at that point believed to be my corpse; to thank me for the services I had rendered her and the need to escape that the current state of my body was forcing on them, she put her head down next to my face and, unable to contain herself, stamped it with the mark of her teeth. I heard the word *vicious* spoken several times, by the voices of the doctor and nurses who took care of me, by the two policemen who came to take down my statement and by each one of the scant handful of visitors who condescended to make an appearance in my sickroom. And yet any relationship between that word and the Nubians was inconceivable to me. Why had Boo given further vent to his rage even after he'd obviously put me out of commission? His first aggression was sufficient to ensure that the session was over, and since I hadn't kept my part of our bargain, they would have been free to go at that point, and I would simply have been deprived of the show because I'd wanted to take part in it. Perhaps he lost control of himself or suddenly understood that he was never, never going to be able to do that for a living and was better off looking for a quick way out; he could create a reason that would free him from having to give the Doctor any kind of explanation by doing something that would force him to run away. Or maybe it was just my bad luck to have been the one who ended up paying for all the broken plates that had been piling up for a very long time in the deep, dark room where Boo told himself his own story, a story that did not begin with his arrival in Spain but much earlier, when a group of white hunters carried off the handsomest man in his village and took him across the sea to exhibit him at a zoo.

The Doctor kept me fully informed of her detectives' progress. But all the information she provided was subsequently corrected by further information which contradicted it. One day they'd been located in a town in Ampurdán, but the next day they'd gone into hiding on the coast. I did not attempt to make the Doctor understand that she should spare me these updates. I imagined them walking at night along an endless highway and throwing themselves down in any convenient ditch to sleep by day. I had no doubt that they'd try to go back to Málaga, where Boo could give his manager and the mafioso with the scars some convincing excuse and be forgiven and admitted once more to the ranks of the gladiators; it's not easy to reject a specimen like that.

I finally left the hospital, still very much a convalescent, my whole body one long, continuous pain, as if I'd been run over by a wheel made of reinforced concrete. When they took the bandages off my nose, almost back to its natural size after seventeen days, it felt as if they'd transplanted a boxer's atrophied proboscis onto my face. Even my voice had lost much of its timbre— and almost all its decibels. I practiced in front of the mirror to try and regain my seductive, nocturnal tone, but what came out of my mouth was the voice of a telephone operator on a bad day. The first thing I did when I got home was check on the Leica. I discovered that the only thing missing from my house was my camera; that was all they stole. They could have picked up quite a number of other valuable items as well, but that wouldn't have had the same symbolic impact as taking only the camera, which

I never saw again; they probably sold it to some driver who stopped and gave them a ride for part of the way, a truck driver who took pity on them and wasn't afraid to pick up two well-dressed black hitchhikers.

I spent two days dragging myself from the living room sofa to the bed. Nothing I tried would give me any peace of mind or erase the Nubians from my thoughts, neither some soporific TV program to lighten my sorrows with the ridiculous things the idiots taking part in some trivial discussion would say, nor reading three more pages of one of the books my mother had rebound with fabric from her favorite dresses. Then the Doctor called to tell me the news. They'd been caught. They'd been handed over to the police, who, without going through any but the most unavoidable formalities—and perhaps not even those— had seen to their repatriation. In a few hours, the Doctor summed up, they'd begin getting sick of Africa and learning their lesson. I asked if she'd seen them, whether she'd had a chance to talk to them.

"Are you out of your mind, or is it just the effect of the drugs you have to take because a building collapsed onto you? I don't want to see so much as a picture of them. I'm a lot easier in my mind now, though I will tell you I've spent some very bad days, my body trembling with fear, thinking that insane criminal might take it into his head to come settle his accounts with me, too, just imagine. The day after I found out what he'd done to you, I called a locksmith, who put ten bolts on my door, and I haven't hired a bodyguard only because I'm not that paranoid, but I really should have; someone as desperate as that might well be capable of any kind of outrage—I know I don't need to tell you anything about that, though I still say you share in a good portion of the guilt. How could you possibly have decided to stick your nose in where nobody expected you to? You should never have spent that money on the Nubians. Of course the board of directors—which is to say me, because as you know around here everyone does what I say and no one argues—has decided to reimburse you the total amount you paid for the show that you never had a chance to enjoy. If you'd asked for a sadomasochistic scenario, we wouldn't have reimbursed you, of course—on the contrary, we would have asked you for eight hundred euros more. Don't get so mad; it's a joke! But listen, let's talk about you: tell me how you are; you know we still have lots of business to attend to in Mali; have you been watching the TV news? The famine there is making excellent progress, and there are scads of mouthwatering trophies just waiting for us to find them, so come on, hurry up and get well, go to Mali, and forget this whole nightmare; you poor little dear, we nearly lost you because of that stupid brute, you can't imagine how awful I feel about this whole story, but it's just that I fell in love with him the moment I saw him in that picture—I said to myself: he must be mine, or rather, ours; the man is a gold mine—and now we've seen how that plan came out, backfired on us badly. But I still say it's because we didn't have time to train him, the first little test came out badly, and that boy is very immature, still just a little boy after all, and he messed up badly. But it's over now; we won't talk about it anymore; they must be on their way back to Africa by now. So fuck them."

So deep-rooted was her incapacity for pity that she refused to allow them to travel together, though nothing prevented her from having them both repatriated to the same place—there was no reason the police would have any information about where the two Nubians came from, and she could easily have said they were both from the same country; the police often ran into the problem of detainees who wouldn't even say what country they should be sent back to, and most of the planes jammed with repatriated illegals landed in countries where the Africans aboard them had never been before; it was all the same if someone who came from the Ivory Coast was repatriated to Mauritania, both countries were definitely in Africa, and hence provinces of the same dark cellar—but the Doctor specified that Boo should be handed over to the Sudanese authorities, which was tantamount to sentencing him to the unimaginable agonies of an Islamic jail, and Irene to the government of Mauritania. It didn't seem to bother the Doctor at all that she had not only condemned them to return to places from which they had fled, but had also separated them, just to keep from giving them the satisfaction of at least going together into the hell where she was sending them.

Now I'll let a year go by, a year like all other years, with its Miss Universe Pageant and its league championship, its tedious parliamentary debate on the state of the nation and its attacks by militant separatists, its various natural catastrophes and its "and the winner is . . . ," its domestic violence statistics and its thousands of highway deaths, its erudite Sundays in crowded outdoor cafés and its careless Mondays when hungover motorists fail to brake for crosswalks. It wasn't a good year; it wasn't a bad year. I scouted pieces here and there, more women than men—I guess I'd lost my taste for taking risks with men, and one natural aftereffect of the beating I got from Boo was a disinterest in saving masculine lives. My statistics suffered a little from this, though no one said anything to me about it; perhaps they understood why I no longer demonstrated the same impartial efficiency I'd displayed in the past. I bought myself another camera, a Rolleiflex— I felt I was ready to make the transition to the larger format— and my pantheon album grew to include eighty-seven portraits. I would need to buy another album soon; there wasn't much room left for the new people I was saving, the first volume of my great work was becoming so bulky. I stopped fantasizing about the future and began fantasizing about the past, making a few corrections here and there, tentatively placing a few notes at the bottom of the page, jotting down comments in the margins of my experiences, embellishing with hand-painted fictional tints the real facts that darkened my archives.

I didn't travel much and had dinner twice with my brother, who showed up each time with a different girl. I approved of both of them and began to understand my brother's strategy for survival: he would feed off of whichever woman he was with. The first girl who showed up with him was a liberal and a theater person prone to making impassioned declarations, and my brother suddenly started talking as if he had read every word of Chekhov and gained much from the experience; he agreed that it was natural for his girlfriend to feel desire for other men and said it wouldn't matter to him if she had a few romantic adventures as long as she told him about them. Meanwhile, his second companion, an older woman, seemed to have recently emerged from a cloister, but only in order to become a member of Opus Dei, and in her company my brother had no qualms about defending the church, justifying the very worst idiocies of the Catholic right wing, and assuring the rest of us that permissiveness in all its forms, sexual and otherwise, was one of the lethal cancers that would ultimately kill Western civilization. So my brother had chosen to accept my father's last words as a commandment which he would faithfully obey; he would rather be in poor company than alone. Maybe I should have learned something from his example, but every time I tried, every time I took a devastating look back to see the desert into which my past had been transformed, as if Attila and his unstoppable cavalry had galloped across it, I would say to myself: it's still too soon; I can still hold out alone. In the meantime I had again developed an interest in youth soccer, junior soccer, tiny tot soccer; whenever I walked toward a field where a group of children were playing a game, I knew I would be the only spectator there who didn't know anyone. Everyone else had come to see their son, grandson, or nephew, but I'd come to see all of them.

Sometimes I even sat and watched an entire tedious training session, and at moments I saw myself back in the middle of the field, giving orders, scolding the stragglers, encouraging the clumsiest ones. And I really enjoyed it, however inept they were, however few decent plays they managed, however idiotic their coaches seemed, yelling out orders they thought were professional but which were in fact completely inappropriate—think defense, defense, they would yell when their team was ahead; take your time, take your time, they'd advise a player who was taking the throw-in—and I was suddenly flooded with all the best memories of my glorious era as a boys' soccer coach. I recalled what I sometimes said to them in the locker room—because they would all show up for soccer practice wearing the jerseys of first division teams with the name of their favorite player across the back, and they all dreamed that they *were* that favorite player and behaved on the field like that favorite player: if a given boy's favorite player were a bellyacher who boasted about never letting the referee get away with anything, always giving him a piece of his mind and earning a yellow card, his little imitator would do the same, and would also celebrate a goal exactly the same way his favorite player did—I would say in the locker room that we were there to have fun and nothing more, not to win the championship but just to have a good time, and they would gaze at me in disappointment, exchange a few glances among themselves—some coach, they must have thought. I would scold them for imitating the behavior of professional players who were none too exemplary, the ones who wasted time, the ones who said that the important thing in soccer is the outcome, and they would once again give each other those looks and sometimes they must have been sure they were in the wrong locker room—or maybe I was. I know a lot of them were glad when they found out I'd be leaving, I'm sure of that. I spent many hours watching kids play soccer, while I played with the idea of going back into coaching as a way of reconstructing the only period in my life when I could remember having some kind of gentleness around me. But I would immediately toss the thought into the pit of unachievable futures, dismissing it with a weary wave of the hand as if it were an insect that was pestering me, and I even grew angry at myself for having indulged in the luxury of formulating and analyzing it, as if there were any need to weigh the pros and cons.

Luzmila was transferred to New York, where she would become one of the assistants to the director of that branch, a position of considerable responsibility that would liberate her from having to cross the globe in search of pieces. The Doctor managed to reconstitute her collection of books with uncut edges; she found out, don't ask me how, that the elderly Cuban who was her main competitor had died of a heart attack and his children had sold the library they inherited to a bookseller with a stand in a plaza in Old Havana. She seemed to grow more and more tired of herself or of everyone else, and more disappointed that the organization no longer appeared to expect her to rise to a higher rung on the ladder, or to be useful in a more important post. Perhaps with Luzmila's departure for New York the Doctor worried that her days were numbered and that her former protégée had left for the organization's most powerful branch only in order to make ready to return to Barcelona in the not too far distant future and take over the Doctor's position.

I made two very important discoveries over the course of the year. The first was the power of sunflower seeds to promote a state of complete inner absorption. I became a fanatical consumer of sunflower seeds. Every night I broke open a new bag, grabbed a handful of them, and let fly. I ate them mechanically while my mind wandered off to far-flung stratospheres, to stories that left behind not even a faint, foamy trace afterwards, and curious episodes from the past which I scratched and scratched at until they were completely disfigured. I might spend an hour eating sunflower seeds without any intrusion from the external world, my pleasure undiminished by any dark thought. While I was eating sunflower seeds, I did absolutely nothing else; if the TV happened to be on, I would only become aware that I hadn't registered a single thing about the program after I emerged from the nirvana in which I dwelled for as long as I was eating sunflower seeds. I would turn into something that looked like a robot but which, nevertheless, deep inside, was busy reinventing itself in some alternate dimension of the time-space continuum that was better than this one, or acted as a corrective to this one. Little by little, the sunflower seeds become a marvelous successor to the interviews I used to grant myself every night before I fell asleep, except that instead of granting interviews and presenting myself as an astronaut or movie star, in my sunflower trances I acted out the roles, I played the parts, or else I planted dozens of trees in the desert of my past which gradually took on the vigor and beauty of an orchard.

My second discovery was Nietzsche. Not Nietzsche himself but his main character: the superman. I became convinced that in our own time the superman Nietzsche described could no longer be someone enraged with the world who hides away in a mountain cave honing his rage on the backbone of each morning, letting out barbaric yawps to boost his own self-security. Rather, in our time, a superman is someone like me, someone unaffected by other people's sorrows and miseries, someone able to remain at a distance from the shadiness and pettiness that surrounds him, and who uses them for his own purposes and pays no price to his conscience for doing so. And that led me to reflect on the startling abundance of supermen in our time. In fact, any man who gets up at seven a.m. and endures an hour of traffic to arrive at a poorly paid job where he will exert his brain mightily each day in the full knowledge that whatever he decides or does, whatever he's told to do or tells other people to do, does not matter to him in the slightest—and then, having cast into nothingness and oblivion a day of which not one second will remain in his memory, endures another hour of traffic to return to a house full of strangers, wife or husband, children, where the only thing that matters to anyone is what TV program will be on for their evening's entertainment—this man, too, is a superman, has no option but to be a superman, has been forced, like so many others, like the vast majority of his neighbors, colleagues, acquaintances, and enemies, to become a superman, in order to survive. And the fact that he doesn't know he is a superman is the final proof that he is one. This minimal, intimate discovery made me so happy I changed the password on my e-mail account to Zarathustra—until then it had been Omniscient Narrator.

As you know, I had often wished for the presence of an omniscient narrator who could whisper news to me of the adventures of the Nubian royal pair whom I was having a hard time completely exiling from my head, banishing from my dreams and barring from the realm of absolute calm to which the sunflower seeds procured access for me. If royalties really did have to be paid for the private, sensual use of someone's image, I would have owed them both a fortune. I wanted an omniscient narrator to reveal Boo and Irene's whereabouts to me, but I don't know whether that was so I could learn the end of the story or as a way to heal the livid bruises that the occasional attack of guilt still left on my soul. That, of course, was before I made a pact with myself: the only thing I could do was accept my situation as a superman. Stephen King says somewhere that every story must contain a transformation, a metamorphosis. And as I examined the various phases I'd gone through, recounting them to myself one by one—and to recount is to enumerate, that is, to put in order—I convinced myself that such a transformation had finally been achieved within me. My former weaknesses (exacerbated by a consciousness that feared the crushing weight of a reality where other people remained human beings, and preferred to reduce them to mere ghosts or holograms acting out a splendid play in which the point was to do all you could to be in the public eye and enjoy yourself while knowing full well that whatever happened on the stage was pure fiction) would never return to send me to the edge of an abyss of anxiety, would never again harm me with the sharp talons of questions for which there was no answer. You might say it's a rather minor victory for me to have concluded that I'd become a superman. All I know is that it was good for me, and that's quite enough.

The proof is that my bouts of nocturnal itching magically disappeared from one day to the next, and my desire came back, fresh and vigorous, and I satisfy it as often as I can—always with the female pieces I scout, and once in a while, I will admit, with the Doctor, whose newly recomposed collection of books with uncut edges I have not laid a finger on. But never again with a man—though how can I keep from thinking of a man when I'm with the Doctor, knowing as I do that the moment she closes her eyes she's pirating the image of some man to whom she doesn't yet have access, and using me to give herself free flight on the trampoline of unfettered fantasy? And how can I fail to take advantage of that knowledge and do the same, imagining that the person I'm really penetrating is not the Doctor but some specimen I have scouted but placed off limits because I intend to stick to my resolution about never doing it again with a man?

Stephen King advises beginners to keep the best they have for the last, and I've followed his advice. I've reserved the incident I view as my final concession to the man I once was for the end of my story. One night, when I was in the Canary Island of Fuerteventura—it was high season for shipwrecked immigrants— the phone woke me up. Before answering, I said to myself, of course: Moisés Froissard Calderón, twenty-nine years old, La Florida 15, apartment 3B, superman and consumer of sunflower seeds. It was my contact in the Guardia Civil calling, a contact whose name I'd gotten from my man on the Gaditana coast. They'd picked up three dozen refugees from a small boat that was about to go down into the ocean waters; most of its occupants didn't know how to swim and would have drowned. They were lucky: not a single death. This particular Guardia Civil, knowing I'd already emerged empty-handed from three or four consecutive harvests, wanted to give me a little encouragement and told me, "One of them is really impressive. I know you're going to take him."

Very soon I was among those present at the station. My eyes started burning from the smell of disinfectant that filled the small room where the piece that was certain to interest me was being kept away from the others; there was no ventilation but the door, which I left open. And there he was: Boo, curled up in the corner, his face buried in his arms, haggard, shivering, more vulnerable than I'd ever seen him before. My contact left us alone after giving me a pat on the shoulder to congratulate me on the amazing find he'd placed in my hands. Boo and I stared at each other awhile. I noticed he was making an effort to hold back his tears; I don't know whether he was in some kind of pain or it was just the effect of the disinfectant which got into your eyes and made them tear up. Even so, he held my gaze, doing everything he could to control the chattering of his teeth, tensing his jaw and shrugging off the blanket he'd been given to protect himself from the cold that had saturated him through and through.

I offered him a smile that was not returned. After repeating the question to myself several times, changing it from one form to another, prefacing it with a few comments then deciding to do away with any kind of prologue until, to keep my voice from cracking, I ended up stripping it down to the maximum degree, to a single word, I finally decided to ask it out loud.

"Irene?"

The Nubian didn't answer. He continued to concentrate all his strength on keeping his teeth clenched and tensing his body so the shivering that was racking him would be less apparent. This time he was in my hands, though taking him with me would be complete idiocy; there was no place in the Club for the Nubian—or maybe there was, in New York or Paris or Berlin, but not in Barcelona, of course, not as long as the Doctor was in charge there, impossible to imagine that she might give in to pity, moved by the substantial profits the acquisition of the Nubian, with the proper training, could earn her—but I could take him away with me, get him out of there to keep him from being repatriated again—but maybe they wouldn't repatriate him; maybe they'd lock him up in one of the castles scattered across the Canary landscape where they keep refugees while waiting to decide what to do with them or to find out what they're escaping from. I came up with that last theory only to free myself from the responsibility of taking him with me, trying to reassure myself in some way that even if I left him there—and my contact's surprise would be great indeed if I said I wasn't interested in this one—he wouldn't necessarily be repatriated.

"I'll be right back," I said in answer to the absence of any response from him and my growing sense that the Nubian, when he saw me, thought I was a ghost returned from the beyond to demand some kind of explanation.

I looked for my contact and asked him to show me the others. He was annoyed; the others, according to him, weren't worth looking at: "You should trust me, man. I've learned to tell when someone's going to interest you and when they won't; I know how to recognize the type you're looking for." Even so, he took me to the room where the other shipwreck survivors were being held. A quick glance told me there was nothing there I could use, and I didn't see Irene, either.

"That's all of them?"

"That's all. Unless you're interested in the pregnant women."

Then I knew that Irene had been on board that boat and that she, too had been saved. She wouldn't be repatriated; pregnant women were the first to be rescued by our emergency services and protected by our judiciary. I did some mental math and realized that however pregnant she was—I mean, however many months she'd been pregnant for—this couldn't possibly be the same pregnancy she was about to terminate when she joined the Club as a model. This child must be Boo's. Circumstances were offering me an exquisite revenge: to have Boo repatriated while his Nubian princess and future child remained here, bereft of everything but their hope that the boat wouldn't sink on its next journey. What happened to the first child? Did she manage to get an abortion, or did she give birth to it? How long had she been pregnant this time? I wasn't curious enough about any of these questions to oblige my uniformed friend to introduce me to the pregnant women he had taken in. This deficient curiosity was one of the most significant signs of my gradual transformation into a superman. The less you want to know, the greater the capacity for invention you acknowledge within yourself. I went back to see Boo, who was standing up now, his eyes fixed on the empty space I'd left behind when I exited the room previously. All I said was "Congratulations. I hear you're going to be a father. That's terrific."

There was something indefinably beautiful and pure in his eyes, a black light that could no longer arouse any fear in me.

"I wish you the very best of luck," I told him. And disappeared.

I rejoined my contact and said, "Of course I'm going to take him with me. That's some piece. Next month I'll thank you for him with a little something extra and a box of cigars. The best piece I've ever scouted. Just let him go. I'm not going to take him with me right now because he speaks Spanish and knows where to find me. It's all arranged."

"But," the man said in bewilderment, "that's dangerous; with these people you never know. He might just escape altogether; I don't want you coming back and telling me you never got him."

"Don't worry. There's no danger. Let him go. All you need to do is open the door and leave it open. There's no one outside right now. There's no danger. He knows what he has to do, I've already told him; there's no problem."

"Whatever you say. You're the guy who's paying so you're in charge," he replied. And he went off to free the Nubian prince while I went back to my car, opened my cell phone, punched in the Doctor's number, knowing she'd have her phone turned off then, and left a brief message: "It's time. I'm quitting. I'm not going to save any more lives."

And I remembered a passage from *Zarathustra :* "I learned to fly. Since then I don't need pushing in order to move from a spot." Of course I knew it was a lie, but that kind of lie can console you if you're prepared to allow yourself to be consoled. I opened the glove compartment and took out the tape I'd recorded in my parents' bedroom. It was time I gave in to the temptation to listen to it. Side A had nothing on it but the insolent sound of silence: a monotonous soundtrack with not a second that could possibly be construed as the breathing of a ghost, the lost syllable of an impossible sentence, or a message thrown into the ocean of air in search of a tape on which to make itself real. But halfway through side B I thought I heard a voice coming through the mists. Asserting its own existence against the white noise in the background, it bellowed a three-syllable word, each syllable somewhat separate from the next, the only vowel a repeated, drawn-out *a*. It sounded like an Arabic word: *Amaya,* or something like that; maybe my father, from his purgatory, wished to express his support for the well-known flamenco dancer of that name, though it seemed unlike my father to waste the opportunity to let the living know something about his defunct state by speaking the surname of a female dancer. Maybe he'd said *papaya;* perhaps that was what he missed most, papaya juice, which I'd never known him to drink. Or maybe it was *batalla,* to define, by that word, what death is—a battle—thus refuting the notion that it is simply a wasteland or a realm of peace and relief in which the perplexities of life are nullified at last. Or he could be saying *la playa,* by which the deceased may have been expressing his desire for the sea or seeking to compare the place where he was with the beach, as an illustration, to give his listeners a precise idea of what it's like to be dead. It might also be the only audible fragment of a lengthier statement: for example *vana ya.* The rest of the sentence would have to be reconstructed on the basis of that fragment; perhaps it was an apothegm, declaration, or dictum about all things being in vain now. But I discarded every one of those possibilities when I rewound the tape to listen to the voice from out of the mists again and realized at once what it was saying: *canalla.* Now the word was diaphanously clear; I couldn't believe I'd been tripped up by all those other possibilities and it had taken me so long to recognize it. I wasn't upset, not in the least. On the contrary, a quick, broad smile spread across my face. *Canalla.* Of course. First I stared up into the sky, which looked as if some frenzied individual had been scrubbing at it with a dirty eraser, then I looked at myself in the rearview mirror. Approving of the insult, happy to be called a scumbag, I said: Moisés Froissard Calderón, La Florida 15, apartment 3B, *canalla.* I almost felt like having business cards printed up with the information.

ABOUT THE AUTHOR

JUAN BONILLA was born in Jerez, Spain, in 1966 and is a columnist for *El Mundo,* a Spanish daily newspaper. He is the author of three novels, four short-story collections, and a children's book. He was awarded the prestigious Biblioteca Breve prize for *The Nubian Prince.*

ABOUT THE TRANSLATOR

ESTHER ALLEN has translated a number of books from Spanish and French. She is codirector of PEN World Voices: The New York Festival of International Literature.